a safe girl to love

CASEY PLETT
a safe girl to love

ARSENAL PULP PRESS
VANCOUVER

A SAFE GIRL TO LOVE
New edition copyright © 2023 by Casey Plett

A Safe Girl to Love was first published by Topside Press in 2014.

ARSENAL PULP PRESS
Suite 202 – 211 East Georgia St.
Vancouver, BC V6A 1Z6
Canada
arsenalpulp.com

The publisher gratefully acknowledges the support of the Canada Council for the Arts and the British Columbia Arts Council for its publishing program, and the Government of Canada and the Government of British Columbia (through the Book Publishing Tax Credit Program) for its publishing activities.

Arsenal Pulp Press acknowledges the xʷməθkʷəy̓əm (Musqueam), Sḵwx̱wú7mesh (Squamish), and səl̓ilwətaʔɬ (Tsleil-Waututh) Nations, custodians of the traditional, ancestral, and unceded territories where our office is located. We pay respect to their histories, traditions, and continuous living cultures and commit to accountability, respectful relations, and friendship.

This is a work of fiction. Any resemblance of characters to persons either living or deceased is purely coincidental.

The following stories have been previously published in slightly different forms: "Other Women" in *The Collection: Short Fiction from the Transgender Vanguard* (Topside Press, 2012); "Twenty Hot Tips to Shopping Success," under the title "The Young Man's Guide to Wearing and Shopping for Women's Clothes for the First Time," on *McSweeney's Internet Tendency*, January 31, 2011; "How to Stay Friends" in *Plenitude*, Issue 3; "Lizzy & Annie" as a self-published zine (2013), with illustrations by Annie Mok.

Cover and text design by Jazmin Welch
Edited by Catharine Chen
Proofread by Alison Strobel

Printed and bound in Canada

Library and Archives Canada Cataloguing in Publication:
Title: A safe girl to love / Casey Plett.
Names: Plett, Casey, author.
Description: Short stories. | Includes new afterword. | Previously published: New York: Topside Press, 2014.
Identifiers: Canadiana (print) 20220412561 | Canadiana (ebook) 2022041257X | ISBN 9781551529134 (softcover) | ISBN 9781551529141 (EPUB)
Classification: LCC PS8631.L48 S24 2023 | DDC C813/.6—dc23

For Jessica and Rigel, who answer knocks and calls
and for Donna

"I loved that dream of a girl, the Beautiful Girl, calm and wild as water. I loved her like I loved the Psychic Girl, another paperback myth, because she was a safe girl to love, a fantasy that I could own. When I grew up and began to meet so many different real girls. I met beautiful girls, calm and wild, who had grown up beside trees and pools of water and I hated them instinctively. They hurt my feelings. I had thought these girls were imaginary, but no, they were real, and I could have been one too, and possessed that water-fed grace. I didn't know who to be mad at for not giving me a river."

—MICHELLE TEA, *THE CHELSEA WHISTLE*

CONTENTS

Other Women

My mom picked me up fresh off the red-eye and we went for donuts. It was the day before Christmas Eve. I told her all the fun parts about living in Portland and she listened and hummed and marched her way through a Tim Hortons dozen. When I asked her about life at the hospital, she said well, thanks for asking. It's just fine. I was silent for a bit so she would know I wanted to hear more, and then she told me a story about how another nurse had misheard a 99 code and went pin-balling through the hospital halls to find a patient not at death's door, as she had thought, but sitting with her newborn grandchild. That's funny, I said. Yeah, she said, running a hand through her wispy hair.

She didn't say anything about gender the whole day, which was nice of her. It was my first time home in Winnipeg since I asked everyone to call me Sophie about six months ago, after I moved away last January. I wanted my visit to be a Christmas the same as any other. Mom's been trying to call me Sophie, but it's hard for her.

She left to work a shift around two and I called Megan. Dude, where the fuck have you been! she said.

Putting in mom time, I said.

Gayyyyy! she said. Megan says that a lot, though she's slept with more women than I have.

Dude, she said. I moved to Corydon, I live by the Blue Cactus now. It's great. I never have to worry about driving drunk. Meet me at my place though. I gotta return some bottles. If you wanna help me?

Megan always asks me to run errands or do housework and stuff with her, which I like. I like that hanging out doesn't have to mean coffee or dinner or drinks or some bullshit. We met in Grade 9 math and bonded over stuff like Philip Roth and Papa Roach, and we hung out for the first time when she asked me if I wanted to come over and help make dinner for her great-aunt. That was ten years ago.

When I got to her building she was already outside, carrying bags of bottles to her car. I rush-hugged her and she dropped the bags and we teetered back and forth on the sidewalk with our boots creaking on the snow like rocking chairs. You look so good, she said. You look so good.

Thank you, I said. You do too, you really do. Merry Motherfucking Christmas. She pulled me tighter and released.

Megan looked the same, actually, though I've always thought she looked amazing. Thicket of blueberry-blue hair. Water-green eyes the shape of grapes. Still refused to wear a coat appropriate for living in the middle of Canada, layering on padded hoodies instead.

We went upstairs to bag the rest of her bottles and take a shot of rum before heading out. It's my roommate's, she said, I need to get another bottle for him when we're out. Remind me.

Right before we left she said okay, sorry, I have to ask. Do they look like man boobs or are they real girl-looking boobs? I didn't want to answer. I'm only a year on hormones, but even though I'm a B cup,

I'm also six feet and they still seem small. They do look like girl boobs if you see them without clothes though, so I said, do you wanna—? and she said yes before I could finish. I felt like a dopey teenager flashing her, but I feel like a dopey teenager a lot lately.

She nodded in this approving way. They're girl boobs, she said. Nice. Shit. I want to take pills to grow my boobs. I said sell you mine. Five bucks each. She slapped me around the middle and said, you're such a fucking pusher! She laughed at herself. Then there was a key in the door and I had to straighten my bra. A short guy walked in with snow stuck to one side of his curly hair and his U of M parka.

Hey Mark, Megan said. This is Sophie. We drank the last of your rum. I'm getting another bottle now though.

Oh cool, he said, in a high, lilting voice. Hi, I'm Mark, he said.

Sophie, I said. I stuck out my hand and he shook it awkwardly. I made a note to pay attention to whether men and women shook hands with each other. All these new social cues are confusing.

You fall down? Megan asked, nodding to the snow on his side.

Yeah, he said. These three big guys came up to me and told me to give them my parka, so I started running. I tripped after about two blocks. I don't think they tried to chase me though.

Yay Winnipeg, I said. Yeah, whatever, Megan said. Let's go.

You got a girlfriend in the States yet? Megan asked in the car.

No. You got a boy?

No. Boys don't like me. I said that couldn't be true, that she was beautiful, and she said well thank you, in that way you might tell a guy on the street that you've got no change on you, sorry, so sorry.

Megan and I never dated, but we did have sex once, my first year of university, when we were really high. We just pretended it hadn't happened in the morning. She said, good luck on your midterm, and I said, have fun at work, and she kissed me on the neck and left. Then I tried to fall back asleep in her bed but I couldn't, so I got dressed, took one of her shirts, and left. I wish I hadn't lost the shirt, this stretchy bright-green thing. I wonder how it'd look on me now that I have boobs.

Your heat not work? I asked Megan. It was thirty below outside, and it didn't feel much different inside her car.

'S a piece of shit. Takes a while.

Blech.

Eh.

HOLY FUCK! she screamed and braked. *SHIT!* We were in an intersection, and a red sedan on the cross street had braked too late for driving on snow and ice and was skidding sideways into our path. *OH SHIT*, I yelled, and then the sedan's back door collided with the front right corner of Megan's car. We slammed forward in our seats and stopped and there was a terrible mass clank of bottles in the trunk.

You okay? Megan said immediately.

Yeah, I said.

Good. She got out of the car. *YOU FUCKIN' BRAIN DAMAGED OR SOMETHING?!* she yelled. The driver was an old man with a red toque sliding off his head, staring slack-jawed at Megan.

She strode over to the car and he got out and straightened his toque and said he was very sorry, oh shoot, he was very, very sorry, and Megan said yeah, you better be. Then all businesslike she said, Come on, let's get out of the road and do the insurance. Can your car go?

He said he thought it could, and we skittered over to a side street. He sounded like a nice guy. We actually buddied up to him by the end. There wasn't much damage anyway since we'd both been going twenty klicks on impact. Just some dents. The guy shook our hands and said he was so sorry he caused such a nice guy and gal a hard day. Megan grunted and didn't say anything and then he left. It's petty, but I wish she had. Just said something like actually, we're both nice gals. Nothing nasty. Instead she looked at me and rolled her eyes. Then we checked the bottles. Only one had broke.

I don't know why I can't just say for myself: Actually, I'm not a guy. I get this awful image of being like a little kid saying Look, no, I'm reaaaally a girl. I promise. I super promise! I wanted someone else to step up and say you're wrong buddy-o, that there is a chick, she's no man and you should get your eyes checked.

Winter coats make it hard to see my new body shape, too, I guess. I used to love that about winter.

By the way, said Megan, picking up on my mood, I know this is kind of random, but I really like how your freckles have come out now.

Thanks, I said, blushing. That was nice to hear.

We returned Megan's bottles then went to the Blue Cactus and got hammered. After a couple hours Megan got a text and said shit! I need to get rum for Mark.

Where'd you meet that kid anyway? I slurred.

Friend of a friend. Why?

Never seen him around before.

Yeah, I don't really know much about him, actually, she said. I've only lived with him like two months. And he doesn't talk that much.

She threw back the rest of her Blue Hurricane. He's from the country. We gotta start walking.

Fuuuuck, I said. I shot the last of the vodka soda I'd just ordered.
Thatta girl, she said.

Mark! Megan said, throwing back the front door.

Maaaaaaaark! I said, following her with the liquor bag.

M-a-a-a-a-a-a-a-rk! we both sang together, on a third, then a fifth. Old joke. We used to sneak up and surprise people in high school like that. Mark looked up from the cello he'd been playing. There was a pipe full of ash and an Altoids tin on the table, and his eyes looked like Superballs floating in tomato soup.

Got your rum, roomie! Megan said. I gave the bag to her and she slammed it onto the table.

Oh cool. Thanks, he said. What are you ladies up to? He enunciated his words precisely and clearly in a way that made him sound almost but not quite British.

We shrugged. I gotta get home in a bit, I said. There's no fuckin' way you could drive, is there, I said to Megan.

She laughed and said, I don't think I could read.

Okay, I said. I did want to get home before my mom did. I didn't like the thought of her coming back to an empty house on my first day. I still had a couple hours though. Megan put on *Eternal Sunshine of the Spotless Mind* and Mark packed a bowl for him and me. It cool if we smoke? I said to Megan. She murmured sure. She used to smoke a lot but gave it up around a year ago.

Megan fell asleep in the first ten minutes of the flick and Mark and I started taking shots of the rum. We didn't speak through our respective hazes for most of the next two hours, except to say things like holy shit and what the fuck. Neither of us had seen the movie.

When it ended, I had half an hour before my mom got home, so I tried to wake up Megan, but she just kept smacking her lips and turning over in her chair.

I gotta get home, I said.

She snort-laughed into a cushion. Are you kidding? I can't drive.

Dude! I said, more angrily than I meant to sound. I have to get home!

We'll die if I drive, so that won't help you.

Megan! I said. Jesus Sophie, she said, her face not lifting up from the cushion. Just get Mark to do it. Her blue hair was covering her face and her outer hoodie was blue and she looked like an angry drunken Skittle. I told her this. She told me to blow myself.

Drive? Mark said. Sure.

No! It's okay, I said. I'll just call my mom. I went into the building hallway. I was disappointed. I liked being in Megan's car.

I called the hospital and they told me she was busy but they'd tell her to call me back. I went back into the apartment and Megan was gone. Mark was playing his cello. I tilted my head in question and looked at the empty chair.

She went off to sleep, he said. Are you getting picked up?

She's gonna call me back, I said. I slouched against the wall. Walking had reawakened the booze and the weed and I was getting the spins. Hey, I'm sorry to bother you, I said, wincing. Like, I'm sorry, but can I steal the couch from you? I sank down the wall to the floor. I really need to lie down, I said.

Absolutely, he said. He picked up his cello. Go for it.

Thanks, I said. He disappeared down a hallway. I rolled over to the couch and slithered onto it from the floor. Then I dozed off.

I woke up to Mark tapping my arm. Sorry, he whispered, I just thought you might be glad to have these when you woke up. He was sitting cross-legged on the hardwood floor. Next to him were a thin pillow and a green-and-black blanket. Next to those was a large tumbler of ice water, and next to that was a bag of Old Dutch ketchup chips. Sorry, he said, seeing my eyes meet the chips, it was the only food I could find that you don't have to cook.

I laughed. Aw. You're nice, Mark.

He stuck his arms out and palms up in an aw-shucks gesture. Oh, I'm not that nice, he said. You just have to get to know me first. I said ah. I took the pillow and blanket and sat up covered. Then I drank all the ice water.

I'll get you some more, he said.

Aw, no, it's okay, I said. I lay down again.

It's no biggie, he said, you are very welcome here. He came back with a refilled glass. I thanked him.

So what do you do, Mark? I said, looking at him sideways from the pillow. I liked saying his name. It sounded crisp.

I'm an engineer. Or that's what I study, at least. I'm a civil engineer, like the kind that designs bridges.

I know what a civil engineer is, I said. It came out meaner than I meant it to.

Oh, cool. Well, I am one of those, he said, unperturbed.

Well, look at you, eh? I said, trying to sound nice. A pot-smoking, cello-playing, civil engineer.

He laughed, a quick, two-toned treble laugh, like the sound of getting a coin in old Super Mario Bros. games. *Ba-ding! Ha ha!* Heya, he said, doing the aw-shucks gesture again. I try my best, honey. What do you do?

I am a master of the shipping and receiving arts, I said. Books specifically.

Oh, cool. That makes sense.

It does?

Yeah, he said. I was wondering, because of your figure.

What?

Well, from a distance you just look skinny, he said. And you are skinny, he said quickly.

This was a lie, I was one ninety-five. But I appreciated the thought.

But really up close you can see your muscles, like, you're quite toned. But it's subtle. It's work strength, not gym strength. He paused, looking thoughtful. You look really good, he said suddenly. You pull it off. You look tough and pretty.

I blushed. Thank you, I said softly. He smiled and said just the truth.

Suddenly I really wanted to know if he was straight or not. I wasn't into men, but I wanted him to be into women. He burnt a hole through my gaydar.

He did make me feel pretty though, regardless.

My mom called back. I took out my phone and it rubbed against the five o'clock shadow on the cleft of my chin. I stopped feeling pretty.

Hey, my mom said. We got a few patients in at the last minute who need a lot of documentation, so I'm going to be late coming home. Normally they wouldn't do this, of course, she said. But they don't have to pay me overtime because I have the next few days off. Anyway, so. Don't wait up for me before you go to sleep or anything.

Okay, I said. I tried to use as few words as possible. I'm at Megan's now, I said. Mark mimed asking if I wanted to sleep here, tilting his head toward his pressed-together hands, then pointing toward the couch.

Oh, okay, Mom said, her voice characteristically blank. It was hard enough to suss out her feelings even when you weren't drunk and high. I wondered if she was mad. She didn't offer to give me a ride, so I guessed she didn't care if I came home or not.

I might just stay here, I said. If that's okay? I'm really sleepy.

That's fine, Mom said. We could go for lunch tomorrow if you'd like. I said that'd be great and then we hung up.

Thank you, I said to Mark.

Oh cool, yes, of course, he said. His eyes had contracted enough by now that I could see they were a deep brown. They'd looked so black before. Do you need anything? he said.

No, I'm fine, I said. Thanks. You're nice. I laid my head down. He got up and waved goofily. Goodnight, Sophie, he said.

Thanks for the hospitality! I yelled quietly as he closed his door, but I couldn't tell if he heard. I heard him stumble over something in his room and say ow fuck before his bed creaked with weight.

⚘

Mom and I spent all of Christmas Eve together. We went to Earls for lunch, then to the Forks to go ice skating. I kept speeding up, and then I'd see I was losing her so I had to wait for her to catch up. You Americans are always trying to get ahead, she said. We laughed. I started sweating from all the exercise, so I opened my coat and let it fly around my arms and the air felt deliciously cold.

We went to Robin's for donuts and coffee afterward and that's when Mom asked me if I felt safe down in the States. I said mostly I did, why?

Well, it's America. She paused. And there's your new lifestyle.

Yeah, I know, I said.

She looked at me hard. I hope you do, she said. There are certainly a lot of—she paused—rude people out there.

Yeah, I know, I said. I'm alert, I promise. I've been fine. Portland's safe and it's really friendly to people like me. It's safer than here actually. I paused. Last night, we didn't go out or anything, we were inside. She said well, that's good to hear, and took a double chocolate and broke it in half.

It's not true. That everything's always friendly. I was at a bar a few weeks back and some guys threatened to throw a knife in my face. Someone yelled *fuckin' faggot!* when I was walking home the other day. I moved to Portland partly on word that it was a queer-dripping liberal dream, but I wish I'd researched geographic specifics before I signed a lease on 104th and Powell. Honestly, I just feel lucky no one's tried to punch me yet. Or stab me. But Mom doesn't need to hear any of that.

She took the trans thing pretty hard. It wasn't bad when I came out to her a couple years ago, admitted I wore dresses, told her I was just thinking about transitioning. She'd listened and frowned and said, okay, well. I think you make a fantastic son, and I certainly hope you can learn to love yourself as a male.

So that was a relief. It was when I told her last year I was going on hormones that she said oh lord really softly, and then kept excusing herself to go to the bathroom 'til finally I said, Mom, just bring the Kleenex box here, I know you're crying, it's okay! Just *please* can we talk about this? I don't know why that was so important, why I had to talk *right away* when she just wanted to go cry alone and process. There was a long silence and I asked her what she was thinking. All of the things I did wrong, she said. She didn't say much else because she was trying to think of something positive to say, because my mom doesn't know how to say hurtful things to people she loves. She finally said well, your acne will get better. Will it? I said. She said yup, 'cause you'll have to take spironolactone, and that's something they often use to treat acne.

It was hard after that. She stopped signing her emails *Love, Mom*. Stopped going out in public with me. Those were rough months. Another reason I moved to the States was because I thought we might never be close again and the idea of staying in Winnipeg with the ghost of her memories on every corner made me nuts. I vomited once, just a little in my mouth, alone in my living room, over the thought of losing her.

We got a lot closer after I moved, though. She even called me her daughter last month. That was really nice.

We spent the rest of the day at home. Read books, chatted. I helped her clean the bathroom. We were eating takeout for dinner when she asked me what I was wearing to church tomorrow.

Our family always met up at my grandparents' on Christmas morning for coffee and pastries before church. We've done it every year since they moved to the city when I was five. My mom and I weren't religious, but we went to church on Christmas. Family.

When my mother was eighteen, she and my dad renounced the church and eloped to the city from a town south of here. Three years later they had me, and two months before that she booted my dad out of the house for reasons that neither of them will tell me. I don't see my dad that much. He lives in the BC Interior somewhere. He moves a lot.

Their families were Mennonites, not the kind so hardcore as to shun electricity and cities Amish style, but enough that apostasy was kind of a bridge burner. My grandparents didn't talk to her again until I was born, and only then for my sake. They thought it was too terrible for a boy to grow up without a family. Those were my grandfather's words, anyway.

I told my mom I had this eggshell-coloured dress I wanted to wear. Hmm, my mom said.

Will that be okay? I asked.

Well, I don't think your clothes will be a problem, no, she said.

∂ℓ

So, she said as we were driving the next morning, have you given any thought to how you're going to deal with the church crowd?

No, I said. I'd been more worried about my grandparents. I really loved seeing them. They'd half raised me. Mom was always working, and I was always at their house. I didn't know how they'd react to me. I emailed them months ago, asking them to call me "she," but they never said anything back. Mom says they haven't mentioned anything to her about it.

But the other churchgoers hadn't crossed my mind. Um, I said, maybe I'll just take the cue from Grandma and Grandpa? If they think anything should be different?

Well, she said, I'm not sure they'll know what the best course of action is.

We sat in silence for a while. Should I not sit with you guys or something? I asked.

Well, that would certainly take a load off their minds.

Sure! I said. No problem.

We pulled onto the street of their townhouse. My grandpa was shovelling snow on the driveway, a dot of a red parka floating on white in front of the beige row of houses. He waved to us with both his free and his shovel-clasped hands when he saw us.

Hello there, Lenora! he said to my mom when we got out of the car. He hugged her and then shook my ski-gloved hand and said: Hello! Welcome! Glad to know you can still brave it up here, even if you are an American now! We laughed and my mom tittered.

Inside, Grandma hugged us and said oh, it's always just so nice to see Lenora and her child! Mom and I both bobbed our heads and said you too!

They sat us down in the living room for coffee. My grandma said oh crumbs, I forgot the shortbread. My grandpa made to stand up and said, I'll get it, and my grandma said, no no, you sit here and visit, and then they both stood up at the same time.

Well, I guess now we're both on the hook, my grandpa said, and my grandma laughed and scratched the inch-long scraggle of hairs on his head and they walked into the kitchen. Don't worry! said my grandpa, I'll supervise her! and my grandma laughed again.

I've always liked my grandparents' house, drab as it is. It's cozy. I like to lie on their burnt-orange couch and read by the window that looks onto the street.

We ate shortbread and drank coffee and visited. Grandma kept straightening the trays. I asked when the rest of the family was coming and Grandma said oh, Tim and Jeni and their kids are going to meet us at church, and it turns out Helmut and Mary couldn't make it. They said the pipes froze out in Kleefeld this morning and they didn't think they should leave.

Oh darn, that's too bad, my mom said quickly.

Oh, I said.

It certainly is cold! said my grandfather.

It's nice they haven't called you by your old name, don't you think? my mom said as we drove to church. Yes, I said, it was nice. My old name, which I hate hearing, is Leon. I've started to get this weird visceral reaction every time I hear it. Or even see it on a piece of mail or something. Too many bad memories, I guess. Not of anything specific, just unhappiness. Boy body. All that. It is nice that they haven't called me Leon, but I hope I can hear "Sophie" soon. I'm just glad I'm still welcome in their home, though. Means a lot.

Church was fun. I may not believe in God, but I like Christmas services. Everyone's in a good mood and the sermon's reflective and peaceful.

I sat in the back and brushed my hair in my face so my grandparents' friends wouldn't recognize me. Then I slipped out as soon as the service was done. One of the ushers gave me a funny look as I was putting on my coat, so I turned away from him. Then a thirtyish woman making her way into the fellowship hall walked right by me and whispered, I like your dress. I smiled at her, then went to sit out in the car. I turned on the radio and sang along to "O Holy Night" and "Hark! The Herald Angels Sing" while texting *Merry Christmas* to everyone in my contacts.

Megan texted back. *Merry Christmas you wild bitch, how's the fam?* *Theyre not bad*, I said back. *Hows your dad?*

Hes great, she said. *Mark is over he couldn't get home cause theres a big storm down by Winkler. Dad loves him. They might run away together.*

Ha awesome, I said. *Hey btw random q but is Mark straight or no? He threw my gaydar into a tizzy.*

idk, she said back. *Im curious too. Will try to ask him. He says Merry Christmas btw.*

Merry fuckin Christmas to him too!

My family came out after not too long. Thank you for waiting out here, my mom said, that was very considerate of you.

Back at my grandparents' house, I met up with Aunt Jeni and Uncle Tim and their two kids, Bernie and Cheryl. Bernie, who's twelve, asked if I could do a puzzle with him. I said I'd do my best and he gave me a thumbs-up and said well that's all I can ask.

We poured the pieces on the coffee table. Bernie connected all four sides in the time it took me to fit in ten pieces, so I decided to reform my position to one of moral support: Go for it, Bernie! Yeah, you can find that piece! You're Puzzle Player World Champion! He smiled and gave a thumbs-up and scratched his dust print of a moustache.

I got a cup of coffee from the kitchen and waved to my mother and my aunt, chatting at the table. I looked out the window and saw my grandparents and uncle stepping out to play in the back-yard with Cheryl, the younger one. She was squealing and my uncle started chasing her and making monster noises: *GARRR GARRRR ahhhhhh!*

I piled up a plate of shortbread for us. When I came back, Bernie had fit in what looked like another thirty pieces. I sipped my coffee and brushed crumbs from my dress and continued cheering. Then Bernie said hey, um, can I ask you a question?

Sure.

It's sort of a personal question, he said. You don't have to answer.

I grinned. Bernie was super, super polite. Sometimes I found it grating, but usually I just thought he was cute.

Why did you choose Sophie? he asked.

I smiled. That's totally okay to ask, Bern. I've just always liked the name, I said. I sipped my coffee and propped my chin on my hand. I read it somewhere a few years ago and it just seemed right. It's not much of a story.

Okay, he said. That's cool. Maybe other people don't think it's cool, but I do.

I grinned. Hey thanks, Bernie. Really, thanks.

You're welcome, he said. He fit in another puzzle piece. I think part of my head will always think of you as Leon though.

Oh, I said. I tamped down an urge to throw my mug through the window. Well, give it time, I said.

I don't know, he said. He asked for a sip of my coffee. I heard, belatedly, how sad the kid's tone was. He looked worried. I wondered what his parents might have told him.

Well, I said to Bernie, what if you thought of it this way: What if I've always been Sophie on the inside, so actually I was never Leon all along, it just looked that way?

I saw his gears turning as he thought about this. Hmm, he said. Wait, what?

Never mind.

Maybe it's just because I always liked your name, Bernie said. Then he said, I like Leon, in this next-to-inaudible voice. He was looking at the puzzle piece in his hand when he said it. It's like a romantic name, he mumbled. He saw my face and then he said but Sophie really is nice too. He gave a thumbs-up.

I do like Sophie, I said, trying to smile. Then he said, hey, so do you go on dates?

I knew he meant did I date boys or girls, but I didn't want to have that conversation now, or here, so I scooped up my phone and coffee and said hold on and left the room. I walked into the garage where my aunt Jeni smoked her Du Mauriers. I do love my name. I read it in a book when I was fourteen and have never wanted to be called anything else since. I don't even remember the book. It's really not much of a story. I took my notebook and pen out of my bag and lit one of Jeni's cigarettes and wrote Sophie Sophie Sophie Sophie Sophie over and over, Sophie Sophie Sophie Sophie Sophie Sophie Sophie Sophie Sophie Sophie Sophie Sophie. I was starting on the other side of the page when my mom and aunt opened the door and I looked up and saw them watching me smoking and writing on the cement garage floor in my eggshell dress. Oh, my mom said, and for a second she looked scared, and then a heaviness coloured her face, like sandbags had dropped through her irises. Oh hey, my aunt said, I didn't know you smoked.

Dear Lord and Heavenly Father, my grandfather said as we bowed our heads and took each other's hands before dinner. We come to you on this holy day, the birth of your son Jesus. We come gathered in thanks, hope, and gratitude. We are thankful that we have so much of our family here, that you have blessed us with their presence, and enabled us to sit down to the meal we are about to graciously receive.

We are especially thankful you saw fit to guide up from America our grandson Leon—

No, Sophie, I said.

I know you're not supposed to interrupt prayer but I couldn't help it. My grandmother took in a sharp breath and my mother said hey now in this quiet and angry voice and I said I'm sorry.

My grandfather paused, as if he were deciding whether to address me or not, then moved on to pray for somebody else. I opened my eyes and saw that everybody else's were still shut, except for Bernie, who shut his eyes as soon as he saw I'd opened mine.

Lastly, my grandfather said as he finished, we thank you for this food and ask that you bless it to our bodies. Amen.

I leaned over and apologized to him as soon as we started eating, and he just frowned and said, well.

No one called me either Sophie or Leon for the rest of the day. The one indication that the whole thing had happened at all was when I went to grab a hair tie from my coat pocket and found a large, neatly folded slip of paper sticking out of my boots. It had my grandmother's handwriting on it: *Trust in the Lord with all your heart and lean not on your own understanding; in all your ways acknowledge him, and he will make your paths straight. —Proverbs 3:5–6.* I folded the paper and stuck it in my bag. I didn't want my grandmother to see it in the trash but I didn't want my mom to see it either. The one time she'd gotten audibly squirrelly about gender stuff in the last few months was when I mentioned to her that I'd gone to this march in Portland for trans rights. She made this exasperated noise and started giving me this big talk about brainwashing and cults and stuff like that. I got a little annoyed. I told her that just because a group of people get together to make the world better it doesn't automatically make them a religion and she said don't ever be too sure about that.

᪥

You need to stay here again tonight? Megan asked.

If you don't mind? I said. I'd rather not have to leave early, I wanna see everyone.

Of course, she said.

We were headed to a Boxing Day party at Tyler's, a friend of ours from high school. It was the one time I was going to see all our old friends; I was flying back to Portland the next day. Tyler was my only other close-ish friend besides Megan. We'd known each other since Grade 1. We stuck fingers in each other's ears in choir class.

Megan and I were pre-gaming in her living room with rum and Cokes. Cello music was coming from Mark's room. Thanks, I said. Then I sucked up a breath and said hey, do you know how Tyler or the rest will, like, react to me?

I don't know, she said instantly. They were kinda angry when you sent that coming out email months ago.

Angry? I said. Nobody responded to it except Tyler and he said he'd do his best; he didn't sound angry. Angry?

Don't worry about it, she said. I told Tyler that if anybody gave you shit tonight I would fucking murder them.

I smiled at her. Really?

Of course! she said, sounding offended I might have expected less. Bitches gotta go through me before they get to you, she said. That's what I say.

Aw, I said, grinning.

Just feel it out, she said. They might be weird, but I think they just don't understand.

Nobody ever can understand, I said. I meant it in a simple, fact-stating way—of course they can't understand, no more than I can understand Tyler's taste for liver and onions—but Megan looked irritated when I said that. Yeah, that's a great attitude, she said.

I meant, like, I don't get why people have to understand, I said.

Let's just go, she said.

I put on my coat and she layered on her hoodies and we walked down to her car, not speaking much. I started to get jittery. I checked my makeup and ran fingers through my hair. I thought about the awkward dinner my mom and I had had at Earls a couple hours before. We'd talked for ten minutes about converting my old bedroom into her office; it was that kind of awkward. When we got the cheque she'd said, so, I wasn't sure whether to say this or not but I think I will. You know that Uncle Helmut and Aunt Mary didn't actually have frozen pipes, right?

I put my hands around my Diet Coke. I did wonder, I said. Yeah.

They didn't, she said with finality. But it was nice of your grandparents to say that, I think. Wasn't it?

I guess so? I said.

Well, she said. I just think we had a really nice Christmas.

I think so too, I said.

We picked up a twelve-pack and got to Tyler's new place. He'd gotten a sweet job with MTS and had moved into this nice Victorian by himself out by Wolseley. The house was huge. Little window-laden turret and everything. Some girl we didn't recognize let us in and we went to the kitchen to drop off the beer.

This house is wild, Megan said. The kitchen was huge and had the oddities of a guy living by himself for the first time: well-used microwave, cupboards empty except for boxes of granola bars. The fridge contents were beer, Kraft Singles, milk, sliced turkey breast, three heads of broccoli, and a jar of Cheez Whiz.

Tyler came into the kitchen as we were cracking beers. He'd cut his thin red hair so short it looked like someone had sprinkled powdered carrot on his head. He'd lost weight, too. Hey Leon! he said, smiling big. Damn good to see you! He shook my hand.

I hugged him and winced at the same time. Actually, I said, it's Sophie now.

Right right, he said jovially. So how're you? How's the US of A? Feel like a Yankee yet, eh?

Yew be quiet, I said in an exaggerated Southern accent. Ah own yew and yer mayple-syrup-drinkin' land.

Hello? Megan said. Do I not fuckin' exist over here?

You bitch, Tyler said. They hugged. Tyler poured us shots. Cheers, he said. You'll always be a Canuck to us.

Cheers!

We drank. I looked into the living room. I didn't know a lot of other people at the party.

So how are you? I said. Hear you got a new job?

Yeah, he said. I work with Sam Wiebe, actually, remember him?

He gave you a swirlie once? Right?

Oh! I still give him shit for that. He's cool now though. Never thought the guy'd turn out to be an engineer though, eh?

Yeah, weird. Hey, you're looking good, man, I said. Different. I like the hair. He nodded and said thanks. There was an awkward silence so I said, I mean, I know I look a little different too. Got some growth in the chest, hips are a little wider—

He laughed really loudly and awkwardly and looked around and then said hey, be cool, all right?

What? I blinked. He slapped me on the back. Megan had left to talk to someone else. Look, I'm cool, okay? he said. Just like, don't … He looked frustrated and trailed off. Don't be gross, he said.

Sorry, I said, I didn't think I was being—

Look, he said, I'm cool with you. Doing whatever, like, I don't get it, I mean, if this turns you on, whatever. But there are people here tonight who wanted to kick your ass, okay? I talked to them, they're cool, but just like, relax, be normal, it'll be fine. Okay?

Uh, okay, I stammered. I worried a lot about safety, but I didn't think I would here.

Cool, he said. Okay, sorry about that. Want another shot?

Sure, I said. I thought I saw some people down the hallway staring or pointing at me, but it might've been my imagination. I did finally recognize a few people. Old friends from high school. I waved, they waved, then I cheersed Tyler. Someone in another room started yelling that the Jets were definitely coming back to Winnipeg, he'd just heard it on the way over. Everyone started whooping. I never even fucking liked hockey.

Megan found me in the corner of the kitchen about half an hour later, on my third shot and second beer, listening to a theatre kid named Jesse I'd avoided since high school talk about how the Boston Tea Party was an example of performance as protest. Megan interrupted him. Hey, she said. She raised her eyebrows. How you feeling?

Ummmmmm.

You wanna go?

Maybe? I dunno. How're you doing?

We can go, she said, nodding.

Thank you.

I chugged the beer then found Tyler. He shook my hand and said hey, don't let us keep you, good luck down in the States.

Good luck in finding out what turns you on, I said. I meant it to sound like a joke, but it came out sounding mean. I decided I didn't regret it. Jerk, I added. We went outside and I lost my balance on the porch steps and fell-sat on the top stair. Then my butt slipped off the ice and I clattered down to the sidewalk on my ass.

Way to go, Megan said, tightening the Velcro on her leather gloves. They looked so fancy contrasted with the four hoodies she had on.

Fuck him, I said.

You are hammered and you're a dick, she said. She hoisted me up and guided me toward her car.

I'm not a dick, I'm a bitch, I said.

Stop it! she said. We were silent for the walk to her car and then for most of the drive back to her place until she said, so you want to help me clean my kitchen?

Mark was rewatching *Eternal Sunshine* when we got in. This movie really got to me, he said later.

Megan put on the Yeah Yeah Yeahs. I did the dishes and the counters while she got the floor and Mark eviscerated the fridge. She and Mark started catching up to me with the rum. It was nice. We got in a groove. I started singing and I realized my range had gotten higher from talking in my female voice. It's nice to hear you sing again, Megan said. Cool, yeah, you have a good voice, said Mark.

Aw, you guys, you're really sweet, I said. That's really, *really* sweet. I got emotional saying this. I hadn't sung in a long time.

I felt awkward after that so I said do you have any beer? I'd been drinking water and was starting to feel less sloshed.

That rum was the last of the booze, Megan said.

Daaaaaamn, I said.

We kept cleaning and then Mark said hey, I'll be right back. He was gone for ten, fifteen, twenty minutes and then came back ruby-faced and holding a twelve-pack. I hugged him and told him he was my new best friend. Then I wrote NEW BEST FRIEND: SOPHIE on his arm with a Marks-A-Lot. He laughed for a long time after I did that. We finished cleaning and sat around the kitchen table, drinking and talking and bullshitting. Megan kept the music going. She and I bumped legs under the table and kept them there. Mark mentioned something about an ex-girlfriend while telling a story and I drenched myself in the "pretty" compliment all over again. After an hour Mark stood up and said goddamn I need to lie down, and he wobbled off to his room.

Megan went to the living room, then came back with Mark's pipe and the Altoids tin. Haaaaa, she said. You wanna smoke a bowl?

You sure? I said. Megan was a serious pothead before she quit. Quarter-ounce-a-week serious. I once saw her make a bong with a Gatorade bottle.

She waved her hand. I'm fine, she said. I can cheat once for an old buddy. That's not bad, is it?

I wasn't sure if it was bad or not, but smoking sounded too fun so I said let's do it. She turned around to walk and crashed against the fridge. Ho shit, I'm hammered, she said. I laughed and helped her up, then fell against her.

We went to her room and got good and baked and watched *So You Think You Can Dance Canada*. Megan got two cans of ketchup-flavoured Pringles from her closet. We were at the bottom of the first can when I started laughing every time the French judge said something.

Duuuuuuude, I've totally forgotten how the Québécois speak, I giggled. Kay-bec-wahhhh.

You! Megan said. You are a fucking Yank now! You're like George W. Bush with a machine gun, and, like, a baseball glove. Filled with apples.

Quiet! You! I said, almost laughing too hard to form words. I can send a fucking tank up here! I'll do it! Do you think I'm fucking joking?! She laughed so hard that tiny triangles of Pringle landed on her blankets and she slapped me playfully and said shut the fuck up. Then she didn't take the hand away, she kept it resting on the skin of my stomach and started rubbing it, even as we both turned our heads back to the screen. You're so soft, she said. I put the tips of my fingers on her arm. She turned her head to face me. We kissed, not in a furious or hard way like the last time, but slow, savouring—slow enough that I could feel the glide of the white-soft hairs on her cheek. She slid her hand over my face and whispered you are so fuckin' pretty. I shivered and whispered thank you, thank you, God I missed you. I had missed her. She put one hand on my hip and the other on my shoulder, then seamlessly pushed me down into the mattress while sliding her right leg over mine. She sat up straddling me and her blue hair blended with the TV light—her head looked like it was bleeding blue, blue falling in disconnected rays down her shoulders and her white cotton shirt. She leaned down and kissed me harder, running her hands up and down the length of my sides, and then her fingers were hovering above my right nipple.

Can I? she asked softly.

Yes! I whispered.

She smiled pertly, lifting an eyebrow. Are you sure.

God please Megan—

She twisted my nipple and my head hit the mattress and I cried, *Hanh*, that noise resembling a goose honking. *Hanh*. Harder, I said, right before she put her hand over my mouth and said: Quiet. I strained against her with a fraction of my strength and felt all of her muscle push me down.

Then she twisted again. Harder? she said. Yeah?

Hanhhh—my voice came muffled through her fingers.

We were down to our underwear when I slid my hand past her belly button, into her panties, and she put her hand on mine and said here. Stop. She placed my hand by my side and then put her hand in my underwear and said mmm, I see this is still here.

Sometimes, I said timidly.

Hmmm, she whispered. She started touching me lightly, two fingers sliding up and down my atrophied penis. I whimpered. She was really good at this. I put my arm under her and kissed her neck.

After a minute or two, though, Megan started looking frustrated. She started jerking harder. She looked unhappy. Are you okay? I asked. She stopped, flinging her arm back to her side. So what's wrong, she said, do girls just not do it for you anymore?

What? I said. No, it felt really good. What do you mean?

It had felt good, but I knew what she meant, I hadn't even gotten half-mast. Hell, third-mast. That's been the deal for a while. Even when I orgasm on my own, which isn't often, it hasn't gotten all the way up in a long time.

No! I protested. It felt good, it felt really good, you're amazing, I said desperately.

I didn't feel anything from you, she said.

It's the estrogen, I said. It makes it really hard to get hard. It never happens like it used to anymore.

She looked really discouraged, then she raised her eyebrow and said well I guess I'll have to do something you haven't been used to in a while. She kissed me and then kissed my chin.

Oh, I said, and then I didn't want her touching that part of me, I hated how she talked about it. Like if my dick didn't seem happy then I couldn't be. I wanted to have my hand inside her, making her come, I wanted to sleep with her chest against my back, I wanted to lift her off of me and say my penis isn't me. Her kisses reached my belly button. She took my cock in her hands.

No, I said.

Shhhhhh, she said.

No, I said, more forcefully. She took it in her mouth and my head was on the mattress again. *Hanh.*

Then I said but. Just but, in this feeble voice. She reached a hand up and put a finger on my lips. It felt male and unnatural but my nerves had exploded in crossed wires of black pleasure and my dick inflated like it never had since estrogen entered my body. I moaned no, no, God, yes, no, fuck. My hands curled around her bedposts and I slid into my booze-and-pot haze, pressed further into her mattress and back, back into maleness, back into boyhood, I travelled years into the past and remembered Leon, saw his body again through my eyes, breathed in his throat and left quarter moons in his palms,

I grunted and groaned through his deep, rolling voice and said oh fuck, God I fuckin' love it.

Megan took her mouth off me and smiled and said yeah? Hmmmm. Yeah? I was ice pick hard now. A condom appeared in her hand, and she said Sophie, Sophie, oh my baby, Sophie.

And then I was back, Leon like a malevolent imp hovering on the bedpost. Exhumed but not gone. Oh, I said. No. No, I'm sorry Megan. No.

Shhh, she said. Sophie, I got you, baby.

No, I said. Stop.

Shhh, she said. I'm gonna take care of you.

Stop, I said. She put her mouth on my cock again. The crossed-wire pleasure surged and I sat up and scooted backward. No! I said. Please! My mouth and eyes scrunched up. Please! I'm sorry! I can't.

She looked at me with bloodshot, frightened eyes. You can't? Did I—

I can't, I said. I'm sorry.

She bowed her head. I could only see her tangled blue hair. Then she looked up hurt, furious. No, she said. I'm sorry, don't *worry*, I won't *bother* you again tonight. I think she was about to cry. She whacked ineffectively at the Pringles shards on the bed and yanked the blankets over her as she lay down.

I put my clothes on and sat on the floor, hugging my knees. Scattered tears slipped out of my eyes. I'd trusted Megan.

I sat there crying for a while, my head between my knees. After a bit I looked up at the empty space next to her on the bed. I was so tired but I couldn't get into bed because if I even accidentally touched her again I didn't know what I would do. I thought of the couch out in the blackness of the living room, and if she would bother to wake me up before she was gone.

Earlier that afternoon, Mom had gone out on an errand and I'd gone in her bathroom for cosmetic pads. Her old tape deck was on the counter. I leaned over and read the label through the window of the player: *Leon Choir Christmas 2001.*

I had a solo in that one. I hadn't sung for a long time; I was a bass and I got too self-conscious. My mom and Megan had both said, always, that they'd loved hearing me sing. They both came to that concert, when I was in Grade 10. The two of them sat in the third row and cheered when I had my solo and we all went out to Earls afterward. Megan had just dyed her hair shiny black and my mother started telling her how to keep the colour in. And then Megan kept my mother laughing and she even ordered a few glasses of wine and Megan had to drive her home, the only time I've seen Mom need to call on a DD. They really got close that night. Megan kept asking about what I was like as a little boy and Mom told her I'd built forts behind the couch with blankets and pillows and laid down covered and cramped for hours, and I made patterns on my bedroom wall with boogers. Megan clapped and laughed and asked for more and somewhere in the night I stopped being embarrassed and propped my face up with my hands and elbows on the table and listened to the two of them go on in the booth as they moved on to talking about religion, piano lessons, tampons versus pads. I drank glass after glass of Dr Pepper and listened to them bust each other up. It was like watching the daughter and mother neither of them had. Or thought they didn't have. When Mom and I got home, her still tipsy, she said you've known Megan for a year now, right? And I said yup, and she said: I think she loves you.

Megan did love me. And I have always loved her. She was the only person in high school who knew I was a girl and one night when I was sixteen and called her at two in the morning she said to me, Leon. Leon. One day everyone will call you Sophie. And I'm going to be so fucking proud of you when they do.

We never did want anything romantically from each other. The other time we had sex was just because we were high. But my mom always wanted us together. Megan was the only friend of mine she ever really trusted. Mom asked about her again today, at dinner. She asked if Megan had gotten the Safeway gift card she'd sent her for Christmas. Mom gives her one every year.

Eventually I got up and looked outside. An old woman was carefully plodding through a parking lot in heels, leaving stiletto heel and sole marks in the snow. We were two floors up but I could hear the crunch of her shoes. I looked through Megan's closet and took a stretchy bright-purple shirt before leaving.

Mark? I said, tapping on the door. He opened it and a cloud of weed smoke blew out after him. Woah, hotbox galore, I said. He grinned sheepishly. Hi, he said.

Hi. Megan went to sleep so I came here, I said.

Oh cool, he said. His room was mostly bare. There was a poster of *Ghost World* beside his dresser and his cello was lying on the floor along with a few books and a pair of shoes. I bent down to look at his bookcase but only noticed a Studs Terkel collection before losing my balance. I fell onto the bed and burped.

Excuse me! I said, embarrassed. I looked down and saw the same green-and-black blanket he'd given me the other night. Mark, your blanket is awesome, I said.

Oh thanks, he said. He sat on his desk chair and smiled awkwardly.

The hell are you doing over there? I said, lying on my side, my face almost buried in the bed.

What? he asked, his face in a stupid hardened smile.

Come here, I said into the bed. He did and I sat up and took his face in my hands. I thought of the sluiced confidence with which Megan had gripped me and laid me down. Do you want to kiss me? I said brightly. We made out messily, wetly. I'd made out with boys a few times before I transitioned, but it was different now. I liked this more, the smoothness of my body melted into the roughness of his. I kissed him hard. He worked his hand up under my shirt. I realized I didn't know if Megan had told him. I hadn't wanted to ask. I never liked finding out that I didn't pass.

Hey, um, there's something you should know about me, I said.

I know, he said softly. It's okay. I think you're wonderful.

I'm sorry, I said, feeling stupid.

Don't be, he said, kissing me suddenly and ferociously. You. Are. So. Beautiful. Don't. Be. I thought he was going to rip through my teeth with how hard he was talking and kissing, and I kissed him harder and said thank you thank you thank you thank you and took off his shirt. I felt for his dick and he stuttered, seized up, moaned. It felt nice to hold, it felt nice to worry about somebody else's dick. He started getting hard and holy shit Jesus, he was big, like really big.

God, you've got the fucking Chrysler Building down there, I said. He blushed and smiled and said well thank you. I kissed him and gave an extra hard tug and he gasped.

Soon all the clothes were off again. He reached into my underwear and I pushed his hand away.

No? he said.

I stopped stroking and rested my hand on the tip of his foreskin. No, I said firmly.

Oh, he said, looking sad. Okay. I just—

No, I said. No. No. No. He looked sadder.

I'm sorry, he said.

Well, I said. Maybe. I started stroking in fits and starts. Maybe, I said, maybe it depends (stroke) on how hard (stroke) you can fuck me (stroke). So (stroke). We'll just have to see (stroke) how much of a (pause, stroke) man you are, and we'll (stroke) see (stroke) what I can be for you. He convulsed and kissed me and pulled down my underwear.

I didn't care that I hated the words I was saying, and I didn't care that I was lying and that I would never let him near my dick. I refused to give up what I thought was my power and I didn't care what I had to do to keep it. I wanted him to split me open. I reached onto the floor to grab Megan's condom out of my pants, then I kissed his cock and unrolled the rubber. I took his shoulder and guided him to a standing position, then said lube? He said oh wait! He wheeled around to open a dresser drawer, his wrapped penis boomeranging with him, and came up with a small full bottle from a brown paper bag. I smiled and bent over his bed, then found out that that didn't work. I was too tall and the bed was too short. It only came up to my knees. I looked at him and laughed. Your bed sucks, I said. He looked concerned. Desk? he asked. I turned around and swept everything off. Notebooks and sheet music and Wunderbar wrappers swirled over his floor as I bent over. I heard him lube up and felt him pushing his dick around the inside of my cheeks, trying to get inside.

For some reason, it only struck me then how short he was; I had at least six inches on him. In my head, I saw this short skinny boy fitting his huge wang into this tall tall girl's behind and it seemed pathetic but in this lovely, wonderful way. I put my head down so my hair brushed the desk and giggled to myself really softly.

Then he got in. I gasped, a deep, shuddering, guttural gasp. I thought it sounded really male and I worried about it fleetingly but I don't think Mark heard it. I breathed hard and groaned. It felt so painfully, jarringly good. I gripped the corners of his desk and moaned yes, oh God, pull my hair. What? he said. Pull my motherfucking hair! He gathered a handful and drew his arm back. I gasped again, face toward the ceiling. For a few minutes I did nothing but concentrate on him inside me on the bottom and pulling me on top, saying Mark, Mark, God you feel so good. I felt only him and the coolness of the desk on my hips and I didn't think or feel anything else.

Then I started to get sore. He was really going for it.

Hey, slower, I whispered, and I think he really tried, for a minute or two, at least.

Twenty Hot Tips to Shopping Success

(Hint: Love Your Outfit, Love Yourself!)

1) Decide on the store where you will be shopping. The best ones are either large second-hand thrift stores like Buffalo Exchange, or midrange mall department stores like Old Navy. Someplace where the employees will be too bored, high, or pretentious to bother you with assistance. Avoid higher end places even if you can afford them; they're too small and their employees are too annoyingly helpful for any reasonable sense of anonymity. Similarly, avoid bargain basement boutiques even if you're dirt poor and have to save up for the thrift store, as you will perish under a stampede of price-savvy single moms while you fatally pause, attempting to figure out if you're a size 16 or a size 18.

2) Arrive outside the store. Casually peer inside. Walk around the block and/or mall floor. Rub your arms nervously. Repeat a few times. This will build your confidence.

3) Go home. Particularly if you are in a mall. Any security guard watching you will think you are casing the joint, and not only that, but doing an awful job of it. Dig through the cupboard for some noodles and a jar of Prego alfredo sauce. Lift the jar up and put it back down. Decide you will never fit into the clothes you desire with habits like these. Take out some whisky instead. Pour a double shot into a tall glass with some Diet Coke. Have a few of these. Convince yourself you probably never really wanted women's clothes anyway. Maybe it was just a phase. Stagger into your clueless roommate's bedroom and challenge him to wrestle. Lose. Go to bed.

4) Wake up in the late morning with renewed determination. Go to the store immediately. Discover an intense hunger en route. Get a burger.

5) Arrive again in front of the store entrance. Pop half a Xanax. What the hell, pop another. Glide into the store on a cloud.

6) Look at the skirts section. There will be women there who appear at ease, or at least they will to you. Feel a rather bloated maleness. Finger the last Xanax in your pocket.

7) Go to the women's pants section. Decide this will be a way to ease into this mysterious part of the store. Try to figure out your size. Remember that sizes on women's clothing seem to follow no rooted

system of measurement. Grab a bunch of different sizes of jeans, as well as a pair of Dickies. Scurry into the dressing room.

8) Find that none of the pants fit except for the biggest size. (The Dickies in particular give your legs and belly the appearance of a smokestack belching out a melted gumball.) Look at yourself in the mirror. Decide that even the pants that fit look terrible. Go back into the store. The skirts section will now look appropriately inviting.

WARNING: DO NOT UNDER ANY CIRCUMSTANCES GO TO THE DRESS SECTION. DO NOT LOOK AT THE DRESS SECTION. DO NOT THINK ABOUT DRESSES. MEN GATHER FAT IN THEIR BELLY, WOMEN IN THEIR BUTT AND THIGHS; THEREFORE, SKIRTS WILL BE THE EASIEST FOR YOU TO PULL OFF. THERE'S ALSO THE BROAD SHOULDERS FACTOR. SO STOP LOOKING AT THE FUCKING DRESSES, UNLESS ONE OF THE FOLLOWING THREE APPLY: A) YOU ARE TINY OF FRAME AND WEIGHT (IN WHICH CASE STEP 8 MAY NOT APPLY TO YOU; ALSO, YOU ARE AN ASSHOLE); B) YOU ARE RICH IN SELF-ESTEEM; C) YOU HAVE A LOT MORE XANAX IN YOUR POCKET.

9) Stride over to the skirts section. Be bold. Hold your head up. Summon some classic male entitlement. You are a Paying Customer. See a clerk's head turned slightly, looking at you. Feel your throat close up. Say "*Huuurk!*" Retreat to the men's pants section. Feel simultaneously comforted and bored by the sizes that follow a rooted system of measurement.

10) Leave the store. Take the last Xanax.

11) Devise short yet complex stories in case someone asks you why you're trying on women's clothes. Enjoy this step. Be creative. "My girlfriend and I are the same size, and I want to get her something nice," or maybe, "Well, I'm a clothing designer, actually, and I think men need to really *feel* the clothes if they're going to design them to be worn. This is part of my job, actually."

12) Weigh the ludicrousness of these statements. Sigh. Go back into the store and check out some skirts. Don't look up. Concentrate intensely. Hope fellow patrons think you are a store employee examining merchandise. Attain a deep seriousness. Discover you have terrible gas. Regret that burger even more than you already have.

13) Find something you think is nice. A brown, soft cotton knee-length thing that will drape in a flowing, subtle manner on your body, maybe, swishing around over a pair of tights, perfect on a cool fall day. Or something white, made out of impossibly thin fabric, with bright-green flowers and green lines running along the sides, narrow at the top and widening out to just below the knee, like something you might have seen a girl wear to the park in high school, sitting cross-legged and laughing with the skirt barely draping her knees, while you sat in huge jeans that seemed to billow around your legs, perspiring in a thin sweatshirt (you've never liked showing your bare limbs), feeling that clumsy bloatedness again. Watching the skirt's thin white zipper sway by her right hip as the lower inch of the skirt flutters in a light breeze, looking with a confused, implacable desire that only much later did you recognize as envy.

14) Anyway, find something like that. Take it to the registers. Pick up a pair of black socks on the way. You will not be sure why, but it will make you feel better. Try to pick the cashier who seems most disinterested in her general surroundings. Ask rapidly if you can have a bag. Find that the bag is already clutched in your hands. Run out.

15) Go home. Take the alfredo sauce out of the cupboard. Boil some water. Find your roommate playing video games. When he asks what you were out doing, laugh with exaggerated hysteria and tell him you were nailing chicks. Such banter is unusual for you. If your roommate comments on this, inform him that he is a fag.

16) Lock yourself in your room. Strip down to your underwear. Look at your blue plaid boxers. Every young man in America seems to own boxers just like these. Take them off too. Look at the skirt. Catch a glimpse of your body in the mirror. It looks dirty. Go take a shower. Wash every part of your body carefully. Decide to shave your armpits for the first time. When you're done, do your legs too. Get up to the top half of your thighs before the hot water runs out. Discover a small number of cuts and rashes when you towel off. But other than that, enjoy the smoothness. Don't look in the mirror. It's not helpful. Depending on how strongly you feel about this whole thing, it may very well not be helpful for a long time. Run your hands up and down your legs in the still-steamy room.

16a) Your roommate may inquire, "The fuck are you doing in there, watching *Lord of the Rings*? I'm about to take a shit in your closet!" while pounding on the bathroom door. If this is the case, remind him of the fact that he is a fag.

17) Get back into your room. Without underwear, step into the skirt. Slide it up your legs and zip up the side. Walk around. Let yourself even twirl, perhaps. Fall back on the bed. Get up again. Sit down cross-legged. Admire the spot where the skirt meets your shaven knee. Think about going out like this. Be afraid. Put your head in your hands.

18) Hear your roommate knock on your door. "Hey man? I ate your noodles and your alfredo sauce. I'm sorry. I was hungry. We can go for burritos if you want. My treat."

19) Open the door. See his eyebrows bounce in surprise. Tell him, "That sounds great. I gotta change though." See him nod. Come back out in a T-shirt and jeans. Hear him say, "You've seemed kinda shaken up the last couple days." Nod.

20) Get to the burrito place. Order. Think about underwear. Think about those stupid boxers. Wonder if you could try on a friend's bra to figure out your size. Ponder whether you have the guts to do that. Decide you can probably at least buy some underwear. You can do that. Receive your burrito. It smells delicious.

How Old Are You Anyway?

The weird thing was that Lisa could never remember her age.

As in when the men on the cam site asked in text chat, she'd tab over to check her profile, then type *24* and be done with it. Though a couple times she was asked live on cam, and she had to pretend it was some airhead-cute brain fart while she discreetly tabbed over again. She felt dumb about that. *Even the ditziest of girls don't forget their age, dumbass.* When she'd started, she hadn't even been sure what age to put. She was twenty-seven but what was the lowest she could get away with onscreen: Twenty-four or twenty-three? Twenty-five seemed ancient (for the site) and twenty-two seemed like, *no way anybody's going to believe that.*

But besides all the dudes wanting free stuff, the work itself was mostly pretty easy. They wanted her to humiliate them and talk about shoving her cock down their throats and see her come. Funny thing, though: They all claimed to want to be dominated. But they never really wanted to be told what to do. Tonight she'd earned thirty bucks in one go calling a man a worthless piece of garbage shit slut whore while miming fucking her laptop, and after he came and she obediently set about brewing an orgasm, he got aggravated she couldn't do it instantly: *Come ON jerk off faster bitch*, he'd said.

And then, with the guy after that, again with forgetting her age.

She did one more show then logged off for the night and changed into pyjamas. She cranked the knob on the radiator then opened the window and lit a cigarette. Her cock throbbed as she smoked and she reached for some vitamin E lotion. She hated that part. She could get into character and such on cam, but the reminder and pain of her pulsing junk afterward was—well, at the least, it was annoying.

Outside someone was yelling and brushing snow off their windshield. She shut her eyes and stretched her arms. She, herself, liked being told what to do. Though it'd been a while. She moved a hand to her nipples and pinched them. She tried to picture someone squeezing them or holding her down but she couldn't focus. When she finished her smoke, she rolled over and went to bed.

Sometimes this winter if she stayed up really late she'd wake up just before it got dark again. The sun went down so fast in this city. Day to day, she usually only left her building right before she started work, and these months Lisa could go days without being outside in light. She'd usually get a king can from the vendor on Sherbrook, and a lot of days it was the only time she went out. It worked out okay. She didn't have many friends who hadn't been her ex's around here, and she was fine with it. She'd never much liked being around people. Even before she transitioned and they started not liking her back. She was fine with being alone and fine with the cold and fine with the tiny minutes of sunlight she got a day. For now she was absolutely and totally fine.

One day she was getting her mail in the hallway and saw a woman lugging a package up the front steps. Lisa opened the door for her and the woman said thanks. Lisa didn't recognize her. She looked late thirties and was very tall, had burnt-red hair and a face that appeared icy and scared, like a bird under glass. Lisa was drawn to her like a kitten. She said hello, and the woman blinked and opened her mailbox and didn't respond.

And Lisa actually kind of liked that, because some people were so goddamn polite in this city you had no idea if they hated you or not. It had been like that with her ex. Lisa'd had no clue how hated she actually was.

Did you just move in? Lisa tried again. I'm Lisa. The woman looked up for a flash, said, I'm Tam, and left.

That night it got down to forty below. After Lisa logged off, she boiled water then threw it off the back fire escape. She wanted to see if it'd make ice before hitting the ground like she'd always heard it would. But she couldn't really tell; it all looked the same hitting the snow. Fuckin' Jesus! someone yelled.

The next day she went to the vendor early, around five-thirty. It wasn't as cold out but it was completely dark and the streets were glaring ice. She was trying to light a smoke when she saw her ex's cousin in the parking lot. The one who was from … Altona, that was the name of her town. Lisa'd forgotten her name but she remembered the town. It was the cousin her ex figured was probably drinking in basements every night and maybe maybe here's hoping was a dyke. Basically the one cousin her ex had hope for. (Her ex had a lot of cousins.)

She thought about saying hello but then Lisa saw the cousin pointing in Lisa's direction and laughing and saying something to her friends. Lisa instantly turned and went around the corner and walked back up Sherbrook to her building. The cousin could've been laughing at anything, Lisa knew. She probably didn't even recognize her, winter clothes bundling and all. But still she was like *whatever, not worth it, who cares.*

There was still rush hour traffic she could see over on Maryland. That always startled her when it was this dark.

She wasn't exactly minding the long nights in winter—but she had liked how things were in summer. She'd started camming in June, after her ex had moved out, and when she'd take a break around ten-thirty the sun would still be making purple and orange through her curtains and on her bed. (Her bed was beautiful, a faux wrought-iron frame and cherry headboard; it was the one thing she'd splurged on this last year.) She would hear guys playing basketball over in the park, then kids drinking on the playground when the bars let out. And that was nice. It jibed with her. Like it felt as if she was still just enough part of the world.

Back in her apartment, she cracked the king can and decided she'd start work early tonight. Like what would it matter if she got on at six instead of eight. Maybe she'd get some new customers and maybe she'd even be done early. So she gave it a try and they were all the worst. Every guy either wanting stuff for free or ass-to-mouth, getting pissy when she tried to sweetly say: Sorry honey, no, or: Sorry honey, not until we're in private together—and they'd type, *who do u think u are. idiot.* She could usually handle that stuff okay, like whatever, because they balanced with the nice ones, but every guy tonight was like that. Toward the end one guy wanted her to take off her panties and stick every bit of them up her ass. She had them almost all the way in when he logged off. She wore a fancy kind with lace and bows; it hurt pulling them out.

Somehow she ended up with a lucrative night though, and when she checked numbers at ten-thirty she was over a hundred and fifty bucks. She logged off and dressed and went right out and up Portage to the liquor store that was open late, picked up a mickey of CC and had one of those nights, stumbling between every part of her apartment from bedroom to living room to kitchen to washroom and laughing to herself for no real reason and rubbing a pound of cream into her scarlet dick and accidentally breaking her special whisky glass and crying intensely exactly once and watching video after video on YouTube and refreshing Facebook fifty times and trying to clean up the glass then trying to read and eventually falling asleep with her broom in the doorway.

She was about to start work the next night when she smelled her ex. Nothing triggered it, no old piece of clothing or anything. It was suddenly there as if Natalie had just left the room. Lisa lay back instantly and Natalie's face appeared, suspended in midair, her eyes blank and her sandy hair bobbed and small.

Natalie used to sit on her in the mornings. She would roll over and straddle Lisa's hips and pin her arms up. It wasn't a prelude to sex but it wasn't just nothing either.

Natalie touched her face, stroked her arms, kissed her eyes and the bridge of her nose. Lisa breathed in sharply and deep. She let Natalie press her lips on her face. She arched her back and tilted up her head, her skin fuzzed.

She opened her eyes and saw the empty ceiling. *Oh Jesus.*

Her lips retracted. She tried not to cry. She succeeded. The smell was still there. *Okay stop,* she thought to herself. *Work. Start work. No. No, not now. Start work later. Just a few minutes later. Do something else first. Leave the bed. Absolutely get off the bed. The mail! You need to get the mail.* Getting the mail seemed like a responsible thing that was both important and emotionless and very doable. Hastily she tucked her dick and threw on a sweater and some baggy jeans.

Downstairs, a dude and a girl were coming inside with bags of beer as Lisa was flipping through her mail. The air that followed them was so cold and unexpected that her body spasmed and she dropped her cheque.

Sorry, the dude said. He picked it up.

Lisa blanched. She had this sudden thought that they could see through her clothes, and her mind went *shit my fuckin' slut-ass WORK outfit and my DICK*—but then the guy said heyyyyy! You live upstairs from me, hey?

Lisa said nothing.

Number 30? the guy said.

She nodded and the guy said well hey then, I'm Miles. He had a beard and sunglasses and one of those thick Canadian accents that Americans always failed at imitating. I'm Lisa, she said.

He reached out his hand and shook it gently. Hey, I dunno if you drink or whatever, but I guess we got some people over, you wanna come up and have a beer?

Oh, Lisa faltered. I—thanks, but I gotta work, she said.

Whaaat? It's nine o'clock! said Miles. Oh, you're probably in school, hey. I bet you're smart. You look smart.

What? Lisa said. No. I'm. I'm—

Miles was smiling at her and the other girl was looking kind of bored.

Well, I did make a lot of money last night, she thought. And as much as she liked her hermithood—it probably wouldn't exactly hurt to make neighbour friends. She didn't have to stay long. Fuck it. What's your apartment? Lisa said. I'm just gonna go change.

Miles's face scrunched. Change? he said. C'mon, you don't need to change, you look great. Miles nudged the other girl. Doesn't she look great?

Yeah! the girl said. Definitely! It was like she sounded enthusiastic and bored at the same time.

See? Miles said. Don't get so down on yourself, now. You're beautiful.

Lisa almost laughed when he said that. Not because she didn't believe he thought it. She did. That was just it. She could feel how much he thought his words mattered. Thanks, said Lisa. I'll just be right back down.

But then the guy kept going at it. I see you got some makeup on, he said. Don't tell me you're gonna put on more, and that sweater? That's a great sweater! Who cares if it's not skin-tight or whatever; I don't! Do you know something? Can I tell you something? I was talking about this with a buddy the other day: The most beautiful women I know, the most gorgeous women you've ever seen, all of them hate how they look, fuckin', they all think they gotta spend an hour in the bathroom I guess. But they're beautiful. And you're beautiful. It kills me you all just don't see how beautiful you are. Hey?

Even though Lisa was internally rolling her eyes, there was a time when she'd said those same things to her own lady friends. In high school mostly, before she figured out her own stuff. It was the most surreal thing to hear those thoughts regurgitated. Like, she'd not only forgotten she used to think that, she'd forgotten some guys thought like that at all. That idea. Like if everybody just always wore big comfy clothes then everyone would feel okay.

Thanks, Lisa said blankly. Okay, let's go. She didn't have it in her to argue. She followed them up to the second floor and down the hall.

And then in Miles's apartment: There was Natalie's cousin. She didn't see Lisa because they walked in right as she tried to shotgun a beer in the kitchen, and she fucked it up and spray went everywhere. Awww Jesus! Miles yelped. And instantly Lisa was backing out the door and stammering, I left—some water—boiling—I'm sorry, I forgot ... She knew it sounded dumb but she was already closing the door behind her. It was a bad idea. Of course it was a totally bad idea. She should've just gone home.

Then her mind started doing backflips. What if she'd just drawn more attention to herself? Fuck, the cousin probably didn't even fucking see her! And something Natalie always said, coming to Lisa now like a loud TV from another room: *Come on, it's the city, it's 2014! No one gives a shit, Lisa! I know you've had some bad experiences but I seriously think you also have some paranoia to deal with.*

Lisa?

Adrenalin filled her and she spun around and there was the tall woman from the mailboxes. (Tam? Tam.)

Hi.

Tam was wearing a fitted black cocktail dress. It was sleeveless and Lisa could see cascades of freckles up and down her arms. And she was wearing brown nail polish that was chipping.

What happened, said Tam.

Huh?

Tam pointed behind herself, back to Miles's place. I was in there.

Oh.

There was silence for a second. I had to leave, said Lisa.

That's a shame, Tam said.

Lisa smiled. It is, she said.

Going home?

Yes.

Tam coughed then said, well then, uh, may I walk you to your door?

Lisa cocked her head. Once, many years ago, she'd had a friend who'd just kissed her out of the blue without warning. She kind of felt now like she did then. Like she was too surprised to know what to make of it. And this time too part of her felt fear—real fear, scared for immediate well-being fear—and she didn't know why. But she felt herself pushing it down and beckoning Tam to follow her anyway, through the hallway and up another flight of stairs.

You know Miles well? Lisa said awkwardly as they walked down her floor. Her baggy jeans and sweater felt like tents.

He's my nephew, said Tam.

Oh, said Lisa.

We're only fifteen years apart, she said quickly, in a way that made her veneer slip a little.

Ah, said Lisa. What do you do?

I work for the city. In water. Tam made a gesture with her hand that said *and you?*.

I don't do much, Lisa said.

They were at her door. Tam coughed again. Well, she said. This is probably the part where, if you'd like to, you invite me in.

Lisa smiled and felt electricity in the small of her back. She gazed up at the taller woman. Her balance shifted to one side of her body and she felt her mouth grow small. She was still kind of scared, but compartmentally so, like she knew at this point she was going to just ignore it and ride 'til the end.

I would like to invite you in, she said. Just wait here, for a second, if you would? I'll be back in just one second.

Tam nodded. By all means, she said.

Lisa went into her apartment and straight to her bedroom. She closed the laptop that was still open to the cam site and stowed her toys back under her bed. She turned on the lamp in the living room and turned off the overhead light and the floorboards of the entrance-way receded into dark. Her body was crackling for her to drop the baggy jeans and the sweater but Lisa kept them on. Her brain was jumping like a small animal.

My water's stopped boiling, she said when she opened the door.

Huh? said Tam, then walked in and cast her eyes around. Nice place, she remarked. Lisa snorted.

Tam saw an ashtray in the living room. You smoke in here, she said.

Yeah, Lisa said, embarrassed.

I'd like a cigarette then please, if you wouldn't mind, Tam said.

Oh, Lisa said. Well yes, sure.

Lisa retrieved two smokes and gave them to her. She lit Tam's then lit her own. Tam blew smoke toward the ceiling. You're not from here, are you love, Tam said.

Nope, Lisa said. I grew up in Ontario.

Toronto?

Sarnia.

Not a lot of people here from that far in Ontario.

Nope, Lisa said bitterly. She got her ashtray and Tam extended her smoking hand to tap as Lisa was holding it.

What brought you here? Tam asked.

Ex-girlfriend.

Ah. I'm sorry. Tam nodded and didn't say anything else. Lisa liked that. Tam suddenly looked fidgety and pulled the hem of her dress to cover her knees.

Lisa blurted that's a gorgeous outfit.

Tam looked down and examined it. Yeah? I thought so. As she bent her head, her deep red hair fell down her front and over her chest.

Lisa heard herself saying it looks really sexy on you.

Tam looked up, smiling full-toothed, bright and glowing, and she said well thank you, miss. And the way she looked at Lisa felt she didn't know where this came from but there was no other word for it—so kind, so incredibly incredibly kind, and Lisa said can I do anything else for you? only half-stifling a growl that had swelled in her throat, at the very same time that Tam cocked a big grin and said tell me Lisa, do you have any beer?

She got one for her, but when she put it in her hands just took one swallow, then set it down and kissed her.

Lisa melted into the bigger woman's arms and rushed to kiss her back, and Tam stopped and hissed no, slow.

Lisa nodded. I'm sorry, she said, and Tam said good and crushed out her smoke. Tam kissed her again and Lisa crushed out hers. Lisa closed her eyes and felt Tam kiss farther into her mouth. She felt Tam's fingernail go up her side and Tam's lips on her ears whispering: Beautiful. Lisa kissed her face, and her cheeks, and her earlobes, her neck, while Tam guided her fingernails deeper into Lisa's body and whispered, beautiful, beautiful. Her arms seized as Tam took hold of them and steered her into the armchair in the little living room, pushed Lisa down and straddled her. Tam took off Lisa's sweater—paused then grinned at her negligee, and felt a nipple through her top and twisted it just a little. Small shots of fire went through Lisa's body and she rocked on the chair. Yes? Tam said.

Yes, Lisa gasped. Tam pinched her nipple hard and Lisa heard herself make a guttural, low, chesty sound. Mmhmmm, Tam said. She pinched Lisa once more then took her negligee off. Lisa closed her eyes again and felt Tam kiss her chest, softly now, airy and delicate, raindrop kissing. Lisa could smell Tam's armpits breathing sweat and feel her thigh muscles contracting on her legs. So missy, Tam talked between kisses. I've gotten. The feeling. Since. I saw you. That you like. Pain.

Lisa nodded. I do, she said.

Tam smiled. Do you like being told what to do?

I do. But—

Tam stopped. Yes?

I just have to—I have to tell you something. I, I.

Tam waited.

God, I'm sorry, I'm just. Okay. I'm trans. Like transgender.

Tam kissed her ferociously. Who gives a shit, she whispered. She ground into Lisa and pulled her up to a sitting position, then said so then. Do you want me to tell you what to do?

I do, Lisa said hoarsely.

Are you sure? Tam said.

I am.

Are you *sure*.

I am.

Tam grabbed her hair and pulled her forward and twisted her nipple hard, *hard*, and sheets of pain went across Lisa's chest and spread through to the ends of her head and legs. Her body bucked against Tam's and her face smushed against Tam's collarbone and she could count the freckles faded into her body. Lisa could smell traces of Tam's body lotion beneath her sweat and she could feel her cheeks dampening as they pressed against Tam's skin. Tam laughed kind of maniacally and said, I *knew* it! She twisted again and Lisa felt fingernails along the back of her neck and then Tam held her body like this. Lisa strained but couldn't move. She was strong.

You're nothing, Tam said. She took Lisa's head by her hair and squeezed her flesh like it was Play-Doh. You're nothing you cunt, she whispered. She bit on Lisa's lower lip and twisted both her nipples so hard all of Lisa's muscles went slack and her vision flickered. She lost touch with her arms and her eyes and she only felt Tam's fingers on her nipples. Her mouth opened and closed like a fish in a boat. Then Tam twisted harder and no she needed to yell stop—

—and then Tam said mmmmm that hurts doesn't it, and released.

Lisa exhaled. She felt blood flooding around her body.

Tam ran her hands up and down Lisa's torso, grinding into her, but softly now. You're so sensitive, she cooed. You feel everything, don't you.

Hurt me, Lisa said.

Tam grinned.

Hurt me, Lisa said.

Tam ran her hand up Lisa's side and grabbed her hair again, brought her ear to Tam's mouth. Shut up, Tam said. Don't say anything. Don't make a single fuckin' noise. She slapped Lisa across the face and Lisa bit her mouth so tightly she thought she tasted blood. Tam slapped her left cheek, then her right cheek, then got up and beckoned for Lisa to stand. Bedroom, she said.

Lisa obediently led her in and Tam saw the bed. Nice, she said. Lie down.

Lisa obeyed.

Shut your eyes, Tam said. Stay still.

Lisa obeyed. She heard Tam unzip her dress, then move around in her room. Lisa heard a clink and then Tam straddled her on the mattress and the end of a belt went around her left arm, then through the frame, then the right arm. Test please, Tam said. Lisa moved her arms and they didn't go far. Tam laughed. Lisa's eyes were still shut. Tam jerked her forward by the hair. Don't open your eyes! she yelled. Tam stroked her right cheek for more than a few seconds, enough that Lisa relaxed her breathing. Tam slapped the cheek hard and then the other and it was like a fuzzy blanket was burning across Lisa's skin. I'm sorry, Lisa said. Tam started punching her tits, right then left. She stopped feeling the belts or the cool of the sheets and only felt Tam's fist on her tits and her mouth as her tongue and lips entered Lisa's and bit her lips and her teeth and dug her nails into her nipples until her skin felt like hot rain. They were slipping on each other with sweat and Lisa could smell the wetness of her pussy, and Tam put her hand on Lisa's throat and she started to squeeze, lightly, like she had at first with her nails.

Lips against Lisa's ears again. Open your eyes, she heard. She did, and inches in front of her was Tam's icy freckled face, her burnt-red hair, her furious eyes, her hands still over Lisa's throat. Tam leaned in close and whispered, do you trust me?

Yes, Lisa whispered.

Tam kissed into her. You look so fuckin' pretty like that, she said.

Thank you.

Tam kissed her again. Beautiful, she said. She tightened her grip. Beautiful. She articulated the word slowly and clearly. Lisa's sight was blurring and grey stars of floater light were moving across her vision. Tam's hair fell over her red-spotted face; her eyes were still ice but her smile, Lisa thought, her smile was so lovely. Tam tightened more and now Lisa almost couldn't breathe and she made a gulping noise, barely sucking in air and Tam laughed, lifted her body forward, and placed her pussy over Lisa's mouth. She ground into Lisa's lips and tongue with a hand on the bedframe and the other on Lisa's throat. Her pelvis spasmed over Lisa's tongue and her free hand slammed against the wall.

When she was done, Tam said can you hear me? Lisa's eyes flew open and her voice came fluttery.

Yes. Yes.

Tam kissed her on the forehead, untied the belts, lay down next to her, and traced the marks she'd left on the smaller girl's body. There were red crescents on her breasts from Tam's nails and dots and lines criss-crossing her skin.

Lisa lay still for a very long time with Tam's arms folded around her. She didn't kiss Lisa or try to talk or anything like that. It was nice. Then Tam touched her hand to her ass and lifted it up and slapped her lightly and the rest of the world came back to her.

That was kinda dangerous, wasn't it, Tam said later. They were still in bed, and Tam's chin rested on the top of Lisa's head.

Lisa nodded. Yeah.

Woulda made a terrible impression on the neighbours if I'd choked that pretty young girl on the third floor to death.

Lisa raised her palms up and down in a *hey what're you gonna do?* gesture.

Tam laughed. Gotta be careful, still. Hey how old are you anyway Lisa? Tam said, bemused.

Isn't that what everyone wants to know. I'm twenty-seven, she said, touching her scarring face.

Really.

You know, Lisa said, my father used to tell me you were never supposed to ask a woman her age.

That's funny.

Yeah.

They stayed silent for a few minutes and Lisa's thoughts kept drifting away. She considered when she'd have to start working the next day, if she'd still have marks and what would that mean, if and when she'd see Tam again, that she needed to clean her apartment, shop for food, deposit her cheque—

I should tell you right now, said Tam, that while I'd like to see you again, I'm not going to sleep here tonight.

Oh that's fine, Lisa said instantly. I'd like to see you again too. But that's fine.

Though, she realized, she didn't actually know. If she wanted Tam beside her tonight or not. Whether she wanted her bed shared or to herself.

It used to be clear to her what she wanted from her partner's body. Especially in her first years of girl puberty, as she had learned to listen to the pulse of her own. The feelings of touch that had acted as dark but clear lantern-lit maps. But right now she was feeling the traces of those directions steadily floating away. She tried to sense the nerves in her aching skin. She tried very intensely to pay attention to what she was being told. It seemed incredibly important to know this. She searched intently for the feel of her body and what it could tell her to do next, and next again. The older woman felt Lisa tense and then pull her closer.

How to Stay Friends

Go to dinner. Do not go to a coffee shop. Coffee shops are where wilting friendships enter hospice and die pathetic deaths. Go to dinner. She likes Thai.

Arrive in your orange dress at that semiclassy place in the Village where you used to go on dates. Be ten minutes late. She is not there. Get a table and order the second-cheapest bottle of wine, as always was the routine.

Stand and hug her when she comes in a pencil skirt and new purple glasses and what you swear are smaller bags under her eyes. Remember she works in a design house now. You love her outfit, and you say, "I love your outfit!" Her palms will go on the sides of her blouse and she will scan you up and down like a bookshelf. Hold still. When she says, "Not looking too bad yourself, lady!" blush. Sit down. It's been six months.

"What do you always get here again?" she asks.

"Pad see ew. I don't even know what other kind of Thai food exists." Do not remember what she gets either; it is pleasant equal emotional footing. Emphatically set your unopened menu on the side. Two men seated a foot to your right are complaining. There has been, they say, a summer re-emergence of whores in the neighborhood. One of them snorts loudly enough to sound like he's beatboxing. Cross your eyes and mimic wiping tears. She will laugh—it sounds the same as ever, short and soft, flowering and lusty; if pouring cream into coffee made a noise it would be her laugh—and she will tuck a lock of hair behind her ear.

When the waiter comes with the wine, all of you will be confused as to who is going to sample it.

When you glance at the menu before the waiter takes it you'll remember she always ordered curries.

When the silences hit, talk about your work, the huge renovated bookstore in Park Slope with the NO STRAND BAGS ALLOWED sign in the window. Leave out the anonymous missed connections ads popping up for you on craigslist in the m4t section, always with a headline that misspells your name—*Blond shemale Minurva bookstore babe*—and which continuously grow in content. Last month it was a marriage proposal, this month a threat to eliminate other potential boyfriends. Talk about hilarious co-workers instead. A forty-year-old shelver with a square beard-moustache brings weird-ass foreign snacks to share every day. "So haggis-flavored pita chips are a thing, by the way. He'll come up on the floor and shove them in everyone's face. 'Have a sheep gut Minerva, come on I got 'em on sale, don't be such a fucking *American*, huh?'" Imitate the cheerful-yet-resentful lurch his upper body makes as he walks around the store. You are great at these kinds of theatrics. She laughs and her purple glasses nudge down her nose. She will say you still got the funnies. Don't ask what this means. The men beside you share a kiss.

Her hair's no longer chin-length short but it's still coloured black. Her eyes are still sunken and her nails are still eggshell white.

When she messes up pronouns on the second bottle of wine, correct her only a few times. Be bashful and apologetic when you do. Don't sound sad or exasperated. Don't feel sad or exasperated. In a voice reserved for teaching intelligent sixteen-year-olds, she will say, "You have to understand, it's hard and it takes time. I really am trying. It's just a reality, it's very difficult for me." Listen empathetically and flawlessly. Be grateful she's expressing her feelings so honestly. Smile sadly (this is important) and say, "I know, I'm sorry," and take a sip of wine.

Let the next few slips go by. Don't escalate and don't be a nuisance. It's like letting a dad drop some f-bombs without shaking the swear jar, like not confronting your drunk roommate when he doesn't flush a shit. Wait. Swear jar. A pronoun jar! You could rattle it and say, "Quarter!" and flash a winsome goofy smile. People would chuckle and dig in their pockets and say, "Boy he's a … *she*, sorry! Ha ha! She's a hoot!" and everyone would think it was funny and it wouldn't even matter if no one had change and you wouldn't ever make anyone uncomfortable again.

When your pad see ew comes, eat it rapidly until you remember you supposedly have a new metabolism. Look down and see a bulge against your orange dress. If she is staring at you when you look back up, smile hugely and tell a joke that involves cocks. Leave the last third of your food unfinished. On the TV above the restaurant's bar, a stand-up comic you vaguely recognize is waving his arm a lot and stomping around a stage.

Share a mélange of news about old friends. Enjoy this part. A few people went back to school and some have moved in with their parents and many are working the same old shit jobs. One girl is an assistant to an editor at HarperCollins. A guy from Occupy rallies concluded he could organize workers in Mexico. A writer with suburban visions of small-town paradise moved to Iowa City. A couple is pregnant but can't afford the kid. A former co-worker can't shake blow.

As for her, she says, her job's okay. She hopes she can get promoted soon. She's saving money living in Bay Ridge and she's still playing rugby.

She will comment on your skin. She will comment on your skin a lot. She will say, "*Lady*, I would trade places with you in a *second* for that skin!" One of the men beside you snorts again as he gets up to pay, and the other man looks at him with what later you realize is intimidation.

Smile bashfully and bathe in the compliment while resisting an urge to shriek and sob. Imagine a comedy sitcom about hysterical trans women where now you would stand up, yell, "The fucking *hell* you would!" kick over your chair, chug the whole bottle of wine, punch Snorting Man as he's paying, then steal his wallet. The second episode could be about pretending to seduce the craigslist guy, then punching him and stealing his wallet.

Consider how the world would react to this if that were actually shown on TV.

Say, "Aw, thanks," and take a sip of your wine. She will smile, then frown and say, "We've gotta teach you about lipstick though. It needs to be subtler. I know you've said before you don't want to look like a drag queen, but it really is the look you're giving off right now."

Nod and say, "You're right. It's totally fine, thank you for telling me and being honest." Mean it a little, hate yourself a little, die a little.

She will look hesitant and then she will blurt, "You just look a little ridiculous with it."

Nod. Say, "Okay," and eat the rest of your pad see ew. When she offers you the rest of her curry, say no. When she asks if you're absolutely sure, say no.

When she suggests going to a bar, agree enthusiastically. An old standard is a block away and alcohol was always a consistent shared interest. Although, you *have* been drinking less in these last few months; a peaceful and dreamy drinking less, pleasantly and ethereally at odds with the clear-eyed seriousness of the term "sober." Walk along Washington Square Park in the night heat. Your orange dress gets damp, and her glasses slide down her nose. They fall off her face, but she smoothly catches them before they hit the ground. Offer a high-five. Somehow you're both kind of suddenly pleased. Tall, silhouetted figures in the dusk are throwing Frisbees, and one begins walking casually in your direction.

Flash back to bringing her to hang out with old actor friends: *Hey girl, it wouldn't be rape, just surprise sex!* You would laugh and she would look down and to the side. Stave off the rush of remembering this by thinking of cardboard or rats or mulch or pineapples until your deluged mind is elsewhere. Decide that just because there are memories you can't paper over doesn't mean there are no benefits to pretending they don't exist.

The man is closer. She walks faster and so do you. Reach the bar before he catches up.

Inside, she gets a table and you order drinks. As always was the routine. A TV above the bar is playing that same goddamn comedian and you can hear him now, and he tells a long joke about Facebook addicts and it's dumb but it's funny. Order two Yuenglings.

After you sit down and she goes into the bathroom, check your texts. Yesterday you ran into the Verizon store and changed your number for no real discernible reason. Your mother has now messaged you: *Did u get this?!* Ignore her. Check your face by taking a picture with your phone.

The picture will be grainy but you want to make the effort. You want to look good for her, for so many reasons; you want her to be proud of you, you want her to think you're beyond stunning. Your lipstick is smeared. Wipe it with a bar napkin. It only spreads. Rouge by a drunk child. The comedian on the TV bows and you can barely hear it anymore. The bar is noisy.

Wonder how other women talk with each other. It used to look so easy. Intimate. You know that's dumb. Imagine women both cis and trans telling you that is dumb. Whisper an apology to the empty table.

When she gets back, cover your cheeks and run to the bathroom. Deliberate for a few seconds, then choose the men's. There is no one in there. Lucky duck. When you get back, ask about her boyfriend. Her face will spark. "We're fucking great!" she'll say. "We drink beer and we hang out in the bathtub." Soon, talking further, she says because of him she's finally cut ties with her father. Show your warm surprise, since this is a man whose violent demise you used to envision wantonly and openly.

Her voice will hush as she talks more about her beau. They just passed their first anniversary. Eventually she will tuck a lock of hair behind her ear and say, "I even think I maybe maybe maybe want kids someday," and it will truly shock you, in the genuinely best of ways. You know more than most people just how much she never wanted kids, how she had no faith in her own motherhood, how she'd planned her tubal and it was just a matter of money. But as she talks now about the guy she seems gentle, beautiful, at peace. The look of someone you love climbing out. And you do genuinely like the boyfriend. He's unjealous and sweet, a film tech, who from all you've seen knows exactly when to take her shit and when to throw it back, an understanding of which you achieved *Challenger* levels of non-success.

Think about her plucking a Tucker Max book off your floor, the famous one, the one where he's pointing a finger at a woman without a face.

On the TV, the vaguely familiar comedian has been replaced by John Cleese, who is pretending to solicit a new wife from the audience. He looks old and his tie is stupid in a way you really like.

You had a fight over Tucker Max.

Bring up the last time you hung out. You were two months on hormones and you went dancing in Bushwick and ended the night eating gross Chinese food at four in the morning. Remind her of the guy she flirted with, the guy with the stubble and the open smile. She'll say, "Dude, that night was mega fun." It really was. No one read you as a lady, of course not, but it was an androconducive kind of place and she helped you with makeup and you both looked pretty fabulous and the crowd was great and you did an amazing dance onstage to a weird remixed version of "Sweet Transvestite" that resulted in more than a few free drinks and lots of squeezes to your stuffed bra. Tell her how much fun you had, and when she says, "Like your 'Sweet Transvestite'?" respond, "Yeah, like my 'Sweet Transvestite,'" and feel the taste of the phrase morphing in your throat, running over your tongue and the tip of your teeth as something alien, stripped of zaniness, its meanings both reset and overloaded.

You had a fight over Tucker Max.

When she asks about your mom, whatever the truth is, lie.

When she asks about the acting thing, say, "Yeah, it's going okay." Old issues of *Backstage* are growing in your recycling bin like coupon books, fleetingly considered and discarded.

When she asks about your love life, tell the story about the date who got fired the day you met and pushed noodles out of a bowl and onto the floor as you talked. It's a good story. Leave out her later demand that you eat her out under a street lamp, and how after you did she said she had a boyfriend. Take a gulp of Yuengling and say, "Not gonna see her again, not for all the hogs in the barn!" She'll laugh. She gets a charge out of your country aphorisms. She was raised in an inner suburb with a ratty yard and a mean younger brother.

Tell her no one *actually* says, "Not for all the hogs in the barn" where you're from. Add "Jeepers *cree*pers," which you did hear your grandpa say a lot. She will drain her glass, she will say, "Oh, country boy …" and her face will wrinkle with memory and look like old love.

John Cleese is proposing to a gorgeous woman with wide shoulders.

Let the moment pass. Don't be sad (you're not a boy, you're not). Don't be sad (you really did used to love when she called you that). Don't say anything. It's not a big deal, it's not, isn't it? How can it be a big deal? Your sister won't even speak to you and when you call your mother now, needing her like you never have, she only cries. And it's not like you ever made many lady friends. So. How can it be a big deal? She's been so nice. She cares about you like no one else. She does. She has such a lovely smile. It's like a knowing smirk but it's not condescending, it's like she's sharing a secret. Notice her bangs are razor straight above her brow. She used to let them grow so long. They'd fan out over her eyes as she slept. Her skin in alternating shadow and light from the cars on Eastern Parkway. Glasses of water she'd brought you on the floor beside the bed. Your legs under your chin, the side of your head on your knees.

Sometimes she wasn't actually asleep.

She would say: What?!

She would say: I love you.

She would touch your chest, move her hand, make a soft rustle in the bristles. She'd say: You're good. I mean, you're good. Here.

Grow assured of nothing but how sorry you are. Exist in gyrating states: apology and peace, apology and anger.

Cough and rotate a pepper-flake shaker. Ask, "So what made you give up contacts?"

"I dunno," she says. "I got tired of the upkeep. And glasses always seem so classy."

You nod.

One of you says, "So Bloomberg. Soda ban. Weirdest mayor ever?"

"Lady, you know what this is really going to mean? Dr Pepper speakeasies. Off the Lorimer stop."

"Yeah. Ha."

Your phone beeps with another text.

She squints at some fine print on the bar food menu.

That jacket of hers still slopes a little to the left.

Blurt out the thing about the craigslist ad. Bring up the man who followed you weeks ago to your building, or the one on the subway who yelled, *Lemme suck your dick!* or those kids, or those cops, or, or, or, or—tell her, in a whisper, that you're waking up more and more scared. Tell her you don't know what to do.

On TV the woman's making kissy lips at John Cleese, who's looking hapless and repulsed. When her kissy lips stop, her face becomes glass, unnotable, like an extra. The first comedian is back onstage, laughing, laughing his ass off.

She will exhale and her face will harden and soften at the same time, look older.

If she says, "I'm sorry," listen. If she tells you a story in kind, listen. If she says, "I wish I could protect you," hunch your knees and fold your body in and say you wish she could too. And listen. If she tells you how to use pepper spray or any such thing, small and simple and solid, listen. If she uses the teaching-sixteen-year-olds voice again, if she snorts and says, "Sure you want to do this?" if she bitterly says, "Welcome to being a woman!" if she says, "Hon, I know exactly what you're going through," swallow and shutter windows in your heart. Need her with an intensity that has no exit. Give. Give. Give. And if she says, "But, like, you're happy now … right?" say "Oh, well, of course!" Say you feel great. Say you feel better every day. She'll beam and say she misses her country boy sometimes but she's so so proud of you. You'll shine through. Smile bashfully. Say, "Aw, thanks." Look down into your Yuengling. Tuck a lock of hair behind your ear.

Lizzy & Annie

When Lizzy woke up for the first time on Annie's mattress, the first thing she registered was the carpet, a mottled brown vomitish colour that was like one of her dad's old apartments back in Keizer. She didn't remember it from last night. Come to think, she didn't remember almost anything from last night. She remembered slapping Annie across the face. She remembered asking was that okay? She remembered holding Annie down on the bed by her hair as Annie strained up, trying to kiss her. That Lizzy remembered. Not much else. Not even what Annie looked like. Wait, she was really tall. Other than that, no.

Her head felt terrible. She sat up, faltered, and lay back down. The ceiling was moving. Oh God, and she had to work today, where was she, what was—

Annie yawned, a long yawn, then turned over to face Lizzy, her eyes open. Hey, she said in a tiny voice, you're here.

Umm, yup, said Lizzy.

Annie stared at her in this instantly awake, burning, uneasy way, and Lizzy filled in the silhouette of what she remembered. She had a small nose. Sloping cheekbones. Hair that climbed up over the front of her face.

Good morning? Lizzy tried.

Good morning, Annie said, as if confirming. Do you want coffee?

Lizzy never drank coffee but she said sure, and maybe some water, too? Annie said okay, then stretched her storklike body and sat up and yawned again. She wore a heather-grey T-shirt with a model picture of the solar system and black-and-white-striped cotton shorts.

Then Lizzy realized she was full-on naked and her clit was even a little bit erect, making a semicircle in the blanket. Jesus. Her clothes? She cast around. The desk. Okay.

Annie left and Lizzy got up and put on her panties. Her dress? No. It was tight and polyester; that'd be dumb to sit in in bed. She left it on the floor. She tried to lean back on the bed with the blanket pulled up against her tits but then her stomach ratcheted up its nauseated lurch-crackling, and she moaned a little bit and slid back down. She looked around. No decorations, nothing on the walls. She checked her phone. Twelve-thirty. She had to work at two—

Shit where *was* she? She lifted her head to look out the window but only saw the back of another building. The room was big enough for her to guess Brooklyn or Queens. Her head thumped with pain and she sank back down. She spotted her hair tie lying next to the bed and put up her hair lying sideways. Her hair was short and it made a little Dr. Seuss–like tuft in the back. *Well, there's progress*, she thought.

Annie returned with two mugs of coffee. One had Beethoven's face on it and the other was a solid bubble-gum pink.

How are you feeling? Annie said.

I hurt, Lizzy said. You have ibuprofen?

Annie laughed and said yeah, hold on. She took a bottle from a drawer and shook out a few pills for each of them. *God*, Lizzy thought, *why can't I remember more?*

How you feeling? Lizzy said.

Not too bad, Annie said. A little headache. Oh, your water! Lizzy grunted. Annie left again and came back with a tall glass.

Can I do anything else for you? Annie said.

Lizzy grunted again. I'll be fine. Annie looked so awake. Lizzy wasn't sure if she could stand. Um, I actually have to leave soon, Lizzy said. I have work.

Oh no, Annie said, looking down at Lizzy, incapacitated and still largely naked.

God, get out of here! Lizzy thought. There was an awkward pause as they drank their coffee, so Annie said, where do you work?

The Lower East Side. Where do you work?

I go to school, remember? Brooklyn College.

Oh, right, Lizzy said. She did actually remember that now. She was in her second year. More silence. Her stomach started crackling again. Then Lizzy had an idea. How long's your commute? she asked.

Like, ten minutes. The 2 is right around the corner.

So we're probably in Crown Heights. So, like, forty minutes to work, and then she remembered that too—right, Annie had been talking about how she got some shit on the street here but it also wasn't too bad. Being six foot and a half helps, Annie had said. Then she'd added: Well, sometimes.

More came back to Lizzy as they talked. She remembered:

They'd been at Metropolitan, a gay bar in Williamsburg. They were both there for a reading, then they were in the same circle smoking outside, then they started ignoring the friends they came with.

Annie had grown up outside of Philadelphia. Somewhere in Delaware.

She was a vegetarian, but sometimes she really missed a bacon egg and cheese.

She was studying American history, which she liked, but her big love was sci-fi. And she loved to draw.

She was twenty-six, three years older than Lizzy. She'd spent most of her time after high school smoking weed, then moved up here at twenty-three and started transitioning.

Her parents didn't talk to her anymore except on holidays and to send out cheques from a fund her grandfather had paid into before he died. Oh, and they sent her cards on her birthday.

She'd bought whisky shots for Lizzy almost immediately after meeting her. She'd bought Lizzy a tequila shot not too much later.

She had asked Lizzy to dig her nails into her cheeks.

That's what Lizzy, in the end, could remember. In addition to the holding her down by her hair and the slapping and asking was that okay.

The coffee and water heaved out once Lizzy was on the street. She did make it five steps to a bush, and it was mostly liquid, at least. Some yells went up around her, and someone said it's called a toilet, buddy!

Lizzy sighed. She felt better though, and the ibuprofen was kicking in. Then she hit herself, hard, on the side of her head with her palm. Why had she been such a fucking hungover bitch in there?

Well, she had Annie's number; she could at least call her. She started looking for bodegas that served tea.

∽

Back in Annie's apartment, music was pounding up from the street, and Annie went to open her kitchen cupboard right after Lizzy left. On the left were stacked piles of Fiber One cereal bars, and on the right were blue packages of ramen. She took a cereal bar and made another cup of coffee with cream—two hundred calories altogether—and sat down on the bed with her computer. One o'clock. That was convenient. Only a few hours 'til dinner. She moved her hand to her nipples. They were really sore. She lay down and thought of Lizzy twisting them the night before, harder and harder until Annie's vision gave and the ceiling turned to black sparkling dots.

&

Lizzy made herself wait 'til late that night, at home, to text her. *Hey I just want you to know despite not being a human being this morning I had a great time last night. Let's talk again soon. :)*

She set the phone down and made herself not check it while she cleaned the kitchen. The roaches were back. She scrubbed the counters and did her roommate's dishes, then put boric acid down in all the cracks. Then she knocked on her roommate's door to give her shit. There was no answer, so she went back and cleaned the kitchen some more. She wiped the insides of the fridge and cleaned the basin of the dish rack.

She was scrubbing the floor when her phone buzzed. *Hey*, Annie said, *I did too. I know this is weird to say over text but it's beautiful to be touched by another body like mine. Especially one as sexy as yours.*

Lizzy leaned against the fridge and read the message again, then again. She lifted her hand up and pressed her hair against the back of her neck and thought about Annie's pinned, tear-soaked head straining against Lizzy's muscles.

Then a roach zoomed across the floor and she yelped and went into her room. She waited fifteen minutes before texting her back, *Awww thank you! The feeling's mutual, hot stuff.* She watched the message send, then threw the phone on her bed. *Hot stuff*?! she thought. But a few minutes later Annie sent back a smiley face. So hey.

∾

Lizzy worked at a discount DVD store on 4th Street and 1st Avenue, with a rotating cast of four morose boys just out of college and a friendly manager in his thirties from Montana named Tom with a brown splotch on his face.

Sausage roooolllls! said Tom, coming through the door holding a spotted paper bag. He hoisted himself behind the desk and turned to Lizzy. Lunch tag team?

Lizzy smiled. Sure.

He raised his hand. High-five? Tom said. She tittered and obliged, then walked out and got a tea and texted Annie. *Hey! Busy tonight? Want to do something?* It had been three days since the first night, which she figured was a good signal for interested but not creepy.

Her dad had called so she sat down on some benches outside a coffee shop and called him back. He picked up on the second ring and started talking about his trips to New York in the eighties. Damn! New York City! he said after a silence. Her dad said that a lot, though Lizzy'd been here for over a year. She'd lived outside Salem with him, in Oregon, for most of her life, but her dad was in Central Washington now.

And the East Village even! her dad continued. Well, it's a rough world there, son, he said jovially. Anyone'll knock a chip clean off your shoulder if you give them a chance. Watch yourself.

Lizzy waited a beat, then said, goddammit Dad.

Shit, sorry, he said. Across the street she saw one of the morose boys storm out of the store and light a cigarette.

Good, said Lizzy. Her phone buzzed and she checked quick: *Yes I do. When?*

Her dad had to go so she savoured her tea and looked down the row of benches. *Off at 10 if that's cool* she texted back. A boy who looked about twelve talked on a cellphone. No no no, Lizzy heard him say. I can't do this afternoon, I've got an appointment at four.

⁂

We're closed, dude, said Lizzy as she buttoned her coat outside the store, watching an elderly guy rattle the door.

No, you're not, he snapped. There's people in there.

And that's the manager, Lizzy said. Tom was still closing up.

The guy looked inside. Lizzy noticed he had a skullet. Like if Riff Raff from *Rocky Horror* had an ugly older brother.

I guess maybe you're right, the guy said. But how do you know?

I work here, she said.

Goddamn, sir! he said.

She sighed. I'm—

Tom opened the door, his eyes beads. Is he bothering you?

She looked at him with open eyes, considering her answer. Can you assure this gentleman we're closed? she said.

We're closed, sir, said Tom. And the man walked away.

They ended up at Metropolitan again. Lizzy lived in Harlem but she hated having people over, so whenever the question of sex rose even iridescently she liked to tilt bunking logistics in favour of the other party.

Having deliberated and erred on the side of casual this morning, she wore shorts over diamond-patterned brown tights, a purple zippered cable-knit sweater, and short black boots. Annie came in a few minutes after Lizzy sat down, wearing a long sleeveless black-and-white-checked dress that went to midthigh, black tights, and black Converse. She waved at Lizzy when she came in, then sat down and kissed her, strong but unaggressively.

Once you slept with a girl, Lizzy had always thought, you could tell how it was going to go from there by the first kiss the next day you saw her. Lizzy kissed her back hard and cupped the square of her back, and Annie's muscles slackened and she slouched into Lizzy's arms. When Lizzy opened her eyes she saw a boy in a blue hoodie staring. The boy scampered off when Lizzy saw him. Lizzy smiled at Annie.

How are you? Annie said.

Better now? Lizzy said.

Heh, said Annie. Was work okay?

Yeah! said Lizzy. It's fun. I like my job.

See, that's amazing to me, Annie said. I couldn't do that. I get nervous at jobs, period. I can't even imagine working with the public.

It's not that bad, said Lizzy.

Are people assholes?

Well, sometimes.

What about your co-workers? Annie said. Even though she was speaking pleasantly, Lizzy noticed, her voice had a seriousness that sounded like it never went away.

They're fun, said Lizzy. My boss is really cheery, he's kind of a bro but in like, the nice, innocent way? You know? There are four other guys and they're kind of annoying but they're okay. They're always really moody and they all have beards and the music they put on is really weird. Lizzy laughed. You know. They all live in Bushwick. They're fine, I guess—

I mean, said Annie, do they treat you well.

Oh. Yeah, said Lizzy. They've been shitty a few times but never in, like, the intentional way. They don't give me a hard time. And they ask stupid questions but never, like, maliciously? You know? I'm lucky.

Annie thought for a second.

Don't you find that sad?

Don't I find what sad?

That that's enough reason to feel lucky.

They went to the bar. Annie ordered whisky and Lizzy ordered red wine.

Classy, said Annie.

No, I just really like hangovers, Lizzy said.

Oh whatever! said Annie, and they sat down in a booth and Lizzy kissed her again and again and again.

My roommates are home this time, Annie whispered. And we really don't want to wake them up.

Lizzy nodded and they quietly took off their coats and boots. Annie poured glasses of water and led Lizzy by the hand into her bedroom. Annie sat down on the bed, brushed her hair out of her eyes, and took a deep swallow from her glass, looking at Lizzy over her rim.

When Annie set the glass down, Lizzy shoved Annie onto the bed and Annie squealed involuntarily, and delicately Lizzy whispered shut up, and put her palm over Annie's mouth and dug her nails in, soft at first.

Later, after Lizzy had come in Annie's mouth, Annie slid up to the head of the bed and Lizzy kissed her long, long, then put her hand on Annie's thigh and moved inward. Annie made a noise Lizzy couldn't interpret. So she said, can I touch you here?

Annie took the hand off her thigh and laid it on the bed like a place setting. No, she said.

Oh, Lizzy said. Okay.

They lay there for a few seconds, looking at the white ceiling, then Annie said, it's not you. I don't like anybody touching my cock.

It's okay, Lizzy said. Of course. I respect that. It shouldn't have bugged Lizzy as much as it did, but she couldn't help it, it made her sad. In a lot of ways.

∂

Routine got sort of natural after that. Lizzy texted her about once a week and they made plans for the following day. They'd go to a bar and then Annie's place and Lizzy would beat her up. Annie would make coffee in the morning for them to drink sitting up in bed, and Lizzy went along with it because even though it gave her the shakes, it was a nice thing to share. Sometimes Lizzy asked her if she wanted to hang out sooner than next week, and Annie would say no.

It was probably for the best in the end, especially money-wise, Lizzy figured, since she was shelling out for laser every month and Annie always wanted to go out. Lizzy did like her, she wouldn't have minded seeing her more often, but Annie had brought it up on their third or fourth date that she wasn't really super great with commitment or monogamy and all that stuff, and she got scared easily, and Lizzy had said, that's fine, I'm usually not either, in general, anyway.

She tried her best not to mention Annie to her friends, either, or her roommate or her dad. The only person she said anything to was Tom, who said to Lizzy one morning, hey, you look like you're spazzing out, are you okay?

It's this girl's coffee, man, Lizzy said, tapping her fingers on the counter. I dunno if she just makes it really strong or what.

A girl! said Tom. He punched her arm lightly. Look at you, stud, he said. She cute? And then he'd wanted to see pictures and Lizzy's face burned, and Sarah Jessica Parker walked past the store with a dog so Lizzy made a show about that and then changed the subject.

∽

Euchhh, Annie said, sitting up. Water?

Yeah, said Lizzy. She felt okay though. The hangovers were going away more quickly lately.

Lizzy's phone buzzed as Annie left the room. She got up and hopped over floor debris to her bag. It was a text from her dad. *Guy at the bar last night said something about fags and I told him to shut the fuck up because I had a big queerbag of a kid and I said I'd kill him if he said another fuckin word. I got kicked out but wish you were here we coulda taken his ass.*

Lizzy giggled and began to text back *Right on! What a cum-guzzler* and Annie came back in and said funny?

Oh, said Lizzy, Yeah, it's my dad. There was a silence so she said it's cool, I love him.

That's great, Annie said plainly. Another silence. What'd he say?

She showed the message. Oh, Annie said. Sounds like a forceful guy.

Yeah, I like that about him though. He sort of raised me. No, not sort of, he did raise me. Lizzy giggled. He's so funny, he's just this, like, overzealous Japanese man from Fresno who ended up in the hick Northwest and plays bass in a jazz band. And can never keep his mouth shut. Obviously.

They were silent. I miss him, Lizzy said.

Well, that's good, said Annie.

Lizzy shifted on the blanket. The noise of yelling and the bass from a sound system drifted up from the street. You wanna go out for breakfast? she asked.

They walked up to Prospect Heights and went to a greasy spoon that Annie liked. They had just gotten their food when Annie said shit it's my ex!

Oh no, said Lizzy. Let's duck? But she was already there, a short cis girl, soft butch, with red hair and a sweatshirt, waving.

Annie? she said.

Hey Weetzie.

Weetzie? said Lizzy.

Lizzy!

Wait, you know each other? said Annie.

Yeah, said Weetzie, But I never knew you two knew—

Yup yup yup, we do, said Annie.

What're y'all up to? said Weetzie.

By the looks of things, I'd guess we're eating breakfast, said Annie.

Cool, Weetzie said. That's awesome. She nodded for a bit, then turned to Lizzy and said hey, what'd you think of Rebel Cupcake?

It was fun, said Lizzy.

You go to Rebel Cupcake? said Annie.

Shut up, said Lizzy.

Yeah, said Weetzie. Like, I've had fun there, dude, but I feel like for a queer space it's not always a welcoming environment to trans women, you know? Or—

Yeah! That's bugged me too, said Lizzy, and at the same time Annie said yeah, and that environment actually fucking exists where?

Well, I guess it's just what I see, said Weetzie.

Yeah, that's exactly what it is, said Annie.

Weetzie was kind of unflappable so she kept talking after that, and they bullshitted a bit more. After Weetzie walked out the door, Annie said, I'm sorry, dude, but I can't stand her.

Lizzy was silent. Annie laughed. There was an extra weird energy in her that Lizzy couldn't place. Annie said really, I just hate dyke everything.

Yeah? said Lizzy. She liked being a dyke, personally. They were both silent then Lizzy said well, Weetzie can be pretty annoying.

Oh my gooooooood, said Annie, transmisogyny! How can I be a chaser if I can't read my fucking Post-it-marked copy of *Whipping Girl* at the dance nights where all the trannies go? Lizzy's eyes flickered at the word but she still found it funny and she laughed, genuinely, a lot. Annie made a jerking-off motion and Lizzy laughed so hard her makeup probably smeared. When she looked up Annie was smiling at her, deeply, and Lizzy blushed. She took a bite off her plate.

Is she really that much of a creeper? Lizzy asked.

Let me put it this way, Annie said. The fact that you're a trans woman in this city and she hasn't tried to fuck you blows my mind. Wait, she hasn't, has she?

No.

That's good.

Annie felt her iPhone buzz and she took it out of her purse. Oh my fucking God, she said. She already tagged us on Facebook.

You're shitting me.

Annie held her phone up:

Weetzie Palmer

November 18 near Brooklyn, NY

Mushroom omelette mission turned into run-in with two strong and fierce lovely ladies!—with Lizzy Inada and Annie Simone

Jesus Christ, said Lizzy.

Right? said Annie.

"Fierce"? said Lizzy.

Annie leaned her forehead on her hand. Right? she said.

Y'know, I don't have as much of a problem with her as you do, said Lizzy. But like "fierce"? Not to mention, "strong"? What the fuck?

But you'll take "lovely"? Annie said, sticking her tongue out.

Lizzy puckered her lips and raised her eyebrows. Mayyybe! she said. But seriously. First, I barely know her. Like, I met her at Nowhere Bar once, and then I saw her at Rebel Cupcake the other day.

You go to Nowhere? God, you probably love Hot Rabbit night, don't you.

Shut up.

I know what you mean, though, said Annie.

Yeah?

Well, it's like the word "brave," Annie said. I'm not brave. I'm not strong. And none of these fucking people who want to call me that have any idea how just really, really not brave I am.

Well, I dunno about that, Lizzy said.

Stop it, said Annie. You don't know and I'm not. I don't know about you so I can't say. But I'm not. Most days I just feel really scared and sad and weak. You know?

Lizzy looked at her with half-closed, youthful eyes, then relaxed and nodded.

There's no shame in admitting you're not the beautiful infallible tragic one, Annie said. I don't think struggle makes you a better person. It didn't make me one.

Lizzy thought a bit. She remembered a random girl at Metropolitan months back who'd said you are so inspiring with a mournful sort of smile. All Lizzy'd done was make some offhand crack about leaving her shitty hometown.

There have been a few people, Lizzy said, who make me feel like I'm in someone's idea of a fairy tale.

Annie gave her a deadpan smile. Turns out estradiol actually is magic, she said. They both laughed.

Still, said Lizzy as she speared hash browns. Like, yeah, it's annoying, but there are worse things they could say.

There will always be worse things they could say, kid.

Okay, if you ever call me "kid" again I'm going to dump Nair in your hair while you sleep.

Fine. There will always be worse things they could say, you cunt.

Lizzy flipped her off with one hand and slowly brought food to her mouth with the other. Annie laughed, and Lizzy giggled as she chewed. Smiling, Annie reached out to take Lizzy's gesturing hand in hers.

Woah! Lizmeister?! came a deep voice from behind them. Lizzy dropped her knife in her eggs and mouthed *Jesus Christ*. Hey there Tom, she said, swinging around in the booth.

They made small talk and then Tom took the hint and went away after smiling awkwardly at Annie for a while. The cheque came and Lizzy reached in her bag. Even in New York, life's a small town, she muttered.

Please, said Annie, yanking out her wallet. Lemme.

No, Lizzy said. It's no problem—

Oh shut up! said Annie, laughing. She tossed a twenty on the table and Lizzy stared.

⁂

One night after taking sleeping pills, Lizzy realized she'd been wide awake, scrolling through Annie's pictures online. The first phase of pictures was the present with a lot of pictures in a park, then another phase with straightened long blond-highlighted hair and streaks of eyeliner. Then another phase with her hair like it was now, with a lot of party pictures and cute cis-looking girls on her arm—she wasn't as skinny in these pictures, Lizzy noted, she looked, well, healthier— then a phase with straightened black hair, a set of which looked professionally taken, Annie in a purple bikini and pink eyeshadow on some Brooklyn rooftop with the Manhattan skyline in the distance. And then one picture of her after that with her hair platinum blond—man, Lizzy thought, she definitely looked a little heavier in this one … *oh fuck you Lizzy*—and in this last picture she was playing cards in a room with another girl who looked trans, laughing and holding a glass of beer, and her skin was slightly darker than its usual acorn shade. The picture was dated two years ago and after that there weren't anymore.

Lizzy dazedly cycled through again, from the park, to the straightened blonde highlights and eyeliner, to the party pictures and cis girls, to the purple bikini and pink eyeshadow against the skyline, to the platinum blond playing cards and laughing. Which was the picture on her screen when Lizzy closed her computer and crawled from her desk chair into her bed.

⁋

A couple weeks later they met at the 3rd Avenue L stop. Lizzy noticed a mint smell on Annie's breath, and a stronger, more powerful smell of the vanilla lotion she always used.

They had tacos and margaritas at a veggie Mexican place on 14th Street. Lizzy had prepped the suggestion of this hole in the wall on St. Marks afterward that was quiet and had three-dollar beers but Annie seemed distant to her. She was usually very present when they were together, but tonight—well, she hadn't really said anything different or unusual, but she was rubbing her foot against her ankle a lot and focusing very heavily on food, refilling their taco chips at the self-serve station four, maybe five, times, and her eyes were darting around.

So when they got out onto the street Lizzy softly said hey. Do you just want to go back to your place? Get out of the crowds? Annie let out a long whistle of breath, like she was about to answer a hard question, and for the first time Lizzy imagined it, in the way of a sudden high nighttime wave suddenly cresting and breaking inside her: *Oh no she's going to break—*

Can I come over to your place? Annie blurted.

Lizzy blinked.

Yes, Lizzy said.

I know you don't like having people over, Annie said.

I don't. I don't at all, Lizzy said, somewhat stunned.

I'm sorry, said Annie.

It's okay, said Lizzy.

At least, Lizzy thought, her roommate would probably be out with her girlfriend in Queens.

I'm sorry, said Annie. She looked pained. Are you sure?

Don't give me that, Lizzy said, exasperated all of a sudden. Of course I'm sure. I want you to be comfortable. I want you to be happy! Don't ask me if I'm sure! And though Lizzy wondered if she sounded a little hysterical or angry and had maybe even said too much, Annie just said thank you, thank you, and Lizzy kissed her on the cheek and said hey. Let's go.

Do you want to talk? Lizzy asked as they walked to Union Square, her head already dancing with the roaches and dirt and mustard-crusted dishes waiting at home. Annie shook her head and said, not really, and Lizzy squeezed her hand.

They were on the local train going uptown when the express train crash-rattled up beside them on the track. For a few seconds the trains were parallel, going the same speeds, and they could see across into the car where a man sat in jeans and a short-sleeved button-down shirt. He looked at the two girls across from him, wearing mascara, holding hands, both tall but one a head taller than the other, and the man cocked his head slightly to the side.

Lizzy and Annie, as if staged, cocked their heads in the same direction in unison and looked back at him, at this middle-aged man with grey hair, a leather satchel between his knees. Lizzy raised her eyebrows and the man's lips parted, just a little, then the local slowed down and the express crash-rattled ahead of them in a blur of orange and chrome.

Oh hello, boys! came a yell from a group of men in lawn chairs as they walked up Broadway from the 145th Street station.

Annie tilted her head down and stared ahead. Lizzy turned around and glared at them. The guys cackled.

Don't, Annie whispered.

Fuck him, said Lizzy, louder than she meant.

Oh hey, boys? You say something, boys? said the same guy.

Lizzy was about to turn around and yell something back when a big middle-aged white man with a crinkled kind face about to pass them on the sidewalk saw them and started laughing. He said, these boys are trouble, aren't they? He was laughing so hard he was almost crying. He stopped and widened his stance and spread his arms wide, as if going in for a hug. Lizzy and Annie had been walking close to the street, and they tried to brush past him but he almost danced in front of them, not letting them through. He was a large man. He started gesturing to the men in the lawn chairs who were laughing too and Lizzy looked down the street and saw cars coming fast one street down and she grabbed Annie's arm and pulled her into the street and ran around the laughing man and back onto the sidewalk then turned around, backpedalling north and yelled in her deepest, most growly voice, *FUCK YOU ASSHOLE DON'T TRY SHIT YOU FUCKING PIECE OF FUCK.*

Then there was a bunch of shouting and somebody started running toward them and the two of them turned around and booked it up Broadway. There were lots of people. Lizzy wasn't sure how many ran after them but none of them had seemed in too great shape and she only looked around once and everything was kind of a blur. They got to 148th and Lizzy turned a corner and unlocked the front door of her building, and just said to Annie, fourth floor, then they ran up taking four stairs at a time. When they got inside the apartment, lock bolted, chain on, Annie started to cry.

Why did you do that?! she said.

Lizzy stood there, mouth open. She'd been about to laugh. I'm sorry, she said.

Annie leaned against the hallway wall and sank, sobbing, down to the floor. *Whywhywhywhywhywhywhy would you do something like that*?! she said. *Why!*

I'm sorry, Lizzy said.

WHY?

Lizzy looked at the door. She didn't answer for a long time. She got down across from Annie on the floor and tried to hold her hand, but Annie shrank away. She kept looking at the door.

Then Annie said, I know, that's the thing, really, I know. She pressed her hands to her head and continued sobbing.

Lizzy banged her head, once, against the wall.

I'm just so sick of being quiet, she whispered.

Annie nodded into her hands. They sat across from each other in the hallway, not touching, for a long time.

Finally Annie said, bedroom?

Lizzy nodded. She took Annie's hand and led her into the bedroom in the dark—the better, Lizzy thought, with the roaches and all—and flicked on the lamp when she closed the door.

Lizzy had a small room, even for the city, occupied wholly by a full-sized bed and a small desk. And one window, over which she'd put a gauzy purple curtain. She gave Annie a shirt and a pair of thick pyjama pants—the landlord hadn't turned the heat on yet—and they lay down together. Annie hiccupped once or twice. They didn't so much as kiss even, but Annie snuggled up to her and let Lizzy hold her. I'm sorry again, Lizzy whispered. Her lips touched the back of Annie's left shoulder blade, and Annie snuggled closer as Lizzy began to fall asleep, her right arm around Annie's torso, her fingers brushing one of Annie's palms, nipples lightly grazing her back through a small thin T-shirt that Lizzy's dad had bought her, years ago, back home.

Around 4:00 a.m. Lizzy got up to pee and tripped over an empty soda bottle that had rolled out of Annie's bag. Sitting on the toilet, feet hovering above the floor, she alternated thinking about the bottle and watching for the roach that'd run under the sink when she turned on the light.

When she got back to the room she opened the soda bottle and put her nose to it. It smelled of stale carbonation and doctor's-office-grade cleaning supplies. Vodka, probably. Weird, she whispered to herself. Annie was usually so consistent about whisky.

She screwed the cap back on and put the bottle in Annie's bag, then gingerly moved it off to the side, against the wall.

I'm sorry, said Annie.

Lizzy started. Annie was silhouetted against a film of street light filtered purple through the curtain. She was still lying down, one eye peeking up from the folds of her pillow. You're up, said Lizzy.

Just now.

How are you feeling?

Annie laughed in a small voice. Cold, she said.

Sorry, said Lizzy. I think my roommate has a space heater let me—

Hey, just—

What?

Annie sat up. It's okay, she said. Just come back to bed.

Lizzy lay down next to her. Annie kissed her lightly. Lizzy kissed her back, also lightly. Kiss me, said Annie. Please kiss me. Lizzy kissed her harder. Kiss me. She felt Annie's muscles loosen, and breathe.

Please, Annie said next, minutes later, with most of their clothes off and her face pushed into the mattress, her garbled words floating up from lips half-smushed onto the sheets, make me disappear, swallow me make me into nothing make me nothing make me nothing make me nothing mak—

⚭

Hey. kid! The message on Lizzy's voice mail was clear for once, not marred by background noise or intermixed with smoker's cough. Just wanted to give you a ring tell you I'm thinking about ya. I know you don't really wanna come back home for a while, guess I can't fuckin' blame ya, so I was thinking I could come out there and see you! If you don't mind putting up your lame dear old dad out in the big city. We can hit up Avenue B, can show you a few of my old haunts! I mean I think that'd be fun I dunno if you think that'd be fun. But y'know I'm guessing your mum hasn't expressed interest and there's gotta be someone out there looking after you, right? Oh! Hey! Did you say you had a girlfriend? You said you had a girlfriend, didn't you? I mean, that's great, hey, I'd maybe like to meet her. If you're okay with that! See who you rub tits with. I guess I actually don't know if dykes do that—do they? I mean, you are a dyke, right? You tell me! Heh heh heh. Anyway. Gimme a call.

Hi Miss Lizzy, said the text from Annie. *Sorry I didn't get back to you the other day. I'm busy for a lot of this week but do you maybe want to go out next Friday? We'll have the whole night, I promise!*

Lizzy didn't care.

If she could love Annie, Lizzy thought, fine. If Annie didn't love her, well, okay. If this was all it would be, okay. She was lucky to have her at all. Who knew, Lizzy thought, the finite amount of nights in her life when she would sleep with her hand around a trusted body. That trusted hers. It wouldn't be a lot, anyway, would it.

∽

Annie was at Metropolitan alone, reading and running a finger down her highball, when Jenny, a friend from her first days in the city, sat down next to her and tapped her shoulder.

Stranger! said Annie. Jenny laughed and hugged her awkwardly from the stool, then ordered a round of whisky shots.

So whatcha here for?

Reading. For school, said Annie.

Well, that's shitty, because you're drinking with me now, bitch! Jenny said.

Annie laughed half-heartedly and closed her book. I like your haircut, she said.

Thanks! Jenny said, running her hand over the shock of hair on the left side of her face. I just got it. You're in school?

Yeah.

That's incredible, Jenny said.

I know, said Annie.

Hours later, as they were drunkenly saying goodbye, Jenny said you look good Annie. Like, really good, you obviously—well, yeah.

Thanks, Annie said, blushing.

Do you still go see Mia?

Annie rubbed her chin. I actually had my last session six months ago.

Oooh! Jenny said, smiling. I remember when I had that. I'm so proud of you. You—really, you look so good. You look happier.

Annie smiled weakly. It's good to see you, she said.

You too, said Jenny.

They hugged. Jenny pecked on her neck. Call me sometime?

Sure, Annie said. Definitely.

They looked at each other and Jenny giggled. I gotta go, Annie said.

∽

Do you wanna go anywhere after this? Lizzy said. They were at the veggie Mexican place again.

Yes! Annie said. Um. She smiled faux-hesitantly. Ummm. Can we maybe go dancing?

Lizzy smiled.

Pleeeeeeeeeease? Annie said, then pursed her lips and batted her eyes.

At Beauty Bar, on 14th Street, by 2nd Avenue, where the NYU crowd was so unrelenting that the bouncer checked every single ID— he balked for a second at the M and old name on Lizzy's Oregon licence, then shrugged and let them in—the two of them pushed their way inside. Velvet black and white paisley patterns on the wall, salon chairs that reminded Lizzy of a dentist's office lined up on the edges of the room. The deal with the bar was that you could get a manicure in the front room while you got drunk. Then the dancing was in the back. Lizzy noticed some people in the crowd staring at Annie. Then Annie said look, and gestured to her left. A girl with huge breasts hiccupped loudly, uncontrollably, over a something-tonic as her nails turned ice cream white while the manicurist looked unpresent, impossible to disturb.

I have to go to the bathroom, Lizzy said. Midway through peeing she was struck with worry that something might happen to Annie in her absence, but she came back to see Annie in the backroom, dancing in a corner to herself, her long body outlined by the flashing lamps. No one else was paying attention to her, the six-and-a-half-foot girl in the black-and-white-checked dress and black tights and black Cons. Or almost no one, anyway. One or two people nearby, Lizzy saw, glanced over at Annie, and one maybe snickered at her (she thought?), pointed at her Adam's apple (she thought?). She was angry that she had to consider the possibility. She suspected everybody, she realized. Everybody of meanness. Whether the softly snickering girl looking to Annie's right was unkind or not, all Lizzy could do was assume. She had to assume.

And then Lizzy didn't want to go up and dance with Annie. She wanted to lean against the wall and watch her, just for a minute. She didn't want to break the beautiful sight of her. She didn't want to fuck it up. So she did. Watched her, that is. She stood on the opposite corner, touching her back to the velvet paisley wall. She wondered, if she stayed there long enough, if, when, Annie would come look-ing for her, then Lizzy pushed the thought down, underwater, and looked at her lover's body vibrating against the light.

Real Equality (A Manifesto)

Hey everybody! I'm really thankful and grateful to be here speaking at this event. Before I start, I just want to say I think it's so wonderful we all have a forum like this where our community can share in all our *amazing* queerness, and I'm really grateful, I'm just intolerably, unimpeachably grateful for the opportunity. Also, our lovely MC never read my bio because *ha ha ha* I was a little too late sending it to her *soooo* she didn't get it! So that's why she didn't read my bio. I'm sorry about that. I'll read it myself just real quick? Yeah? Right, so: Ahem. "Jilo Bombastier"—that's me—"is a white cis queer woman who lives in the County of Kings. Her passions include social justice, vegetarian Indian food, grumpy otters, and *confusing the hell* out of straight people on OkCupid."

No. Really.

Anyway, okay.

It is *not* enough to be queer and have a queer identity. I am tired of believing that is true. I am tired of the marginalization that we inflict onto our own selves. Sequestering ourselves into gaybourhoods with our gay bars and our gay readings. It's like the world told us, "Hey, you're different, you don't belong here, queers!" and we said, "Sweet, sure thing, straight people! Let's go build bars and readings and culture and identity away from you!" Well, I am through playing right into the bigot's hands and being told what to do by the man's hands. They say we don't belong, then the most radical thing we can do is start belonging.

Take literature. I'm through seeing myself ghettoized by the gay studies section in a bookstore. I say gay literature is literature, no qualifications, no exceptions. When I buy a Jeanette Winterson book, I want to see her right next to Wordsworth and all the Wolfes, and I don't want to see any of those awful illustrations on the cover of naked girls with snakes around their boobs! Hello, how else do you say, "Dykes only"? Why can't we put something on the cover that reflects classic literature?! Like a coffin in the sky! Or maybe a big glowing cock! That's equality! Or others too, I want, I want to see ... Eileen Myles next to ... John Milton! Leslie Feinberg next to ... William Faulkner! Sarah Schulman next to ... David Sedaris! And don't tell me the straight bookstore hegemony doesn't have an interest in keeping us shoved in some corner of their basements next to mouldy anthropology textbooks. I was at the bookstore the other day and this totally straight girl who was just spurting objectification, she asked someone, "Hey, does this place have a section for gay fiction?" and so, deploying my knowledge of radical interruption tactics, I stepped in front of her and said, "Why, so you can feel good about ogling dykes?" And the bookstore's lit-e-hetero-rati kicked me out of the store! For daring to act like a straight person! They saw me as a fly in the ointment they slather over their body wash of fake inclusion!

I had the last laugh on them, though: As part of my new campaign for guerrilla literary equality, I'm dismantling the gay studies section of the bookstore bit by bit by moving the titles into other sections. The other day I got all of Erika Lopez safely over into Thrillers & Suspense, and next I'm going to try to get Dan Savage into the Fantasy section. That's equality! True, pure, refreshing, unfiltered equality! And I have had it up to here with fake equality! Those who came before me did not fight for rights just so I could safely walk down the street with my genderqueer-bodied-licious partner listening to the Athens Boys Choir and eating vagina-shaped cupcakes. Like *please*, can you say, "Separate but equal"?! I just want to be treated the same! If I shave my head, the last thing I want to hear is, "Oh she's been out half a year now," I just want them to call me ugly and unfeminine like any other girl!

Now! Now! Maybe you're thinking you don't want any of this. Fine, I get it, because you know what? Let's face it. Equality is not for everybody. And if you can't fight for it, y'know what? Fine. But I will say this. I have personal, gut-shaking, heart un-cocking, soul-macing reasons for being so passionate. I once had a girlfriend who was trans, who is no longer my girlfriend who was trans. I mean, she's still trans or whatever, just not my girlfriend. I'll call her Julia Serano. That's not her real name. My girlfriend who was trans, she used to say things like, "If I could kill every straight and cis person in the world, I would." And then I'd say to her, "Well, the little girl we're thinking of adopting is cisgender and might be straight, and actually hey! I'm cisgender too! So that does that mean you want to kill both of us?" and she'd say, "Let's talk about your internalized transphobia! And I guess your internalized homophobia too. I want to have this conversation because murderous urges are an important part of my identity and for you to not respect them just makes me feel really marginalized."

Now, first of all, I consider myself a gigantically huge trans ally. When I was in college I had a guy friend who thought he wanted to wear dresses, so one day I surprised him with a bunch of my old pink things from high school! I never heard from him again actually, so I guess he decided not to be trans. Or actually maybe he died. I forget if that one was him. Anyway. Huge trans ally. And back to my girlfriend who was trans, Julia Serano. I really feel like her murderous urges were a result of her own self-ghettoization, she was so "active in the community" and so "big on advocacy work" and on trans culture and identity that it made her so focused on the hate and rage of the larger world, and my heart just wept for her, it just torrented, it gushed sympathy and pity like a fire hydrant. I think that Julia would've felt happier if she just stopped trying to fix all the rage, because it was causing all of her rage. And rage begets rage. Begets more rage. And the rage has to stop somewhere, so let's just … take … the hate … of the world. And hold it. And take it in our hands. And then into ourselves. And just *not let it out.*

Because! If we want to be equal, the only way we're going to achieve true, real equality is if we're equal in culture and identity, and that means not sectioning ourselves off from the world! Not isolating ourselves through things like art! Or books! Or socialization! I want to see a world where a cis straight person doesn't think about the fact that we're queer, doesn't think of us as having differences! Whether we're bringing our partners to the church potluck or getting lasers shot at our genital hair. Where if we talked about queerness, the cis straight person would just be so taken aback that they'd go, "Why are you telling me this?" as they laugh. "I don't think of you differently at all! Shut up! Paint this wall!"

Unmoved by the reality of our experiences and existence, untroubled by the nuance of our histories or desires, content in the knowledge that straight or gay or transgendering, we are all human and therefore we are all the same. *EXACTLY THE SAME.* And that we can't pretend we're different. There is no difference. And if we want to get that, and live it, we have to stop caring about what anybody else thinks. Or feels. Or suffers.

And really: Who better to teach this to the world than us queers?

So let's teach them.

That'd be real equality.

Thanks everyone.

"Life being what it is, one dreams not of revenge. One just dreams."

—MIRIAM TOEWS, *A COMPLICATED KINDNESS*

Portland, Oregon

Adrienne smelled cat urine when she woke up, but because her building was freezing the smell was faint and diluted by icy air. *They didn't call*, she thought as soon as she woke. She'd been desperate for one of the girls to call. She wrapped herself in blankets and got up, shivered over to the window and drew back the cloth she used for a curtain. Pale sunlight lit the room. She stood on her tiptoes to get a better view. She lived in a basement apartment and the windows were small and near the ceiling. *Snow's gonna set in any day now*, she thought. *Then God, who knows how long it'll be 'til I see out of here again.* She heard a car chug-start outside, then the *shkkkt shkkkt* of an ice scraper on the windshield.

She drew the curtain and checked the answering machine on her nightstand to make sure she hadn't missed anything. Then she padded to the bathroom. There was a puddle of cat pee in the corner. She wiped it up and scrubbed the floor, then slipped on her flip-flops (the apartment had been her boyfriend's at first, and after multiple cleanings the bathtub was still gross) and ran water. When it was hot enough she threw her blankets in the corner.

When she got out and went back to the bedroom she checked her machine again. No messages, though she was also like, *what, dummy, like they'll need you to drive at seven in the morning?* She put on clothes and a scarf and combed her breaking hair. *Maybe I'll just do nothing today*, she thought. Yeah. It was her day off from her regular job anyway.

She washed the bathroom floor with Mr. Clean and then went to the kitchen and decided she'd have breakfast. She split an English muffin. The cat nudged her leg. She sighed. "La la la la la la," she said irritably in descending tones. "It would kill you for me to eat first, wouldn't it." She reached under the sink and dumped a yoghurt cup of food in his dish. He gave her a scornful look. "Yeah whatever," she mumbled. She was almost out of cat food. Fuck. Maybe tonight they'd call.

She took a two-pound jar of strawberry jelly from the fridge and leaned against the counter while the muffin toasted. The cat stopped crunching for a second, stared up at her, then went back to eating. He was a big cat. His fur was grey with rounded black stripes, and he had yellow eyes and an awkwardly large chin.

An ant crawled up the wall opposite her. She made a face and smudged it with a paper towel. They should be gone when it was this cold.

She rinsed a plate and pushed up on the toaster lever, then scooped on jelly and climbed into the green armchair in the living room. She was small and the chair was big and she could fit in it easy, curled under a throw rug. Her head made a divot in the chair's back. She really hoped one of the girls would call tonight. She adjusted the rug so it went up behind her and made a cushion.

She slipped back into the apartment around eight—when the woman had said they might call her again—and leaned her frame against the wall. When she stood upright, off-yellow paint flakes were on her coat. She took it off and shook them out and went into the kitchen to heat up soup. Soon she was back in her armchair.

The cat wandered over and lolled on her feet. He was deceptively large; he looked average-sized enough as he walked but when he sat on his haunches his weight spilled from his sides like pudding. He leapt onto the armchair and squished in beside her and the armrest. He filled in the space like caulk. She stroked his head. "So I was a bitch this morning," she murmured.

"Slightly," he yawned. "I suppose I deserved it. I did pee on the floor."

"Yeah," she said flatly. "That was kind of gross. Were you drunk?"

He cleaned the back of his paw. He spoke enunciated and carefully, like a midcentury businessman. "Maybe. You *did* leave the lid down."

"Glenn, *please* go in the bathtub. I'll like that a lot more than you going on the floor."

"Fine. I won't do it again."

"Okay."

"Okay."

She blew on her bowl. "It's frosty in here. Hey! Will you be okay with the winter? Because I could get you a heater." She nodded to him and slurped. "I can do that."

"Not at all, Adrienne. You see, I'm a Norwegian Forest—"

"I *know* you're a Norwegian Forest, dude."

"Well. I just need you to understand. I don't wither easily."

She scratched under his chin. "Tough kitty. You're sure? You tell me. I want you to be comfortable here."

Glenn closed his eyes and sighed out with a high pitch that sounded like a wheeze. "I will let you know if I am cold. I wouldn't suggest worrying about it, however."

She nodded quickly. Then she ate her soup rapidly and he fell asleep.

She tried to crane her neck to look at the phone in her room. She really wished they would call.

She gave Glenn a little kiss on the side. The black stripes on his fur grew when his body rose with his breathing.

She tried to get up without disturbing him but he woke up.

"Goddammit," he said.

She laughed. This always happened. "Whatever, man! Like you need more sleep." She put the kettle on. "Do you want some tea?"

"I've never had tea."

"It warms you up better than rye. You prefer rye? Right? Isn't that what you like to drink? I keep forgetting, I'm sorry ... I always think you like gin for some reason."

He came into the kitchen, leapt onto the counter, and then the fridge. "Piddle. And yes, that is what I prefer. And actually. Sure, I'll have tea. I've never had it."

"How'd you grow up without having tea, weren't your owners all snobby?"

"My former humans drank Scotch and hot chocolate. Well, and rye. But not, in fact, tea."

"Mmm, my kind of family."

"No, absolutely not."

When the kettle went she put a tea bag into a bowl and poured the water in. She was almost out of tea too. Goddammit. She went to check her machine just in case. Nothing. Fuck.

She sat on a chair in her room. Then she picked a pillow off the floor and hunched up with it on her knees. They'd told her what they'd pay per call and she'd counted on making that much soon, but if they didn't call her in the next couple days—

"Adrienne?" yelled Glenn. "This is far too hot. I can't drink it."

She came back to the kitchen and blew on his bowl a bit. "Here," she said, "cool-a-riffic."

"Thank you." He tentatively lapped it up. "Heyyy, wowee." He lapped more and looked up. "This is remarkably tasty. Is all tea like this?"

She grinned and bobbed the bag in her mug. "Nope. There's thousands of different kinds, actually. This one would be called English Breakfast."

"English Breakfast?" Glenn kept his nose in the bowl.

"Yes."

"Do the English really drink this for their breakfast?" He continued lapping, and she drifted to the window where snow had just begun to fall.

"I don't know, Glenn," she said absentmindedly, staring up through the glass where she could almost make out the flakes hitting the ground. "I really don't know."

The apartment door shutting woke Glenn up the next morning. That was disappointing. He liked seeing her off to work. Must've slept through her alarm. Oh well. He would be seeing more of her anyway, with winter coming.

He stretched up from her blanket and hopped to the ground. He sniffed a pair of underwear on the floor. Humans smelled interesting enough anyway, but there was always this faint tangy smell in her underwear he could never place. It made him think of honey and human underarms, but it wasn't quite those things either.

He went into the kitchen. She rarely forgot to feed him, and he appreciated that. His former humans had forgotten a lot.

His mother had only given him and his siblings one piece of advice, as she was cleaning them one morning. *Your humans have one job, she said. To give you food, every day. If they cannot do that right, leave. I am not sure you need to know much else.*

Those old humans had been shits. Still. It had taken him a while to get out of there.

He ate then looked for leftovers from her, but like usual she hadn't eaten breakfast. He couldn't understand that. She had food. He had no problem with humans as a rule—he enjoyed their company more than most cats did, really—but it aggravated him how little they used their things.

In the bathroom he found the toilet lid down. He thought of peeing in the sink to make a point but went in the bathtub, which thankfully was dry.

Back in the bedroom, he saw that Adrienne had left her closet door open, and he padded over to look. He always wanted to see more of her clothes, but they were jammed in tight on the rack and they were sorted by colour so they all blended together. And daily she usually only wore a T-shirt and jeans and the same sweater when it was cool.

He stretched and returned to the bed. He padded over the flowered blanket and plopped himself against her pillow. The phone rang and no one left a message. Adrienne's sheets were a violent purple hue and the colour filled his vision when he closed his eyes.

When Adrienne got home that night she yelled, "It's freezing out!" and took her gloves off with her teeth and went to put the kettle on. "Glennnn!" she yelled. "Do you want hot chocolate?"

No answer. He was sleeping, she supposed. She got her tape deck and the tape with soothing pianos from the living room. When she played it, Glenn wandered in from her room and she brightened. "Monsieur!" she said. "*Cette soir, je faiserais un petit de lait du chocolat. Voulez-vous?*"

He stretched and scratched his neck with a hind leg. "I heard you when you said hot chocolate. As did the entire building. Far too sweet. Tea instead please."

She washed a bowl and laid it on the other side of the stove.

"That is strange music," he said. He jumped on the counter and sniffed the tape deck.

"It's Chopin."

He cocked his head at her.

"It's from a piece I played in high school."

"This is you!" he said in awe.

"No!" she laughed. "I just played it once. And then my boyfriend got me the tape. Of someone playing it better." She paused and thought to herself. "Huh. I'm glad I didn't take that the wrong way."

"Hmm." He went on top of the fridge and settled. "Why isn't he your boyfriend anymore?"

The kettle whistled. "*Him?* Oh I—it just didn't work. Sometimes these things don't work."

"No? How so."

"It just didn't."

"Did he not want to see you anymore? You do not talk about him much."

"I don't really like him, so no, I don't."

"And why's that?"

"I don't know, lots of reasons! This was like a year ago, man, give it a rest!"

His ears flattened. "Oh I'm sorry! I am very sorry."

She sighed and poured his tea. "Oh fuck. Don't, it's okay."

"I am really very sorry," he said earnestly.

"It's okay."

"I am *so* sorry."

She made her hot chocolate then bent in front of her fridge. He lapped at his tea.

"But what was he like?" he said.

She emerged with a Tupperware of beans. "Hmmm?"

"What was he like. That boy. Or what are boys like. I don't know."

She opened the beans and sniffed them. Then she took out cheese slices and peas and put water on for rice. "Well for one, he was young," she said. "Young as me. But he had very old skin, for some reason. His face was so rough. Sometimes I thought I was going to bleed when I kissed him."

"Huh." He lapped at his tea exactly once then said, "And was he fun?"

She set down the bowl she was about to wash. "You're trying to ask if the sex was good."

"Well, not necessarily. Though I am interested in that, yes."

"The sex was good. And he could be kind of a bastard. But yes, he was usually fun."

"So he was fun!"

"Yes Glenn, he was fun."

"Okay!" He was excited. He liked discovering more about her life. "So. What I want to know then is: What does fun mean between you and a boy?"

She stared blankly at the fridge, rubbing her fingers on a bag. Then she smirked and added rice to the water. She washed the bowl and lined up two hot sauces. She finished her hot chocolate and put the kettle on again.

"God, would you just talk," he said disgustedly.

Her eyes flicked at him then back to the stove. Then she settled against the counter. "I used to tell a friend of mine: Girls always say boys are oblivious. You know. And they have the right idea. But they're wrong about the words. What boys are? Boys are innocent. Even if they've been through a lot, even if they're monsters." She opened another thing of hot chocolate. "Boys more like—" She mumbled and trailed off. "They suspend things. Like in that moment there's only their dumb jokes. They're so fucking stupid. Nothing else matters except whatever, like … stupid thing they're interested in. My boyfriend from high school? One of my favourite things used to be going to watch his a cappella group practise. Like they were five guys in this kid's living room or whatever. I went to every single one, and they were so *bad*. I never told anyone I thought this, but they sounded so awful." She laughed and suddenly choked back a sob. "I can't believe I'm going to cry about this. They really couldn't sing for shit. And they would *argue*. About the stupidest things. But I loved watching them. I had so much fucking fun at their stupid fucking rehearsals. It's so dumb. I loved them." She rubbed her face and smiled at him. "It really was the dumbest thing. You know?"

"Hmm." Glenn studied her unblinkingly. "And yet you loved going there. That is certainly quite interesting indeed. Hmm."

She looked up and saw his lack of expression. An image of a particularly emotionless professor from her one semester suddenly drifted into her head.

She narrowed her eyes. "I suppose it is," she said. "Interesting."

She made her hot chocolate and stirred her rice.

"What was this particular boy's name?" Glenn asked.

"Rob," she said, not looking back at him.

"Well I suppose I don't get it. But tell me—" he started, but she just laughed and went to check her messages. She took her bra off and changed into pyjama pants while listening to her sister vent about money. No calls. She sat down on the bed then got up almost immediately and went to the living room to put a movie in the VCR, and sullenly Glenn followed and waited for her to sit down.

The movie ended and she clicked the set off. "Glenn."

He woke up. "Yes? What?"

"I'm sorry I'm waking you—"

"No problem." He yawned and stretched. "What is it?"

"Do you like your food?"

"It is not bad. I have, of course, eaten far worse."

"Okay," she murmured, "I'll buy you different stuff. Just if you want, I'll do that. Just if you ever decide."

"All right."

He licked himself for a few minutes then hopped down and licked her empty bowl. "Adrienne?" he said. No reply. "Adrienne?" Eventually he heard her snoring, softly, in short, irregular bursts. A street lamp from outside was reflecting soft yellow light through the packed snow, onto Adrienne's head and her chair. She looked shiny and small, like a—fairy, that was the word for those things? Maybe it was something else. He hopped back up and burrowed his head in her side. "Okay then," he said sleepily. "I'll tell you tomorrow."

✧

The phone rang hours later around one and Adrienne jerked and unballed herself—Glenn woke and yowled and ran into the kitchen before her feet hit the floor—and she said, "Yes oh God please," and bolted to the bedroom. "Hi? Yes. Yes, I can definitely drive. Six four seven South Greenwood. Okay got it. I'll be there in twenty. Goodbye. Thank you!"

"You're driving somewhere?" Glenn yelled from on top of the fridge.

"Yeah!" she said. "Thank God!" She put on a bra and pants and a coat and boots and was out of the door. Glenn blinked and licked at his empty bowl of tea.

When she got home as the sun was rising she rushed in without speaking, slept for two hours, then got up and went to work without feeding him.

He reminded her when she got home, and she apologized a ton and loaded up his bowl. Soon she got a call to go out and drive again. She didn't stay out as late and when she came back she made both of them some tea but didn't eat. She chatted with him for only a bit before going to bed.

"What is all this about?" he said crossly. "Where are you driving?"

"It's for an escort agency."

"What?" he said, lapping. "I don't know what that is."

"Prostitutes, Glenn," Adrienne sighed.

He kept licking. "You're not serious."

"Absolutely I am," she said, taking off her bra and throwing it in the direction of her room. "Oh hey, in cooler news, I was able to get you some rye."

A couple nights later she didn't go out at all but slept for ten hours. Then left again without feeding him.

"Adrienne," he said when she got in that night, "my food please."

"Oh, right. Fuck," she said in an exasperated voice. She dumped a cupful in his bowl. "I'm sorry. I know that's like—really not cool."

"No it's not," he said and began eating. "You won't let it happen again, I trust?"

"No. No. Promise."

"Thank you."

But the next night she left around three and didn't come back at all until the next evening. When Adrienne stumbled in he simply yowled, "*Adrienne! ADRIENNE!*"

"Fuck I'm sorry, I'm sorry!" she said. She rushed into the kitchen and poured the bag into his bowl until it overflowed, then leaned against the fridge and blew on her hands. She pulled off her hat and gloves and dropped them on the floor. "I'm sorry. I'm sorry. There were all these calls and I had a morning shift and"—she moved to the bedroom. "I'm sorry, I'm a piece of shit, I'm sorry." She kicked off her boots in the hallway. She doubled back into the kitchen and took out three cheese slices, which she unwrapped and ate in succession.

She watched Glenn sink his head farther and farther into the bowl of food. She reached out and scratched his back. He kept eating.

She straightened up and finished eating and had a thought. "Hey!" she said. "Maybe I'll leave the bag out for you. Hey? Can I do that? Let's do that. That way you could even just eat whenever you wanted."

He stopped midcrunch and blinked at her and said, "I'm sorry what."

"Yeah, you know," she said. "That way you don't have to wait for me to get up in the mornings either."

His insides bunched. "I never mind doing that," he said quietly.

"But see that way if I forget you're not going hungry." She took out some rye and swigged a bit, then poured out a saucer for him. "Like, doesn't that make sense? You shouldn't have to go hungry because I suck. Doesn't that just make sense?"

He swished his tail, which had become the size of a feather duster. "Why would you keep forgetting though."

"Oh, I—" She bunched up the slice wrappers on the counter and made a gesture of helplessness with her hands. She was so tired. She put the wrappers in the garbage. She was so incredibly tired. She was already moving to the bedroom. "I don't mean to forget. But also like today, I couldn't come home … I'm just like, I just think it makes sense." Suddenly she was irritable. "What works. That's responsibility, right? What is going to work, what the results are!"

He didn't understand but also didn't really care. He leapt on top of the counter then the fridge and looked at her, coiled. "I'll overeat if you leave the bag out," he said desperately.

"Really?" She was taking her coat off now and tossing it with her hat and gloves on the floor. She reached for a little more of the rye. "You never ask me for more."

"I will," he said. "I will eat and eat and I won't have any control. I don't even like it." It was half a lie, and a rotten one, a shitty one, because though he did overeat sometimes, he wasn't actually worried about it being self-destructive or anything like that. His body was still quivering and his tail was still huge. "Please do not do this," he said.

"Please. Just put food in my dish in the morning. It's not hard. Please. Please. Please. Don't do this."

Adrienne stopped and looked into his eyes. He blinked slowly.

She shuffled to him at the fridge, reached up and put a hand on his back, then on his ears, and scratched him lightly, then scratched under his chin. "I'm sorry," she said. "Know it's not an excuse but I'm sorry. I'll feed you like normal. Tomorrow. Promise." He purred and rubbed against her hand and she went into her bedroom, dropped her jeans, took off her bra, and got into bed. He lapped up the rye then joined her.

The phone rang almost right away. "No. No!" she said as she woke up. "*No-o-o!*" And it came out like she was sobbing but she wasn't, really. "I'm so tired," she whispered to herself and threw back the blankets. "I'm so tired. I'm so tired." She picked up the phone. "Hey. Yes. Yes I can drive again. The outskirts?" Glenn didn't hear her come home and he fell asleep at four.

☙

This went on for a while. Adrienne would forget about him every few days and Glenn would be seething and on edge every morning he checked his bowl. She apologized more and more each time and swore it wouldn't happen again, but it didn't really change. He tried to be patient. He knew she had started a second job, that humans weren't perfect, it didn't mean it would be this way forever. She tried to bring up leaving the bag out again, but he just hissed and that had been enough.

And it wasn't all bad. Adrienne seemed less stressed, for one. Calmer. Even if there were nights they didn't really get to talk. And they did still have fun. When her calls were slow they got drunk late and watched *Keeping Up Appearances* and made dumb imitations.

"OHHH LORDY," said Adrienne, "MY TEEVEE'S GOT ALL THE EXPLETIVES IN IT!"

"JOLLY BAD!" Glenn cackled, lapping at his saucer of rye and missing. "JOLLY BAD BAD BAD BAD!" lurching around and managing the pretty impressive feat of falling to the floor on his face.

∽

"What are those?" Glenn asked one night. Adrienne was cleaning out her bag in the living room and had set a Ziploc baggy of pills on the coffee table.

"T3s."

"Hm?"

"I'm going to go to bed soon," she said. "If they call again, they can find someone else. I have to go to sleep." It was around four and she'd just gotten home after leaving at eleven. On the table she'd also put books, condoms, stray cigarettes, some twenties, ChapSticks, lighters, pennies, nail polish remover, pens, napkins, a small hand mirror, a notepad. She only returned to her bag the notepad, two pens, the condoms, the mirror, and the lighter. Glenn noticed that she was moving strangely, slowly.

She still hadn't fed him that day.

He sigh-wheezed.

"Could I have some food?" Glenn asked.

"Oh shit," Adrienne said. "Yeah. Yeah. Sorry." She moved up jerkily. She was so tired. She was so incredibly tired. She felt every part of her body clunking and straining. She moved to the kitchen in slow steps, bent in front of the cabinet to take out his food, dug in a yoghurt cup and, instead of pouring it, placed it in the bowl. When he went over to look at it, only a third of the cup was filled. He turned around; she was closing her bag, leaving the extra things on the coffee table and heading into her room.

"Glenn," she said, "come with me."

"Hmmm?"

"Come with me."

He followed her to the bedroom and she undressed, pulling her bra out from under her shirt, unbuttoning and dropping her jeans in one motion, putting one knee on her bed then letting her weight fall on the whole thing. She put the blankets over herself and Glenn jumped on them.

She picked him up and placed him on her chest, then leaned forward and scratched him under the chin. She said, "Glenn. You're really ..." She closed her eyes, like she was saying something difficult. "I am grateful. You are in my life." Her head nodded down. She was so tired. It felt like a slow but firm hand was pushing her whole body deeper into her bed. She focused on getting words out and making them sound like words. "But I. Am? Hurting you."

Glenn blinked at her and said, "Oh. Well. I ... Perhaps sometimes. Hmm?"

She leaned her head back onto her pillow, gently and gradually, then sent her hand to rub her forehead. Her skin was so dry the sound it made was rough and quiet. Like a book moved along a carpet. "I'll be better," she said. She laid her hands above her blanket on the sides of her body, breathed in and out deeply, her head further and further in her pillow. He could see her gently sliding away, and she was feeling herself leaving, like the warmest, softest plastic wrap was going around her brain. She lifted her hands once more to stroke Glenn—this seemed to take forever—then she said, "Could you tell me something nice? Just tell me. Something nice. That's happened to you." She felt each of her fingers sink into the blanket then disengage from response. "That's something you could do. That I'd really like ..."

Glenn blinked at her. He didn't know how to reply so he said, "Hmmm," to stall and blinked and waited for her to say more. He was only thinking *I asked you. And you didn't even give me a full cup.* She didn't say more and he turned around and went to eat.

One night, after another two days went by without her feeding him—she was hardly home during this time at all, actually—Glenn gave up and started pawing at the cabinet where his food was but he couldn't figure out how to open it. He butted it and clawed at every edge from top and below but he couldn't do it. He tried for a while.

In the sink there were some peas in the bottom of a soup bowl. He ate those and felt a little better, but then he hacked it all up on the carpet an hour later.

Glenn was right, though, that Adrienne was less stressed. In some ways. Money wasn't as much a worry, for one, and thanks to a few of the girls she could always get someone to pick up for her. Adrienne was grateful for these things (and those T3s were nice). But she was disconnecting, feeling more and more removed from the world, never unsleepy, awakened multiple times a night. She knew she was neglecting Glenn, that not only was he angry about the food but he missed her being around—though, she thought, he always had booze now and nice food and it was always actually in the house—and at her day job too she felt the faces receding, speaking to her like water. She wasn't exactly not okay with this—the work itself was boring and peaceful most of the time (most of the time). Though she did hate the sleep thing. More, she felt like she was watching herself drift further and further from the known world. She never turned down calls, except for that one night, which the woman who ran the agency hadn't been happy about. (She liked the girls better than the woman.) Adrienne knew they liked that she was so reliable. And not only was the money good but like—she felt some pride in that. So she was out almost every night, and she would drive home in wee hours from bungalow suburbs and midgrade hotels back into her part of the city. Sometimes it wasn't quite morning yet, so the streets would be quiet, but sometimes she'd be out late enough to see people on the dawn shift straggling out of their buildings, with parkas and coffees, zipping up their kids' snowsuits and waiting at bus stops. And when she watched them it was like nothing had ever felt less real. She didn't feel sad per se when she saw them, just impossibly heavy, unmoored. Like they were lives she was watching from far away and had been familiar with long ago.

When she came in that night around four-thirty, having taken the last of her T3s an hour before, she swayed and zagged to her bedroom, losing her hat and gloves and coat to the floor on the way and not really hearing Glenn's mewing or yelling or noticing the vomit, shovelling food in his bowl zombielike and only stooping to scratch him once before putting a knee on her bed and muttering, "I fell asleep in my fucking car."

⚭

The next day around eight he woke up as she was showering, but he pretended to sleep. He listened for the sound of the yoghurt cup. When it didn't come and the front door slammed, he went to the kitchen and found her dishes unwashed and—

Okay. There was more food. He just hadn't heard her. Phew. She had cleaned up his vomit too.

After eating he went to the bathroom and found the lid down. He hissed at the bowl, which he knew was silly, but it made him feel better. He sighed. The bathtub would still be wet from her shower. He went back to the kitchen and leapt on top of the fridge. He gave a single lap at the tea bowl from a few nights ago. He wondered if she would remember him tomorrow. It really made him bonkers sometimes, not knowing. Perhaps he should have saved the food—

No.

What he should do, he thought, was go. He should just leave. He could bolt through the front door before she knew what was happening. He could do the same in the lobby. Winter'd be over soon. He could just go.

He swatted the bowl and knocked it onto the floor. A piece broke off.

The phone rang. He paused, considered, then wheeze-sighed and leapt down and went to the bedroom. The phone was on her dresser. It kept ringing. He jumped on the dresser and tried to gently turn the receiver over. God, he hated this noise. He pushed it once and it didn't budge. It kept ringing. He pushed it harder but his paw just slipped over the top.

He tried to lift it up from the bottom but it was too heavy with just one paw. Then he put pressure from the bottom and butted it with his head, and the receiver turned over onto the body of the phone then slid off and over the side of the dresser, where it bounced suspended about a foot off the floor.

"Hello?" came a woman's voice. "Hello?"

Glenn leapt to the floor and got close to the receiver. "Hello?" he said. "This would be Glenn?"

"What?" said the woman. "I can't hear you."

"*HELLO?*" he said again.

"*WHAT?* I don't understand."

"*HELLO?*"

"I can't hear you—where's Adrienne? Can she drive?"

"No!" he tried.

"I can't understand you. You don't even sound like a hum—okay never mind." She hung up.

He blinked at the receiver until the dial tone turned into the alarm-drone sound of a phone off the hook. Then he jumped onto the floor and peed on a pile of clothes.

∾

It was later that night around three that Adrienne came in and bolted a glass of orange juice and looked around the apartment. Glenn didn't seem to be around. Strangely she wasn't tired. She wasn't hungry either; she'd just eaten. She wished she had something to drink, but they'd run out last night and she'd forgotten to get someone to pick up for her. Or get some pot. Shrooms? Maybe. Glenn had drunk the last of the booze too. She put the juice glass in the sink then saw she'd left the front door open a crack. Oh Jesus. She shut the door and locked it.

She went to her bedroom and put most of her money away. She called the one dealer she had a number for. No answer. She smelled the pee on the clothes pile and thought, *Goddammit, Glenn*, and sprayed them with Febreze and threw the pile in the laundry. She tried the dealer again, no answer.

"You know what I don't get," Glenn's voice came from behind her, "is how you can hardly afford rent but you have no problem paying what must be an enormous phone bill."

She wheeled around in surprise. "Glenn!" She picked him up and rocked him in her arms. "Crazy kitty, were you there the whole time?"

He wriggled out of her hands and landed soundlessly on the floor. "You still haven't answered my question. How can you pay for the phone?"

"That's getting better now!" She bent down and scratched under his chin. "You never answered my question," she accused lovingly.

"I was sleeping and then you woke me up, so now I am here. I am also extremely hungry, if you don't mind feeding me again tonight."

"Yeah sure, no problem, of course." She rushed to the kitchen, and then she remembered: They'd run out of cat food this morning. "Shit. I didn't get you ..." She trailed off and put her hands on the edge of the counter. She pressed onto it as hard as she could. She pressed hard enough that purple ridges appeared in her palms when she stopped. Okay. Whatever. She'd go to the store now. She'd go to the store and buy a huge bag. She would do it right now. She threw on her coat and said, "I'm going to Safeway! Coming back with food for days!" She yelled it as if Glenn were in another room. She pulled her boots on, and then she had an idea. "Ooh, I'll get some cough syrup too. Yeah. That's what I'll do." Glenn's eyes bugged slightly.

"Cough syrup?" he said. "What are you going to do with cough syrup?"

"You'll see! I'll be back in a bit!" Glenn turned and slunk into the kitchen and she left. She went up the steps to the lobby and was slammed with cold air and snow as she went outside. She retied her scarf and walked faster to her car.

∽

"Are you sure you are okay?" he said. His glowing eyes zoomed down on her from far away.

"Yeah man…" she said from the floor. "I'll be fine. I'm safe. It just feels so nice down here."

She had been lying there for a long time. He hated taking care of her. It didn't feel natural. He went over to his food bowl and said nothing.

"Fuck off, man!" she said. "I don't get mad at you, Glenn. Do I?"

His tail swished. She sat up to face him, which spurred a churn of nausea. She lay back down and said, "Noooooooo!" to the ceiling.

Then she said, "Okay so I want to talk. We should always be talking? Right? Like I'm thinking about you drinking and your family. Why did you leave that family? I feed you shit and this apartment is small, ha, I'm small. I'm cold. I'm in debt. I am an ower. Ha ha ha that means I don't own."

She stuttered for a bit and then said, "You do not make sense!"

"Oh I don't make sense."

"I'm sorry," she said. "I'm sorry."

"It's okay."

"Goddammit!"

"What! What!"

"I wish I could know," she said, pointing at the moulding on the wall. "I never know when they'll call. I never sleep. I don't know what will happen. And sometimes the guys, they—there's this one girl I worry about so much, she—nope nope we are not going to, never mind. I never sleep. I always worry. I just never know. My goddamn car. I don't even need it to go to work." She slapped the floorboards hard. "Day work," she corrected.

"Here is a thought," he said. "You could sell it!"

"I couldn't visit my family then," she said plainly. "They don't even run Grey Gooses out there anymore. Fuck Grey Gooses."

"See, I find that curious," he said immediately. "Because I must say, you don't speak about your family very positively."

"My parents are bastards. I love my brother and sister. Fuck, I have to call her back."

"Hm." Oh! Glenn had a thought. "You wouldn't drive now, would you?"

"No. They probably wouldn't call me? Now? Though? It's very late."

"That job really does sound so interesting."

"It's really not and I want to talk about it except no." She dragged her fingertips up along the floorboards then put them on her face.

"I just get curious, I'm not trying to judge. I'm just curious."

"No," she said beneath her hands.

"It is nothing salacious or anything!" he said. "I promise."

"Mmmm."

He hesitated then said, "I'm just so curious as to what the escorts are like. What kind of people are they? Where do they come from? What would make them do this?"

Her face went dark. She sat up and panned her head side to side, like she needed to see him from every angle. "Glenn," she said.

"Maybe you don't need to hear every detail about all the sensational things you've found."

"I'm just curious. Like I said, I'm not going to judge. I just want to know."

She looked at him darkly again, and she said, "Oh yeah?" Then she hit her hand on the floor once, twice, three, four times. "Oh sooooo *interesting*!" she said. "You're just currrious! You like stories, huhhh?"

"Don't you?" he said. "I remember you mentioned wanting to be a writer at some point, yes? Maybe this will inspire you?" He was trying to be helpful.

"*INSPIRE ME?!*" she said. She had that way of laughing and yelling at the same time. She lifted her head up and pointed a finger at him. She tried to talk but kept stopping. She made little starts of sentences that sounded like quasi burps. "I'm sorry, I don't like that," she finally said.

His ears had flattened. "Well!" he said. "You talked about wanting to be a writer once! That would be all I meant."

"Heeeeeeere," she said. "You can have allllll of my stories." She bunched her hair up by her head and drew a circle on the side of her scalp. "Here you go. Everything that's happened to me *and* everything I've ever heard. But ha ha it's you, like, you ever open up about *shit*! I—" She hiccupped and looked at Glenn in the face, goggle-mouthed, like something new about him was dawning on her. "*Wow, fuck you!*" she said breathlessly.

She crawled to her bedroom, then up into her bed and pulled over the covers.

"Why am I here?" she said. "I'm so cold. I'm always so cold. I just want to be warm. I would give—" She snorted and chunks of mucus came out and glistened on her skin. "Guhh I'm sorry!" she called out.

Glenn padded in and said, "Oh you're *sorry*, are you."

Adrienne rolled over and fell on the floor. "Fuck," she said, "this is stupid," and Glenn coldly said, "Think, perhaps, about what is stupid," then immediately nuzzled her foot. Adrienne said, "Glenn, this is stupid." And Glenn said, "Adrienne, come on." He tried to nuzzle her neck and accidentally inhaled the awful syrup smell still on her lips. "Adrienne," he said. "Come on. Get into bed. You'll feel better in the morning." She laughed and hit the floor again. His tail bushed and his hair stood up and he said, "Adrienne I will leave you alone if you get into bed! Get into bed!!" She said, "You really mean that?"

She got up and into bed and he lay down on her stomach. When the phone rang she said, "*NO!*" without really meaning to and it sounded like a sob again, like no, please, please don't make me do this. But she picked up anyway and the woman answered and Adrienne said: "Hi. Oh … no … oh no I'm so sorry I can't drive, I drank this … I … okay I'm sorry, no I know you can't keep having—" Then there was a dial tone and she looked at the receiver until the alarm-drone sounded. She spasmed and screamed and the phone squibbed out of her hand. She stared at the ceiling and couldn't cry. She made dry choking guttural sounds from her throat. Glenn ignored them and fell asleep. She watched the faint outline of his body go up and down. Then back to the ceiling. The room was rotating slowly, subtly around her bed like it was trying not to be noticed, and Glenn looked so small. It was like he was shrinking, like she could reach out and clutch his whole body with her hands.

⁂

Glenn woke up before she did for once, around ten, when the sun had been fully up for an hour and the light was fully poking through the snow to the room. He went to pee then checked around the apartment. Nothing was out of place except that her hoodie and coat were bunched up against the front door; other than that, normal. That was good. Once, she'd taken mushrooms and emptied all of the drawers onto the floor. Organizing, she'd said.

He went on top of the fridge and lapped at a few drops of cold tea that were still in the bowl. He looked out the window and the new inches of snow on the ground.

He felt bad about badgering her last night. He felt bad about a lot of things he'd asked about her life since he'd known her, about her past with boys, her job as a driver, dropping out of school, her parents' marriage. He just never paid attention to how she was reacting to him until it was too late. He got caught up. He really was just ferociously curious. And too, he did want to know everything about her. He loved her, she was his best friend, and she took care of him—she would get better about feeding him, of course she would, she was a good human, good humans fed their cats—and she was almost never mad at him, not even when it came to stuff like the piss and the vomit and the broken bowl. And she'd had such a topsy-turvy, fascinating life over her twenty years (was she twenty? around there anyway). He was five, and he'd never see what she had, even if he made it to the age she was now.

Sometimes that bothered him. He realized, looking out the window at the wooden fire escape on the building across the way, that he had to explicitly admit that to himself. And that it was his deal to work on, not hers. Something about her life made him feel bad and insecure about himself. His world was mostly this apartment, and, well, as long as Adrienne was here, that was how it would probably stay. After he'd left his old humans last summer, he'd lived on the street for only two weeks before Adrienne had taken him in, and while nothing too terrible had happened besides awful food and a couple small fights, he'd been terrified enough during that time that he knew he wouldn't be much with the venturing again. It just wasn't for him, not with the safety and love he had here. Irresponsible, erratic, off-the-deep-end as Adrienne could be. He did love her, and he knew she loved him. He wanted to stay. He did. And he wanted to know all about her and her life, her world. He didn't want to be her, no, but he did want to be strong like her, funny like her, alive like her. Know what she knew, see what she'd seen. And he hadn't understood how those desires were not only impossible but also, well, kind of bad. But he knew now, he knew he needed to leave some things alone. He knew he wasn't always the greatest friend. He knew it didn't come naturally to think about what she was feeling. He didn't understand how she worked, how girls worked, humans worked.

He was trying to figure this out. He wanted to be better. He wanted to stop making her feel bad without realizing it. He wanted to stop thinking her world was tragically glamorous when in reality she was just usually in pain. He wanted to not break shit and pee on stuff when he was angry. He wanted to be less insecure around her, and he wanted to deal with that on his own without mucking her up in his bullshit in the process. He wanted to be good to her, on her terms. He wanted her to feel better. He wanted to be a good friend. He wanted to try.

⚘

She woke up sweaty. She had slept clothed under the blankets and now the sunlight from the window was baking her. She remembered the phone call. Fuck.

It was one o'clock. She had an evening shift in a couple hours. Well that wasn't so bad. She'd call the agency tonight too and apologize, say she'd had a bad night but was ready to work again.

She rubbed her eyes and breathed. Went to take a long shower. Put on some mascara when she came out. She dried and straightened her hair. She had so much breakage it was finger-in-light-socket frizzy. *Conditioner*, she thought. *I need to buy conditioner today.* She put on her jeans, a shirt, and a sweater. Brushed her teeth, went to the kitchen to feed Glenn and toast an English muffin. She made some coffee too.

"Hey there," she mumbled when he walked in.

"Oh hello," he said. He looked up once at her and swished his tail. Then he dove at his food.

"Sorry about last night," she said.

"No no, it is okay," he said. "It really is okay."

She drank a glass of water then went into her armchair. Glenn leapt up and squished in beside her. She should really have more people over, she thought as she ate. Maybe her friend Tina from work. "How'd you feel about me having a girlfriend over here tomorrow?" she said. "Be nice if we had some company, huh? What do you think?"

"Oh, well yes, that would be nice!" he said. "And of course, if you would like some privacy or such I can gladly scamper away, that's just no problem."

"Oh no!" she said. "No, no, I'd want you here! Thank you, though. Thanks for offering that. I might take you up on that. Some point."

She scratched under his chin and he purred. "Of course," he said. She finished her food and he climbed onto her lap. He closed his eyes and let out a sigh-wheeze.

"Adrienne?" Glenn said.

"That's me."

"We can try leaving the bag out. We could perhaps give it a try and we could see how it goes."

She looked at him. He had opened his eyes. He was staring straight ahead at the wall, and his usually Zen face was heavy and sad. She leaned over and put her forehead on his. Her hair made a curtain around his head. She was silent for a while, and then she said, "I'm sorry."

He turned his face up and licked her cheek. "It's okay." He thought: *Sometimes mothers are wrong.*

The coffee burbled and she made to get up. He leapt down to the floor. At the sight of her back leg straightening and going upright, he suddenly had a memory.

"Oh say," he said, following her. "I am sorry if this is not an okay question, please tell me if it isn't. But whatever happened to that one friend of yours? The one with the, er, tattoos. I think she worked in an old folks' home?"

"Tracy," she said. She looked up at the window and saw the building across the way. "Hey, they cleared the snow on this side." Then she smiled and took out some cream. "That's an okay question."

"Oh good," he said. "Yes. Tracy. I liked her."

"Me too," she said dreamily, stirring her coffee. "You know what we used to do? This is before you came along. We used to put soap in the fountains at night. We weren't even drunk, it was just like, something to do. Hey? One night we walked like thirty blocks from

137

downtown to her place. In the summer. It was beautiful. She was such a good musician, too. She had one of those velvety voices, y'know? Did you ever hear her sing?"

"Yes," he said. He closed his eyes and yawned. "I definitely thought it was nice as well. It sounds like you miss her? If I'm correct in that?"

"Yeah. God, she could charm the horns off a bull with that voice," she said. He was still on the floor, and she sat down opposite him, her ass on the linoleum, under the window. "And ambition," she said, sipping from her mug. "For all her wildness, like, that girl had gleams, like, conquest in her eye. I always thought she'd be on TV by now. Or at least in a music video or something."

He had questions, but he decided to listen.

There was a little silence before she spoke again. "What happened to her," Adrienne said. "She moved to Portland, Oregon. Isn't that funny? Of all the places."

"Oh hmm," he said. He padded over to her and curled in her lap. "Is that strange then? Well, I am sorry she's gone."

"Yeah," she said. "She was a ball. I get a letter from her every few months. She's always complaining I haven't gotten on email yet. But I guess she's doing well for herself out there."

She drank her coffee, and she petted her cat.

She set the half-full mug down on the linoleum.

She had to go to work soon.

The wind got strong outside. It was snowing again. She noticed for the first time that the wind had two sounds to it, a whistle and a blow. The whistling rapped and seeped through the window and sounded closer; the blowing stronger, but farther away. "I really do hope I see her all famous someday," she said. "I should write her again soon."

Adrienne sighed and leaned her head on the wall. Her eyes fell on cracks in the ceiling that intertwined and looked like diamonds. She drank her coffee. Glenn was starting to fall asleep.

She massaged his fur. She felt unforgiven, needy. Not weak or bad but—unspecial. She saw herself here, in her apartment, the two of them growing, in summers and winters, looking up together to the ground.

She bent down and kissed her cat. She had to go to work soon. She had to get tea and conditioner on the way home.

Not Bleak

Nobody wants to fucking be here except me. I love it here. I could work on that floor for decades and I wouldn't mind. Shelve and talk about books all day—honestly, most days that seems okay. I used to have this whole set of dreams, but now, I dunno, so many of those dreams ended up wrong or impossible. After a few years at this store I still like going to work every day, and sometimes I figure, well, isn't getting to say that a good dream enough? Most people here want to leave; everybody's looking for a better way up. But me, even this morning, when all my body wanted was to look at the shadows on my ceiling and listen to podcasts with the volume low and curl up in my headachey ball in bed, even then I was kinda jazzed to go to work. I know. That's weird.

You know that kind of hangover when you wake up and you're shaking a little. Like you get up for water and when you lie back down your heart's beating like you sprinted three blocks and your skin's worming around. I always feel so connected with my body in that moment. It's so fragile and frail. I feel every part of it. Like when it's putting barricades up against shutdown is when I'm least detached from my body, the most aware and tuned I am to its existence, that all my systems are present, intricate, working beneath my skin. It's not like I like hangovers. But it is a part I don't mind.

It was still the chilly part of spring, and I put my robe over my pyjamas when I got up. In the living room, the guy we were putting up was still sleeping on the couch. He had broken eyeliner around the side of his face—not smeared so much as, like, little sections of it had fallen off. Zeke, his name was.

My boyfriend Liam and I are always putting up people he meets on the internet. Like a queer couch surf for kids he knows from forums. Sometimes friends of friends, but generally randoms. Kids kicked out of their evil families, kids just trying out small-town homo life. Sometimes kids just going between coasts since we're not too far north of the interstate, just up Highway 52. I really love that Liam's gung-ho about that, though once some girl stole our bathroom sink. That was stupid. Turns out bathroom sinks are worth money, who knew.

Once I'd showered and shaved, the kid was awake and stretching and looking around. Most people can't fit on our couch, it's small, but he was pretty short, and beyond that, his body was small, almost unnoticeable. I don't mean that in some stupid *ha ha turn sideways and he'd disappear!* way; he didn't look malnourished or emaciated. More like inherently unobtrusive.

Do you want tea or coffee or anything, I asked him.

No. Thank you very much though, he said earnestly.

Okay. Well I'm going to work, but Liam should still be here for a while.

Okay. Thank you for everything. This is all really nice of you.

Yeah yeah, I said. What're you doing today?

Handing out resumés, he said. I'm going to try the south strip first. I don't know. Do you think?

Good freaking luck! I said. That's what I think. Everyone wants to work in that area. I have no fuckin' clue how I got my job.

Oh. He looked downcast but still earnest. Really?

I shrugged and said well who knows. Besides, you're pretty, that counts for something. Good luck.

I went to my room, got dressed, and put my laptop in my bag. The kid seemed nice, but man, ever since the bathroom sink thing I've been less careless around here. That whole thing had seemed like one of those warnings Christians would say are concrete messages from God: Like, *Look, see what could've happened instead! Now don't be fucking stupid next time, okay?!*

Zeke left our couch after a week, then a little while later I ran into him working at the fair trade store. I didn't even see him at first. He just said oh! Carla! and then there he was straightening a dream catcher. He was wearing a green flower-print dress and full makeup, and he looked so unbelievably pretty. I said hi and was about to say *Zeke!* then caught myself. At our place he'd said he wasn't quite sure about transitioning, but judging by how he looked now—

But then I wasn't sure what to say. All options to signal I hadn't forgotten his name seemed dumb. When I started transitioning, everything everybody said to me seemed dumb, and I guess now, years later, I can't think of anything to say that's not dumb. And too, I was kind of excited to see the kid like this—there aren't a lot of other trans women here.

(And by that I mean I know exactly one. Well, I guess two now.)

Like an asshole I grinned and said: Well then, name?

It's Zeke, he said.

Oh right, yeah.

I like your outfit! he said. He had this way of speaking that was blank and monotone but it was also sort of hopeful.

Thanks, I said.

Do you still work at the bookstore? he asked.

Yup. Just down the way.

Cool, he said. We were silent for a bit. Poor kid looked nervous. Then he said so, I don't know, maybe we should get a coffee sometime?

Sure, definitely, I said. Come by my work, I always take lunch at two.

Great, he said. I live just a few blocks away.

Cool.

Also, he said. I go by "she" now?

Cool cool. I smiled. Congrats?

Yeah! she said. I will certainly take lots of congrats, I think. Yes. I will take a congrats. She smiled big then, so I smiled back and said I liked her dress.

We live in a small town in the part of the country that's north and cold and flat. It has a college so some liberals ended up here and made it a marginally less stupid place to live than most small towns. I guess I don't really mean small town. It's like twenty thousand people. (We're sixth biggest in the state, if that tells you anything.) But I grew up here and it's nice enough and a batch of queers here do okay, so after I left home I stayed. Liam's from west Kansas, and like most transplants there's a lot he loves and a lot he hates, but I've just always been here. When I was a teenager I wanted to leave. But I dreamed about it like you dream of saving the world. I stayed in town, went to school a couple years, dropped out, transitioned. Met Liam, got my job, moved in here. I'm twenty-six now.

When I got home from work, Liam was there with a bottle of Advocaat, this custardy egg liqueur thing I find fucking delicious. We drank most of it and made out and watched a movie, then the girl on our couch came home and started drinking with us. Liam and the girl kissed eventually so I went back into my room with a glass and my book. Don't get me wrong, we're both okay with sluttery (and Lord knows we'd slaughter each other if we shared a room), but Liam's a trans guy so things get a little one-sided. And I can feel awful about my body super fast, so—into my room we go.

The next morning I had the day off. After a Tylenol and coffee I noticed the girl's shit was gone, so I went into Liam's room. He was naked and moaning on the bed and his nipples had that tortured look where they were done swelling and starting to crust. His face was red too.

Hey gorgeous, I said.

UGHHHHHH.

Here, I said. I set a few Tylenols and a mug of coffee on his end table.

Thanks, he said. He downed them and held his stomach, then put his head on the wall. We had wood panelling and his hair was almond brown so it looked like the apartment was eating his head. He said: It's your day off, right?

Yeah.

Good. You're not going to like this, but we have to hunt someone down today.

Huh?

Remember that guy who stayed a few weeks ago, kinda tiny, thought he might be a girl?

Oh, yeah! I said. Zeke! I ran into her yesterday, she's a girl after all. Why do we have to hunt her down?

Oh word, okay, he said. Well I'm pretty sure she stole some of our shit.

What!

Yeah, my passport's gone.

WHAT!

I went into my room and riffled through a box in my closet. Passport was gone. So was my three-month supply of backup hormones.

Jesus Christ! I yelled and walked back to his room. I didn't even notice that, I said.

Yeah.

FUCK! That was like two hundred bucks worth of shit!

Fuck, Liam said.

Wait, I said, couldn't it have been—okay I totally don't remember her name—couldn't it have been the girl who stayed over last night?

Liam shook his head. I would've seen her. Besides, how would she get into your room, she came after you got home. Did you check on that stuff after she left?

I grunted and pressed the wall with my palm. No. But I never do.

Make some more coffee, Liam said. I'll be right back.

He went into the bathroom and I heard him open the window and toke up. He does that for me. I like weed, but even a few hits ruins me for hours and I get weird hangovers the morning after, like, paralyzed bed-strapped warrior-goddess-effort-required-just-to-get-up-and-empty-my-bladder hangovers. I try to stay away from it but I'm bad at self-control, and especially if I smell it I'm doomed. Hence Liam in the bathroom.

The weight of the money suddenly hit me. I didn't have to replace the passport anytime soon, but my backups …

I'd run out of hormones once. A year into transitioning, not the most stable time anyway. A shipment had gotten stopped at customs, then I didn't have the money for more right away, then Inhouse went down a for a bit. Exhausted favours with the one other lady I knew at the time, and in the end I went without for a month. And after a week I'd started smelling like a boy, and morning wood returned and my skin got oily and my body hair came back, growing like stepped-on weeds. And uncontrollable, debilitating waves of rage. That were, in their weird way, worse than anything before estrogen in the first place. It was like getting scooped up and thrown back into a swamp. I blew up at people, got a few warnings at work those weeks, and it was—this might sound stupid, but it was hard to believe anything would ever get better again? It wasn't a good time. I drank close to two bottles of whisky one night. So I hear, I guess; I don't remember doing it. I just remember falling on my bed with the second bottle from the store and then I was in a hospital. I was living in a basement with roommates who couldn't have given a shit and it was only because Liam was checking in on me that he found me on my floor beside a creek of vomit. Eyes in the back of my head, apparently.

Still making payments on one of the hospital bills.

So. I've been careful about backups ever since.

I cried a little and made more coffee and opened a window. I love the smell of the wind around here. Even where we live, next to downtown, here you can always smell grass and country. It was mid-May and the nights were just getting warm and the air was getting sweet and sticky, the kind of sticky that left nipple marks on my night T-shirts and rub marks on my thighs. I don't mind it, really. It felt gross when I was a boy. But it's not so bad anymore. Both Liam and I, we like the stickiness. And the gentle, placid breezes we get around here in the summer, the sweet cool air that rolls in from the north and pushes the eighty-five-degree sweat back up our arms. When the students are gone and the profs go to cabins in Minnesota or Wisconsin. And everybody left descends into a kind of lazy hibernation.

Eh. College towns.

The coffee finished and Liam came back in black jeans and a flannel shirt, smelling like lotion and soap. He saw I'd been crying and rubbed my neck a little.

You okay? he said.

No.

He hugged me and said, she didn't get my T.

Oh fuck you then, I said into his neck.

Sorry, I just meant like. I can pay for stuff for a bit. If you need.

Thanks. I kissed him on the cheek. You know, it could've been just one of our regular friends, we've had a lot of people over.

They're our friends, he said.

So?

And who would take your hormones?

I don't know! I said.

Sorry, he said. Sorry.

He got out mugs and did both of our coffees, four sugar cubes in his and a bunch of cream in mine. He leaned against the counter and looked out the window. His front half always hunched over as he did this. He looked like he was curling himself. My left arm twinged, which it's been doing a lot lately.

Kids aren't playing outside yet, Liam said.

It's still kinda cold.

Young'uns these days, he said. He fingered the ripped mosquito netting in the window. I need to replace these, he said.

Do you want to go to talk to her? I said. We can go talk to her.

I would like to, yes, he nodded. You don't have to come.

Let's just go to her work, I said, and he nodded and shut the window and I filled up the Thermos.

She wasn't at the fair trade store but our friend Doug was working, this trans guy who always wore horn-rimmed glasses and coloured vests. Today's was red.

She left some stuff at our house, I explained to him. We were going to bring it to her at work, but doesn't she live just around here? I could tell Liam was chomping to tell him the whole story but I didn't think it was worth it, and besides, what if it hadn't actually been her.

Yes! Doug said. She's at the Heritage Complex.

What's the number? I said. I lost it.

He looked up her file, then I bought a new bag. It was on sale and I felt guilty about lying to him so he could illegally give me his co-worker's information. Which we needed to go surprise-accuse her of stealing. Oh well. It was a nice bag.

Oh no! Zeke said when we told her.

Yeah, oh no is right, said Liam. He said it like it was a line he'd heard in a movie. And it kinda seems like you took it all.

Zeke shook her head. No! I didn't. Gosh, I'm so sorry that happened, that's terrible, but I didn't take it.

Well you're the only one who's been in our house without us, so then who did? Liam said.

I don't know, said Zeke. Her voice was still blank, but her features softened when I looked at her. I'm sorry, I really am. I didn't take them, that really sucks. She looked at me and said here, I have some extra estrogen actually, why don't I—it's an extra. May I give it to you?

She stood up and brushed her skirt. Let me give it to you, she said.

She went into her room and came out with one of those Inhouse circles of estradiol. Here, she said. I sipped more coffee and took it wordlessly. Then she said, I just don't understand, why would they take those things?

Liam snorted. Are you kidding? Passports are worth moolah like whoa.

Really!

It's a thing, I said. My friend got broken into last summer and it was all they took. Like, they even left her laptop sitting on her desk.

Wow.

Mmm.

I shrugged and looked at Liam. Now look, he said.

Zeke nodded attentively and waited for him to speak. She had on this big T-shirt and a big flowy skirt, like lounge-around-the-house-for-the-day kind of wear, but her hair was shimmery and had that just-straightened look. It was down to her shoulders now. And there were little beginning-to-be-pokey outlines of nipples behind her shirt.

Look, do you not get that we're serious here? Liam said. He was staring at his hands and moving them like he was shaking an invisible Magic 8 Ball. We could call the fucking cops on you! We need our shit back and we can make life in this town really hard for you if you don't do it.

I'm sorry, said Zeke. If you want to call the cops I completely understand, and I'll talk to them, and just, whatever you need, if that helps you, really, no problem, that's just no problem.

Liam made a noise that pretty obviously connoted running out of steam.

We gave it up after that. I really didn't get the sense she'd taken it, and besides, even if she had, what were we gonna do. Were we really gonna call the cops? *That's* a bright idea. Liam wanted to spread word around "the community" as if we were trying to blackball her or something, but I talked him out of it.

It all kind of worked out anyway. One of the managers quit and I got promoted. A buddy of Liam's put locks on our bedroom doors. I ordered six months' worth of backups and scattered them at the bottom of old boxes of pictures.

∽

Then, in the middle of summer, Zeke and I started hanging out.

It was late June, when the humidity really started to turn on and wear on even Liam and me, and Zeke came into my store sweating balls and said hey, I was just looking for a book? The author's name is Lorrie Moore? I read this book by a woman named Miranda July, and someone told me if I liked her, I'd like Lorrie Moore?

Absolutely, I said. She's fucking great, I love her. Start with *Self-Help* or *Like Life*. Don't read her novels, at least don't read them first. I was about to add, *and ignore the way she writes fat people 'cause it's gross*, but then I didn't. Which was weird, because that's my usual postscript to reccing Lorrie, but when I looked in her face I couldn't say it. Which was weird.

(And I didn't say anything about Miranda July. Nobody likes hearing you don't care about a book they love. They can take it with music and movies a little better, I think?) She bought both books and came back a few days later.

She'd liked *Self-Help* but wasn't overly fond with how *Like Life* talked about the Midwest. She asked if I had other recommendations then said, also, if you wouldn't be interested I totally understand, but, I was wondering if you maybe wanted to get some lunch?

It was close to my break, so I sold her Aimee Bender and we went to the diner across the street.

What brought you here again? I asked. You were in Minneapolis, right?

Yes. But I'm not much of a city person, she said quickly.

Oh word. Where are you from?

North of here. It's a tiny town.

Let me guess. I've never heard of it.

You probably haven't. It's in Canada.

Got it. Hey wait! I said. You have health care up there! Why would you live in this stupid country by choice?

Lots of reasons! she said eagerly. But personal ones. As she was speaking she nodded her head like a dog.

I pointed at her with the saltshaker. You are a nutjob, lady.

Shitty thing to say, and ableist to boot, and I kinda meant it too. She looked hurt then laughed a little. Shit, I'm sorry, I said. That was crappy, I'm sorry.

Oh, no, well … She moved her hands and lips as if about to say something else, then stopped. How is Liam? she asked.

Bitchy, I said.

She laughed. I don't mean to offend or anything, but he certainly seemed a little uptight?

Offend? I said. Lady, I live with him and I fuck him, you think I can stand it? Not that I'm better. I hate everything. She laughed at that too. She had a laugh that went in descending tones and came through her nose, like she was trying to be subdued about it.

Our food came (we'd both ordered chicken fingers), and we chatted a bit more but then she did what to me was a very strange thing: She took out Aimee Bender and started reading. She read for a few minutes then I took out my book and read too, and we read 'til we both had to be at work. It was nice. I was surprised how much I dug it, actually. Reading's ordinarily such a solitary activity for me. It's not something I like to share. But it was nice, reading with her.

It became a pattern as we kept hanging out. She wasn't much of a talker, but it was in a way I liked (and admired, because, you know, I talk a lot). For all her nervousness and quirks and shit, Zeke also had this baseline self-assuredness about her that just made you quiet and comfortable. I guess it's not a super rare quality, though maybe it is in trans women. It turned out she'd started hormones around the end of winter, before she'd crashed with us for a bit. (You didn't know if you were a girl, but you were taking hormones anyway? I said. Yup, she said.) So, lovely thing, I got to be around for some of those stages. The fat from her cheeks smoothing her face, her skin sprouting freckles, her hair getting fluffier. Zeke would rarely talk about that either—another weird thing—but she'd smile whenever I brought any of this up to her. She was so obviously guarded, but even I could see some of the weights lift from underneath her. This many years after transitioning I've pretty much forgotten what that feels like, or even looks like: For all the kids we've put up, we've only had a few trans ladies, and nobody fresh on HRT. So Zeke—it really was beautiful to watch her.

Mostly though, we just read and talked about books. I got her into Amy Hempel; we both agreed we loved her but didn't understand her. (I don't even remember the story plots the next day, she said. But she's so beautiful, sometimes I cry when I'm reading her!) I got her into David Foster Wallace and we argued about trans bullshit in *Infinite Jest* (I just don't care, she said a third of the way through it. I don't mind seeing terrible trans characters vilified because they're trans. I don't know why I don't care, I just don't!)

We didn't talk much about ourselves, but I learned a few things about her. She was twenty-one. Left home at eighteen. Was actually born in Nebraska, but her parents were Canadian and moved back when she was a baby. She loved riding her bike. She was starting a garden on her balcony. (She talked a lot about her damn garden when you got her going.) And she'd travelled all over the country, which I wouldn't have guessed. When I got her into Joseph Mitchell, she told me about a night in New York she'd spent smoking on a warehouse roof with some girls from Lithuania.

I didn't want to invite her back home, so the diner and the bar kinda became our places. Liam still seemed butthurt, but I don't think the two of them clicked even before the stealing-accusation thing. Me, I figured that either that other girl had made off with our stuff while we were sleeping or it was someone from town we'd had over, though sometimes I did still wonder if it'd been Zeke. It kinda seemed like a parlour game though, like, we'll never find out really, so who cares.

Oh also, her voice. She switched it around so quick. It was kinda infuriating, actually. She still spoke in that hopeful monotone, but now her voice had this velvety, deep quality. It's a weird game how getting your voice to pass means flipping its perception from high to low. And she made it work so well. She almost sounded coquettish. Except she was reserved and all.

Did you ever find out who stole your passports and your hormones? she said one night.

I shook my head. Nah. It's okay though. I replaced them when I got promoted.

Hey, that's good, she said.

Yeah. I grimaced and drank from my beer. God, sorry again about that whole inquisition thing we put on you.

Oh it's okay, she said. I might've wanted to do the same.

No you wouldn't have, I said. You're so quiet and nice, I don't think you would've barged into someone's house like that.

I said I might've *wanted* to, she snapped. I didn't say I would've actually done it. I grunted and swallowed my beer. It felt nice to get a rise out of her.

A bunch of weeks went by like this. I hung with Zeke during the day and then at home Liam was always putting someone new up. It was a good summer. We got new mosquito screens that weren't ripped to shit, and we left the windows open and let the breezes come in. Liam got a new job at the fusion café and brought home all this delicious food. Work was slow but steady, and all the new hires were low drama. Everyone who stayed with us was nice and pretty, and we found jobs and places quick for a couple kids on the lam. Liam and I only had a couple blow-ups, and there was always good beer but I didn't drink too much, and the days were warm and so were the nights and for a while life was kind of a beautiful haze.

One day, in the middle of August, Zeke came in looking for a gift for her grandfather.

Oof, I said. Well, histories or biographies of stodgy old dudes are what always come to mind for me. But what's your grandpa like? Is it his birthday or something?

No, it's just a gift.

Oh word. So what's he like?

Well, he's a Mennonite, she said.

Ah yeah?

Zeke had mentioned being a Mennonite a few times but never really talked about it. I felt dumb for not knowing, honestly. I've lived around here all my life but never actually met a Mennonite. Though I guess they keep to themselves. Sometimes they come into town. And we've put up a couple of their apostates. I know some wear the old traditional dress stuff like suspenders and kerchiefs and some don't. But that's also, like, all I know.

I nodded like an asshole for a bit then said wait, okay, so what does that really mean?

Zeke snickered—not like, tittered or giggled, she snickered, loudly, and it was weird—and she said oh boy, it means a lot of things. But he's very old school. He used a wood stove to heat his house until he was seventy.

I blinked. He doesn't, like, live in Texas or something, does he.

No. In Canada.

What the fuck?! I said.

Yup, she said. He only started wearing a watch a few years ago too. And he still won't wear it to church.

What a hardy guy, I said.

She snickered again. Maybe not quite the right word for it, she said. But yes. A book. I want to get him a book, just something he wouldn't normally read. But no political stuff. Actually no religious stuff either. I would just get him the wrong thing.

Sure, I said. What's he interested in?

Well I thought perhaps, like you said, something historical would be good? But not about anything too recent and nothing religious.

Would he be into Renaissance history?

As long as there isn't too much political or religious stuff, she said encouragingly.

There's this new thing folks have been liking, and I don't think the Reformation is too much of a factor, hold on ...

It was a book about Portugal by that Columbia professor who'd blurbed basically every popular history book from the last twelve years. It had a gorgeous-yet-subdued picture of a ship on it. She paged through it for a while then said: Thank you! This is great! Thanks!

I watched her as she went to pay. She was wearing a sky-blue cotton T-shirt and black jeans, and even like that she wasn't getting read. You could tell from how they all looked at her. It was kind of amazing.

Though also, like, what a fucking bitch.

A few minutes later, as I was sorting poetry, she came back. Sorry, she said. I forgot that I finished *Inferno* last night. I really liked it. Any chance you might have another suggestion for me?

Lidia Yuknavitch, I said instantly. (I'd been prepared.) It's a memoir. *Chronology of Water*. It's heavy but you'll love it.

I went to our holds stack and gave her the copy I'd set aside. She said thanks and left.

Shit, I thought, *I really don't know what to give her next.*

Zeke always wanted more stuff to read. When she didn't have much money she would scour the dollar shelf, or just ask for recs then check at the library. Nobody else was like that. Like, sure, we have regulars who come in every few days or weekly or whatever, but they're lit folk. People down from campus, usually. Profs and kids alike. Or they're collectors. Or whatever. You know. Book people. Like me and most of the other fucks who work here see some old thing and gush, like, *Ooooh! I've wanted to read that forever!* And that's great but—I dunno. It's different than what people are like when they're just burning for a good read, someone who misses the way they felt when they read *Harry Potter* and they're looking for you to give them that feeling again. Who just want to walk out of the store dizzy to disappear for a while. It can be about anything, I really believe that. *Fifty Shades of Grey* sold to the same people who bought *The Hunger Games.*

Anyway. Point is. Those kinds of customers, the make-me-feel-that-way-again customers, they're never the regulars. They come back between months and years, if they do at all. But not Zeke. She was so persistently bonkers for something good to read you could see it, she was just *hungry* for it. I loved that about her. I hoped her grandpa liked the book. Whoever he was.

I woke up the next morning with patchy-but-hot memories after a night with a thirty-year-old mega-top woman from the Christian college in Jamestown (it's barely an hour away so we see folks from there a lot). She had really gone after me. It was nice. When I moved to get up I could feel every bruise and ache from where she'd touched me. That kind of thing hadn't happened with someone new for a long time. My sex drive isn't terribly high, honestly, not that there are hordes of people lining up to fuck fat trans women in the first place. But she had been so lovely to me. Though my head and stomach felt awful enough that Tylenol and coffee didn't do shit.

Bumping around in the kitchen, trying not to wake passed-out dom lady on the couch, I saw a missed call from Zeke and no voice mail. Made a couple hours prior. Weird. I texted her. *Six-thirty call? What's up?*

In the mirror getting ready to shower I saw some hickeys. I touched them and they only hurt a little. I turned on the water but before I got in I put my hands down my stomach flab and my sides. My skin was aching at such a slight touch. And my ass hurt. Right, that happened. I drew my hands up over my body and held my breasts. My left nipple twinged slightly and I could feel a tiny bit of crust. The bathroom steamed and I got in the shower and stood there with my eyes closed. I held my breasts and stood completely still, holding and feeling the water and my body. When I first transitioned, I used to do that a lot. In the bathroom, with my eyes closed, just breathing and touching my own skin. It's so peaceful. I used to think of myself as lucky, just that in itself, a woman calming herself only by holding her own body. It was nice to feel it still working.

Zeke said to meet for lunch and she'd talk then.

My hangover stuck around for a lot of the morning and my fucking left arm got all tingly again but at least work was quiet. Only blip was some guy got indignant that I wouldn't take a return for a book he'd water-damaged. Shouted he'd never set foot in here again. (Why do they always say the same lines?) Walked out with this dad face looking all stern and satisfied. Then the next customer, middle-aged guy, stepped up grinning and shaking his head saying *yeah boy I used to work in a store like this when I was about your age, well maybe a little younger, boy, some people huh? Let me tell you, we had this one guy ...*

People. They work on a sales floor a few years in college and talk about it like they're old salts for the rest of their lives.

I don't know why that gets my goat so much, although I guess anybody who works customer service is going to develop seventy pet peeves and it's better to just acknowledge this than pretend you don't have them. I dunno. I guess it's just like—when you stop having to live with something day to day, you forget what it's like. You remember the events that happened, sure, but how it felt, day in day out, is different. Even some traumatic things, I think? Like your body remembers it but your conscious self doesn't. Hopefully you don't forget enough to be a jerk. But it happens. Like when Liam says all hopefully that one day I won't be harassed or misgendered by strangers anymore. Like, hey asshole, you haven't been "she'd" by anyone but your dad since you were twenty, fuck you.

So I'm going to be asking you a favour, said Zeke.

Okay.

And I just want to make clear. It's totally okay if you don't want to do it. I will completely understand if you say no, it's just no problem, no problem.

Okay.

So I'll be asking a lot here.

My head was still pulsing. Just fucking say it.

Yes, well, she breathed deeply. You remember my grandpa. The one I bought the book for yesterday.

Yeah, we're old friends, I said irritably, shaking out more Tylenol. What about him?

Well, she said. I'm going to see him in a few weeks. And I won't be going as a girl, unfortunately, but. Given, well, circumstances. You know. I would really rather not travel alone.

I nodded. She was looking me in the eye with no break in her gaze, the way she did, but somehow now it was a little creepy. And, she continued, this may sound strange, but—not only do I not want to travel alone, but, he thinks I have a girlfriend. And it would really make him happy if he met that girlfriend. And so I was wondering if perhaps you could come along with me and, well, pretend to be my girlfriend? Possibly?

I blinked. I swallowed my Tylenol.

Honey, I said—and I enunciated clearly here—you don't want me.

Yes I do.

The blind could read me, Zeke.

Well, I don't know if *that's* true.

I gave her a dark look. Don't fuck with me.

Well Carla, she said. You have to understand. They don't even know it's possible.

She was sounding both reasonable and condescending as hell. *Well*, why *me*? I said. Why not a cis girl? Or if you really want a trans girl with you, there is Sophie, fuck, she looks gorgeous, besides isn't she a goddamn Menno like—

I don't *want* to bring fucking Sophie! she said. Her voice became stilted. Perhaps. Maybe. It's possible. I don't. Trust other people here! Right?

Fuck, all right, all right. I let out a stream of air. Sorry.

Thank you, sorry, she said hastily. I apologize. I did not mean to get so excited.

Uh, you didn't, I said. She'd barely raised her voice.

I know I'm asking a lot, she said. Anyway, just let me know whenever you can, and just, no pressure, that's very okay.

Even if I wanted to, I said, I still don't have a new passport. We never put in for them.

I can pay for the new one, she said instantly.

Are you fucking serious? I said. We'd have to get it rushed. I'm pretty sure that's like a hundred and thirty bucks.

Well of course I'm serious, she said matter-of-factly. I'm the one asking you, so I should do it. If you say okay, I'll do it. Really, she said, nodding her head. I'd have no problem doing that. And I think we could get you a card passport anyway, instead of a full book.

I put my palms to my cheeks. She sat patiently without saying anything more. She was being so nice waiting for me to process. She looked so placid. I wanted to deck her. I imagined her sitting there just as still and unmoving, only with blood coming out of her mouth.

You'd have to tell me what to wear, I said.

I gave up the idea of not being read long ago. And I kinda started dressing accordingly, like, putting all that effort in every morning wearing shit I didn't like just to still get "sir'd" was just … ach. Like, I still shave and put on makeup every day, but I mostly wear jeans and cardigans and my hair's always a fucking mess. And I still get sir'd or the *you a boy or a girl?* crap, and, you know, worse. But I guess, like, now I get an extra thirty minutes in the morning? I dunno. It's rotten and it's awful and I hate it more than anything but at the same time I've gotten so used to it as an ingrained part of my life. It's weird how that works. Anyway, the morning we left, I put on an old loose black dress, this formal thing I'd worn to Liam's mom's funeral down in Sublette. It had been so hot down there, and dry and mean and dead. A different Midwest. Nobody talked to us but it was whatever, we'd hung out with his aunt mostly, this badass chain-smoking woman who had huge glasses and ran a bar and hated everyone.

Makeup was trickier because Zeke told me to be super femme but not be too elaborate about it (What the fuck, I'd said). After shaving and putting on foundation and concealer, I sat and pondered in front of the mirror. I plucked my eyebrows. Then put on mascara but no eyeliner. Then extra concealer under my eyes. I eventually decided on lipstick, muted red, but it took me a while; I haven't worn lipstick in years.

I brushed my hair then eyed myself in the mirror a few more minutes, which was about as fun as punching myself in the face. I flat-ironed and was about to call it good when I thought of my hair clip. Perfect.

I had this pastel-purple hair clip I bought when I was eighteen, way back, on one of those first barely-able-to-even-look-at-the-woman's-section shopping trips. It's got a dumb green dot in the middle and the spring is wheezy and I don't really wear it that often, but it's also kind of elegant and pretty. The tines are curved and ornate in this way that looks like they're made out of bone. Regardless, I feel better when I wear it. I wore it down at the funeral in Sublette too. I went back to my bedroom and opened the junk drawer where I kept my hair shit.

Fuck, I couldn't find it.

I dug through the drawer about five times then just turned the thing upside down and let shit go all over my desk and the floor. Nowhere.

Nothing. I went back to the bathroom and went through all the drawers there. Nothing. Fuck. FUCK. I went back to my room and looked through the crap again. I looked through all the other drawers in my desk even though they only had stuff like cords and notebooks. I looked in places that made no sense, like Liam's room and behind chairs. But I knew, I realized, it was gone. I hadn't worn it for months (I think? Shit, maybe I was drunk), and we're not the neatest of folks. We lose stuff like this all the time.

I actually started to cry a bit. For living in one town all my life, I don't have much stuff and I don't have a lot of mementoes. Or, for that matter, a lot of things I really like to wear.

Zeke texted that she would be there in five. Fuck. Oh fucking whatever. This was stupid. It was so stupid and weak and teenage girly to get upset about this. It was stupid it was stupid it was stupid. I combed my hair again and called it good.

Shit, shoes?

Fuck it, Vans it was.

She pulled up in a borrowed Chevy Celebrity, wearing that green flower-print dress. I hadn't expected her in girl clothes, and I hate to say it didn't help my bad mood.

Okay, so really, I said as soon I got in, how are they going to react when you show up with a transsexual?

He's not going to know you're trans, she said calmly.

Fuck! I said, hitting the dashboard. You can't say that! You don't know! There's at least a very good chance they're going to think I'm a man, and you *know* that.

I really don't think so at all, she said. I don't quite think he has the language for this. In fact, I know he doesn't. Nope, you have nothing to be worried about.

How do you respond to that? I let out a slow stream of breath and turned the rear-view mirror to check my face. Nothing to worry about, I repeated, and realized I didn't really know why I'd agreed to come.

We hopped over to Carrington then went north and then took back roads to get there. She seemed to know where she was going and didn't want to talk too much, so I sat and read and put my arm out the window when we went slow through towns. We stopped once for gas at this sad little station where the numbers on the pumps flipped over like old alarm clocks.

We stopped again a few miles before the border for her to change in a Dairy Queen bathroom. I decided to wait in the car then after a few minutes realized I was hungry. Like starving.

I looked around and just saw the highway and a few rundown houses and a fire station. There were people walking around and a bunch of other cars in the parking lot. I didn't even know what town we were in.

I put my fingers around the door handle, and then realized I wasn't going to open it. I knew without a question I couldn't do it. I'm fine on my own turf usually. Like, I can deal with that stuff, just—who knows? You never know. I've heard such scary fucking stories come out of some of these towns … you know? And, like, even if I didn't have anything to be physically afraid of—which I probably didn't, but probably in the sense that when you drive in a snowstorm you probably won't end up in the ditch—I felt so ridiculous in this stupid fucking dress and my stupid hair and I could already feel every fucking eye on me if I even stepped out in public and hear people snickering and old ladies huffing and some fucking dude laughing and my voice cracking if I even managed to talk at all and I just wanted to fucking walk in there and order some awful food without announcing a freak show or having a fucking panic attack—

Zeke opened the door and I jerked my face up from my hands.

Whoa, I said.

Her face, so naturally drawn to calm, suddenly moved into an expression of glumness. Yeah, she said.

She was in shirt sleeves and grey cotton pants, and her shoulder-length black hair was slicked neatly back. Zeke was on the pale side to begin with—which is saying something for our stupid corner of the world—but with her soft girl-body, already so unassuming, and now passing for a boy, she looked truly ghostly. Like she was a wraith, something you could put a hand through.

Or maybe like a goth kid being made to go to church.

You all right? I tried.

Oh, Zeke said. She flapped a hand up and down. Well.

Wanna go through the drive-through? I said gently. Zeke smiled a little and started the Celebrity. Come on. Let's eat things that are really gross, I said.

Possibly they make quintuple cheeseburgers, she said.

The border was a dinky little crossing, a guy sitting in a shack on one side and another guy sitting in a shack on the other. One car ahead of us in line. I texted *Going under the Canuckistan curtain* to Liam and turned my phone off.

Wow, I said. I always go up I-29. And that's so, like, imposing. And this is like—

Maybe not enlarging your faith in the Department of Homeland Security? Zeke grinned.

I'd finally updated my passport gender and I guess I looked all right, because the agent just gave us a few suspicious once-overs then let us pass. Welcome home, he said to Zeke.

It was hot. I know it doesn't get that hot in our town compared to other places, but God, it was so hot. We were blasting AC and the canola fields were shimmering and those little white balls of fluff were flying everywhere and we drove for about twenty minutes before stopping in this town called Winkler for her to run out and get some pops, and even though there was wind the sweat rolled down me just after a few seconds in the parking lot.

(I sucked it up and got out of the car. Whatever. How bad could Canadians be.)

Zeke's mood wasn't exactly chipper. But she seemed a little better. There was a ten-storey building in the distance and when I said I'd never seen something so tall in a town this size, she said yes, well. It's the mothership of the senior homes, so I suppose you could call it City Hall.

It suddenly clicked to me. Hey, I said, so this is where you grew up, right? You grew up here!

Hell no, she said. I'm from Morden. That way. She pointed across the highway.

Got it, I said.

After leaving town we turned onto a gravel road. We trundled along it for a while before turning onto another gravel road, then finally onto a long driveway surrounded by dirt with a little paint blot of a house at the end and a patch of canola behind it. The colour of the house was robin's egg blue.

My grandpa doesn't farm anymore, Zeke explained. But he rents out the canola field for money.

An old guy needs money? Aren't you all socialists up here? I said. I was joking around but she took me seriously. Well sure, she said. But, y'know, Mennos, they'll never leave any money on the table. There's like this joke? What's a Mennonite's ultimate dilemma? Free alcohol. She looked like she expected me to laugh.

I wasn't really serious about the socialist thing, I said.

Hmm, she said. Well.

We crunched up the driveway and knocked and there was no answer. Just from the walk we were both glossy with sweat, and a breeze came from behind us and fused my dress to my back.

She pushed open the screen door and said: Helloooooooo! Grandpa?

She beckoned me in and shut the door. We were on a landing with a little closet to our right and in front of us stairs to a concrete basement. On our left was the kitchen. The linoleum was bright blue and had imprints of flowers.

Hellooooooooooo? Zeke said. She motioned for me to take my shoes off. There was a ticking from a clock I couldn't see and a half-full coffee pot burbling on the kitchen counter. There was a single plate drying on a dish rack. Other than that the room looked long untouched. Beside the kitchen there was a table with six chairs, then past that was a tiny living room with one chair and one couch that were both fuzzy and burnt red. On the other side of the room was a radio. Zeke whispered oh no and called again: Helllooooooo! then pivoted and went back through the kitchen and down to the basement—God it was cooler down there—but there was nothing but boxes and old board games and a water tank with stacks of softener beside it. Zeke leapt back up the stairs and I clattered after her and we went through the kitchen and the living room again and up another flight to the second floor. It was still so weird seeing her in those huge shirt sleeves and pants and slicked hair. Even as she took charge she looked gaunt, windless. We went up the stairs; they were linoleum too and the colour of honey, and Zeke took them three at a time. On the landing she knocked on a closed door and it swung open but nobody was there, just a little nicely made double bed, and beside it a nightstand with a devotions book on it, and on the other side of the room was a dresser with a picture frame containing only a quotation of just a few lines in Gothic script. The first line was printed bigger than the rest and I could read it: I thanked the Lord for you today. Zeke turned around and said oh no again and then: Hellooooo! and ignored the next door and went through the last one. It was a bathroom with more blue-flowered linoleum and I could see a carpet-covered toilet seat and on the floor the edge of grey sweatpants and Zeke gasped in a pitch so high it was like a squeak and soon her phone was out and calling 911, and downstairs we heard the screen door open and slam shut.

⁂

Pardon me, I'm sorry to interrupt you, the nurse said.

No, not at all! said the neighbour. He'd been coming over to the grandpa's place to visit and now he was with us at the hospital.

Is it—she turned to Zeke—you're Mr. Reimer's grandson, correct?

Yes, whispered Zeke.

Okay, she said gently. As we said earlier, your grandpa's going to be fine. At this point we don't think his bleeding is going to start again. She put her hand on Zeke's shoulder. It's good that you're here, she said quietly.

Of course, Zeke nodded. Her pant legs made a rubbing sound as she shifted them.

Though of course, the nurse said, he shouldn't be alone. Is there someone looking after him?

I come see him every day, said the neighbour.

Oh, that's a good start, okay, said the nurse.

I can check on him more often than that, he added.

Well. That would probably be the best idea! the nurse said. Maybe I'll chat with you about that before you leave.

After she left the neighbour turned to me. So a thousand pardons, he said to me, I'm Abe.

I shook his hand, though I never know if you're supposed to do that when you're trying to pass. Carla, I said. I was trying to talk softly (Airily? Breathily? No, too breathy. Fuck!) It's nice to meet you after all that time following an ambulance together, I whispered.

He cackled. Oh well, he said. How'd Ezekiel keep a lady like you that's lovely *and* funny?

Bribery, I said before I could stop myself. He gave a hoot and elbowed Zeke in the ribs. Zeke gave a little laugh and made a smile for a few seconds then stared back at the vending machine again.

That's when I realized Zeke was actually right: They weren't reading me. It'd been a couple hours in each other's company by now and he wasn't reading me. Jesus Christ, he wasn't reading me. He'd been this close to me and he'd heard me speak in the car too and he still wasn't reading me.

I thought it would feel different.

I thought when this happened so plainly and cleanly it would be a crossed-the-Rubicon moment. But it wasn't. I just felt, like—wary. Suspicious, even. Like they were fucking with me or, even worse, just trying to be nice, like maybe Zeke had told them the whole thing on the phone ahead of time and even called the neighbour and explained very carefully that this was his *girlfriend* and call her his *girlfriend* and you know his *girlfriend* might look and sound like a big gross man but humour her and *don't mess up, okay?*

When minutes later he called me a lady again, I realized: I wasn't able to believe him. Not metaphorically—I mean that I literally didn't have the capacity. It was like if Liam told me he'd just spoken with his dead mother. I'd believe his experience. But I wouldn't believe it was real. I could try to believe it but internally it just wouldn't work.

I had to try really hard not to cry when I thought about that.

So I kept talking with the guy with as few words as possible, and Zeke perked up a bit as I did, and I told him about my job, and he told me he loved being retired but he missed his family, that his daughter was in Winnipeg, his sons were in Steinbach, and his wife was in heaven. But Zeke's grandpa was Abe's cousin, and he lived next door, and that was certainly nice. Abe came over every day to check on him and have a coffee. Your guy's good to his grandpa, Abe said to me quietly, motioning to Zeke. In case you didn't know, he said.

Another nurse appeared and put her hand on Zeke's shoulder. Your grandfather's in room 57, she said.

I only saw an empty bed when we walked in. It was a few seconds before I realized he was actually sleeping in it.

Her grandfather was so thin and weak looking, such a lanky, bony man. His hair was thin and so incredibly short, like a duckling's. He was balled up sleeping on the blankets, wearing the sweatpants and T-shirt we'd found him in. Hooked up to a few monitors. Zeke touched his leg. The slick in her hair was gleaming under the light. A doctor came by and told us Mr. Reimer could go when he woke up. Was there someone around to look after him.

It was around five when we got out of the hospital. He was up and moving fine, just a little slow. Kept apologizing for messing up our trip. We drove him back in the Celebrity and he asked Zeke stuff like nothing had happened.

I liked him. He was upbeat and friendly, but not in the gregarious way older men like that often are. Like, the guy really seemed to just want to chill with his grandkid. Did he have a car now? No, this one was a friend's! How was his job? Excellent, thanks, his boss was very nice! How were his siblings? Doing well, thanks, though they hadn't talked for some time. They were all still out west, yes? Yes.

And Abe the neighbour hmm'd and oh'd but mostly let the two chat.

We dropped Abe off—man, his house was big—then crunched up the gravel driveway again with Zeke helping her grandpa walk, and the wind had stopped and I was hammering on myself from the mosquitoes. Inside, he offered to fix us some sandwiches, then he saw the coffee pot was still on. Oh! he said. Well then, would you like some coffee? Fresh, obviously.

We laughed and nodded yes and he poured us cups. He pointed to the clock setting and said oh so yeah I just got this new thing here, it's got this little … timer thing on it? A little extravagant perhaps, maybe, but. Well. It's useful!

Very useful, said Zeke. It must be nice for your visitors, yup! I know I would definitely appreciate it! The guy said ahhh and grinned and waved his hand.

Then he said, so! The famous Carla! My, well, certainly hope every introduction to our family does not go like this one! I giggled at that and he said yes, well, forgive me for saying so, I just, it's certainly nice to see Ezekiel with such a nice girl!

My brain still didn't believe him. It didn't. But I blushed and said: Why thank you. And I haven't blushed for a while, I'll tell you that.

He changed clothes and we hung out with him for a bit in the living room and Zeke gave her grandpa the book. The rubbing of her pant legs became like background noise. I wondered if her grandpa could tell how uncomfortable she was, or if this was just the version of her he knew. I spent a lot of time looking at the pictures in the place and through a family photo album on the coffee table. I thought I could pick out which one was Zeke when she was little, but everyone looked so similar it was hard to tell.

We left at eight, standing outside saying goodbye with all of us trying to face east and not get creamed by the sun. The mosquitoes were really starting to go at it, though the old guy didn't seem to notice and just idly slapped his leg every few seconds. But the heat had gone down, and the air was warm and sweet.

(Skeeters. That's another vehicle for self-deprecation people love around here. You can buy little magnets at truck stops with pictures of grinning batshit mosquitoes and the words NORTH DAKOTA STATE BIRD. *State bird, ha ha, good one!* God, gag me with a fucking spoon.)

Are you in need of a few shekels for your gas tank there? said her grandpa.

Oh gosh, said Zeke. Well hey, certainly, if you're offering, certainly don't feel pressured at all, I'm doing just fine really but if you're asking if it would be useful—well, yes it definitely would be!

Oh no no no, he said. He pulled out his wallet and gave her a twenty. That's just my pleasure now, absolutely.

Thank you, thank you, Grandpa, Zeke said. She nodded over and over. That's super nice of you, thank you very much.

Aw shoot. Hey, are you getting enough to eat down there in the US of A? he said. Maybe watch what I say, none of my business or whatever, but, maybe thinkin' you certainly look a little pale!

Trying to get some *Warenki* shipped down there, Zeke said dryly.

Oba yo! he said. *Scheenschmakjen?*

Yo, yo! said Zeke. They try to make 'em down there, *schmakjt en oot-yu-rachktah Shpanzuh Futz.* The old guy really busted up at that and put his hand to his face and shook his head and said oh shoot, oh shoot, forgive us Lord, eh? Then he strong-armed her in a hug and said awwww, aww, my grandson, hey, it's so nice you came to visit, that was just really nice, now bless you!

So what was all that about the coffee pot being extravagant? I said once we were driving.

Ummmm, she said. I would suppose he doesn't want anyone to think he's too … She trailed off and gestured. Fancy, maybe. Or worldly, as they used to say.

What.

Remember what I said about the watch?

Yikes, good thing I didn't, like, mention I own a cellphone.

He wouldn't care about that.

Or God forbid he find out about my iVibes.

He wouldn't care about that, she said. He doesn't care as much about others.

No?

Well it's weird, she said.

We turned off the first gravel road onto the other.

I think a lot of Christians can't shake the fear of being judged for certain sins, even if they can shake the fear that *other* Christians will be judged for them.

Hmmm, I said.

I'm never sure what to make of it, Zeke said thoughtfully. On one hand, it's great you're not gumming up others with your bullshit. That's good. On the other hand, if you really believe this certain thing is a sin, isn't it almost selfish to think God would be concerned with your soul but nobody else's?

I dunno, I said. Sorry, I've only been to church like ten times my whole life.

Mmm, she said.

I didn't know you spoke another language, I said.

Low German? I only know a few words, she said.

What'd you say that made him laugh? Shmacks what? Tastes like something?

A stretched spider's vagina, she said, and when she didn't elaborate I realized it was time to shut up.

We filled up in the town then went back over the border and Zeke changed into normal clothes. I turned my phone back on and texted Liam: *BORDER PATROL ON OUR TAIL. SEND HELP.*

I really passed up there, didn't I, I said.

Told you, she said immediately. Those two men, they have no space for us. They literally cannot comprehend that we would exist.

Neither do some people in our town, I said back. But they look at me and still see a fat dude with tits.

She cringed when I said that. Oh. Well. Now. I don't think you're—you look that way. For one, people in your town do actually know what the word "transgender" means. But, like, look. Think about it. To them I'm still a good Christian boy, even if the good Christian boy is this weird kid with long hair who moves around a lot. And so for whatever tiny spot of their brain has space for the idea of trans women, there is zero space for a trans woman either being with me, or looking like you. Who's not in, say, a short skirt and heels or whatever. So if I say you are my girlfriend, to them you're a cis girl, full stop, and they'll just think oh, Ezekiel has a weird-looking girlfriend. And let me tell you, they *really* want me to have a girlfriend.

Weird-looking, huh, I said.

Sorry, she mumbled. Her placid face came on and she was silent and I wanted to hit her again.

Thanks for coming with me, she said at the next town.

Liam texted back: *This is the feds, punk! Your man is dead! Expect twenty-five to life!*

Yeah uh-huh, I said. So why did you come up here again?

It means a lot for him to see me, she said.

Right, but do you actually like seeing him? You were so miserable today.

I was not, she said. Sorry, but you're wrong on that one. Besides the death scare thing I had a good time.

You like those shirt sleeves, do you, I said acidly.

No. Look. Can I tell you something I've never told anybody?

Yes.

I would rather wait for him to die, she said. I honestly don't want to know how he'd react if I came out to him. I don't know if he'd cut me out. Maybe he would. Maybe he wouldn't. But I don't want to find out. I don't want to see him looking at me like a space alien, and I don't want to get letters in the mail about my soul, I don't want to hear from all thirty of my relatives about how sad I'm making him. And I doubt he would cut me out entirely. He would probably still let me in the house, though I doubt I would be invited, exactly. But it's not like I would stop calling and going up there every couple months. I wouldn't care how shitty he'd be, Carla, I'd still go. I'll never not love him, I'll never leave him. He's sick. He's old, I can fulfill one last responsibility as a grandson. That's a thing I can do, I can actually do it. I have to and I will do it.

You've given this a lot of thought, huh, I said.

Everyone else in my family became a worse person when I came out, she said. I don't want him to be a worse person too.

My own parents came around after the alcohol poisoning thing. My mom refers to it as my suicide attempt, though I dunno about calling it that. When you can't remember the act in question, it's hard to know if you were really trying to die. It definitely was a point in my life when I was okay with dying. But I hadn't thought I was in a place to actually attempt. (Can two bottles of whisky even kill a fat trans-sexual?) I really don't know. I think about it a lot. With my mom it's open-and-shut, though. She said it absolutely turned her around; she said she was sorry and she cried at my hospital bed and she even gave me a few bucks for more hormones. My dad and I don't have much to say to each other but we can be in the same room and he doesn't use my old name or anything. I really am glad we talk now. It's just hard to forget it took a trip to the emergency room. I can see and feel my mother trying, I can, and I feel like *such an asshole* for feeling this, but—I still don't really feel like I can trust her. There was a period in my life, right after we started talking again, when I tried really hard. And I told everyone my mom and I had reunited and it was all magical and amazing. The whole thing was kinda twenty-first-century Lifetime movie ready, right? But it still eats at me. I hate it. Like, how can it be love if it takes a close shave with death to see your daughter as a person? I don't see how that's love. I know that's a snarly thing to say, I know I should just move on, I feel so petty for not getting over it, but I don't know how to not hurt about that, I don't. I don't want to be all magically close and loving with my mom again. I just want to forgive her and stop hurting, I want to be calm and forgive, but I can't, I still hurt about it, I can't, I can't, I don't know how.

That actually makes a lot of sense, I said to Zeke.

Thanks.

Liam texted again: *When you getting home?*

Can you really run it out that long? I said.

Who knows. It's kind of terrible to say I guess, but he's obviously not getting any younger.

Yeah I wondered.

We were going through a town. It was nine o'clock and the sun was half set and you knew anybody outside was losing pints of blood by the minute from the skeeters. There was another Dairy Queen on a corner of a four-way stop next to peeling white houses with seafoam trim and triple round holes in the windowsills. We stopped at the stop sign and a teenage girl crossed.

Sometimes, Zeke said suddenly, sometimes I have this very weird vision. I suppose maybe you could call it a fantasy. And I see it all the time. Where he dies soon. As is not unlikely. And I go to his funeral and I am dressed as a boy like usual. And I say my prayers, touch his face in the casket, and hug everyone in my family. All these people.

My parents too. I hug them tight and nobody questions why I'm crying or bawling when I do. They just think I'm crying because we're at
a funeral. And then after we put him in the ground, when we are back
at church, I stay in the hall. All afternoon. Until I'm the last one there,
and the guy who has to lock up the church comes to tell me I have to
leave. And he's family too, I have a second cousin who does that. So I
hug him and tell him I love him though earlier we had to remind each
other of our names. And I change out of my boy clothes in the car
and I don't give a shit what happens at the border and I never go back
again. And everybody wonders what happened to me, they go *oh yes,
there was that nice weird boy Ezekiel,* and they just think, oh goodness
he was always so strange, but he was so good to his grandfather. And
his faith was strong. We liked him. They'll wonder, *oh where did that
boy end up, whatever happened to that strange boy?* They'll talk about
it every year or three years or months or whatever. And they'll just
think: *Oh, I hope he's doing well. God bless him.* And they will. And it'll
be the right kind of prayer, Carla, it won't matter they're calling me
a boy when they do this, it won't, it'll be the rightest possible thing,
and they won't be mad, they won't be worried, they won't even know,
they'll just be hopeful. And they never have to look at me, or see me,
or hear me speak, I won't even make them sad, not a little. They'll just
pray with their little books of devotions and their husbands outside
leaning on their snow shovels and they'll just think *God bless that boy.*
And they will, I know they'll do that. And then none of us have to see
each other. Ever ever again.

Liam and I made love when I came home. I jumped on him pretty
much instantly. He stayed in my bed afterward, which was unusual for
us, but nice. We both dozed, and at one point I felt him try turning me

over in my sleep and I said not now and he stopped. Next morning we both had days off. I made a huge pot of coffee, a mess of eggs, and a stack of toast and brought it to bed. We ate watching movies with my door open and my computer nestled in our thighs. It was Saturday and everyone was mowing their lawns and the smell of grass drifted in with the breeze. It was lovely. We stayed in bed until two, when a kid from Minot was supposed to get in, and, for a few days, stay. Liam quietly put his clothes on and checked his phone, then kissed me on his way out.

⁕

Having drinks with Zeke, I texted Liam. It was a week or so later. *Come hang if you want, I think it'd be nice if you did.* I doubted he'd text back but I thought I should make more of an effort. It'd sunk in since our trip that Zeke could probably use more friends.

She was reading *Consider the Lobster* and drinking beer. You really love him, huh, I said, tapping the book.

He's really smart.

Mmm.

It's funny, my boss can't stand him, she said.

Yeah? That's not surprising, I said. Her boss was the type who wore hemp skirts and purple sweaters. She came in to the store sometimes. She liked that we didn't call our Inspirational Psychology section the New Age section.

Saying that got Zeke annoyed though. She glared at the table. Why, she said, just because she's a—hippie type or whatever.

Please, I said. Stereotypes are true for a reason. Correct stereotypes, anyway.

I'm sorry, what? she said. She sounded both combative and genuinely confused. What do you mean?

I set down my book.

They are, I said curtly. Most people are pretty predictable. Look, you work retail, you have to get that. Eighty, ninety percent of the time, someone walks in and you know right away what their game is. The guys in trench coats with long hair are going to Sci-Fi/Fantasy and maybe History. The middle-aged men in suits are going to Mystery or Politics. The nineteen-year-old girl in the cardigan hasn't fell for a book since her last Brontë and wants something that'll make her feel that way again. It's like how the bro who doesn't understand why you won't tell him your old name will probably call you a faggot when he's drunk or nod like a puppy at racist shit. I'm not saying people can't be unpredictable, and, like, bigots just have the wrong stereotypes, like, look at us, right? What I'm saying is that there are patterns and most people don't break them. Most people just aren't that good or interesting.

When I stopped ranting, her face was contorted into the sad-wraith look that had come when she wore the boy drag. In a small voice she said, is everyone really that bad? I remembered, then, how young she was. Though she was nine months on hormones and I had almost five years on her, in my head she was always a little older than me. In both kinds of age.

Well hey, I said softly. I got, like. Carried away. I dunno if what I said was quite right—

Ladies! Liam yelled, appearing out of nowhere. He kissed me and said, I was just walking by, nice timing. What's up? Hey Zeke, what're you reading? Oh God DFW I *hate* that fuck!

When Liam decides to get over his crap he gets over it. And the two of them ended up getting along fast. He straight-up apologized for being a prick about the stolen stuff and said he wished we'd had her over again at the apartment this summer. Zeke said oh, well! You know, bygones!

Of course, Zeke. Bygones.

We hung out for a bit. I ended up chatting with the bartender, then I headed for the bathroom and of fucking course they were making out in the hallway. Before I could give them shit Liam cocked his head and Zeke nodded pretty eagerly and kicked open the nearest bathroom door handle in a surprisingly smooth and badass way.

I muffled a laugh. Then I put my ear to the door because I'm a goon. There was an unzipping sound and in a breathy voice Liam said I have low dysphoria.

I smiled. I liked to think of the kid getting some, even if it was with my nympho boyfriend. I went to the other bathroom and took a dump and tried to listen in on the other side.

Liam and I are the same height. I've always loved that, I loved it fierce. Five-ten. Bang-o. I love how we look in pictures. We make a good team, him and I.

The two of them were standing at the bar when I came out and I said someone got off quick. They laughed. Then Liam waved to a guy and girl in a corner of the bar and said oh shit! Hey!

It was Doug, the guy from the fair trade store with horn-rimmed glasses and coloured vests (today's was pink) and Sophie, the other Tall Girl in town. We got drinks and went to their table. Sophie was already a couple whiskies in because, you know, trans women. She was talking about going to some party out in the bush. Most of us weren't into it but Sophie seemed to think Zeke was persuadable.

I don't get Sophie. Girl's been post-transition long as I have and had enough encounters with angry men to make anyone scared to go somewhere darker than a hospital, but she wants a bunch of transsexuals to go to a bush party. Search me.

It is nice out, Zeke said. It might be nice to not be in a bar.

You really wanna go out in the fucking bush? I said.

There's a party at our new house, Doug said. We could go in my car.

Sophie nodded. Let's get the hell out of here.

We walked down the strip toward Doug's car and Sophie flipped off a minivan.

What's that about, I said.

Yeah? Zeke said.

I gave that cuntball head once and he fucking choked me 'til I threw up, Sophie said.

Jesus, I said.

Oh my God I'm sorry, said Zeke.

He's a prof now too, Sophie added.

I've served him at work, said Liam.

Ho-leee, said Zeke.

He did help clean up, Sophie said, like an afterthought. But still, fuck him.

Zeke giggled then stopped and said, that sucks. I'm sorry, that really really sucks. Sophie shrugged. Zeke looked pained, as if she had to say something but didn't know what. That's really shitty, she finally said.

Oh, said Sophie. It's okay. I mean. It's not, but. She got suddenly quiet. I was being dumb too, she said.

I doubt that very much, said Zeke, and Sophie fiddled with her bag and smiled at her. How was Winkler? she said. Get any *Rollkuchen*?

I fell back to take Liam's hand and drag on the cigarette he was smoking. Hey, he said instantly, do you actually want to go to this?

Not really, I said.

Do you want to leave? I don't have to go.

I shook my head. I should be there if Zeke's there. It's better if I'm there, I said. I knew that was bullshit but I said it anyway. Liam nodded. Oh shit, he said. Should I not have—

Oh God no! I said. No, I get a bang out of that! Fuck like bunnies, please.

Liam cracked up at that. His head flew back and his hair washed out behind him in a shag of brown. He had a really lovely laugh.

Two guys passed us on the sidewalk. One of them made a face when he saw me and the other said hi to Zeke. She nodded and they slowed their pace. The one guy said no hi?

I nodded, Zeke said meekly over her shoulder.

God you can't even say hi? he said. What kind of human being doesn't even say hi?! he yelled to the street. He was drunk. His buddy put his arm around him and said hey, it's not your fault. I was half-turned with my eyes on them though we were still walking. Hey! the guy said, are you gonna fuck her? Are you? He was pointing at me. Then suddenly his eyes narrowed. Wait, he said, and his voice sounded dangerous. Are you a guy? *Are you a dude?*

Sophie yelled: *Oh fuck you!* at the same time I stepped in front of Zeke and yelled, *LEAVE US ALONE SHITHEAD!*

FUCK YOU FAGGOT YOU WANNA START SOME SHIT! he yelled and hit his arms on his chest. I flipped them off and so did Sophie, and Doug jogged to his car and said hey I'm over here I'm over here. He had that sound of someone freaked trying to sound calm. We went over and piled in and the dudes didn't follow us, they just kept yelling stuff. Doug peeled out in a way that made me almost say geez man, we're not fleeing the Huns or anything. But I stayed quiet.

Then we were driving and the adrenalin ebbed and I immediately thought *fuck, that was so fucking dumb, I might run into them again, fuck! Fuck!* Doug was letting out breath like whooo and Sophie said God *fuck* them! and Zeke was in the front and staring straight ahead. Zeke …

I took this stuff for granted—though I usually didn't yell, I just kept my head down. Honestly, I'd kinda accepted that, passing or not, dudes were going to get on my case for one reason or another and hopefully they just wouldn't be too aggressive about it. I've been lucky I've never been hurt, and maybe I'm getting blasé about it. Or cocky, rather. Or, at least, maybe not the best example.

I touched Zeke's arm. Hey, I said, don't worry about them.

She turned and smiled automatically and opened her mouth but no sound came out.

It's okay, I said. I literally had no idea what else to say. It's okay.

Oh *hell* yeah, Sophie suddenly said. Doug, turn around.

What? No!

Sophie was riffling through a grocery bag she'd found on the floor. Come on, she said.

Sophie! I said. Let it go!

But she was whispering in Zeke's ear and then Zeke nodded and steadily said, that's fine, Doug, turn around.

Doug made a strangled noise and pulled a U-turn, and Zeke and Sophie shifted to face the right windows of the car. We pulled up to the dudes, who still obviously looked pissed, and Sophie stuck her head out of the window. Hey! Hey! We're sorry, she said.

Huh?!

We're sorry, we really are, said Zeke.

You guys were just being nice, said Sophie. *I'm* sorry. I shouldn't have yelled at you. I was just in a bad mood. Really, I'm sorry.

Awwww, said the calmer guy, while the other still looked pissed.

Was kinda *fucked* up, said the other one.

No it's fine, it's fine, his friend said.

Look, hey, Sophie said in a tiny voice, I dunno, we're going to this party and maybe, like, we could make it up to you? Somehow?

They stepped forward and then Sophie nudged Zeke and they sprayed both of them in the face with Silly String.

Fuck you! I yelled then Doug gunned it and drove away.

Fuck youuuuuu! I yelled again back out of my window. We drove away and were yelling and laughing our asses off.

Jesus Christ you guys! Doug said. That was a terrible idea.

Yup, said Sophie.

Yup, said Zeke.

Whatever! I said. When was the last time you did something that stupid?

Girl's got a point, said Liam. Doug shook his head and turned the radio up and it was some dumb alt-pop-country band. Liam took out a flask and said, I forgot to tell you I brought this, and I laughed and we drank and rolled the windows down and beat on the sides of the car with our palms, and Sophie started singing and even though she drowned us out we all joined in, the lyrics something about seeing your ghost ohhh ohhh whatever, and Zeke looked bouncy and giddy like a teenage girl who'd just snuck out of her house for the first time.

Liam turned and kissed me, hard, hard, like he rarely does, and I sank into the seat and pulled him closer by his hair.

⁂

The party was kinda not great.

When we came in the house, the first thing I saw were people in the kitchen playing a drinking game with tarot cards. We were doing a reading, one of the guys said. But then we just decided this would be more fun.

I don't like queer house parties. I actually have a hard time talking with folks at them. I always get this weird feeling everyone's there to hook up with someone else then laugh at me. I dunno. I like to be social but I'd rather have people over at my place. Hosting means you know most of the people and no one thinks you're weird for butting into a conversation.

It was nice chilling with Sophie and Zeke around, though—three trans women in a room, when does that happen—and it was fun telling and retelling our story about the dudes. Why did you have Silly String in your car anyway? I asked Doug at one point.

It's for Halloween! he said excitedly. It's a house project. Instead of putting up decorations outside, we're going to each write a message, something affirming, on our front lawn. Stuff that's body positive and queer friendly. It's something I want to do for the neighbourhood so we can put out something loving as new neighbours. A message out there telling people they are valued and they are loved. And any of us can write one too, not just people who live here, I want it to be a community-building project.

That's the gayest shit I have ever heard, said Liam.

Seriously, said Sophie.

Dude, I said. My folks live around here. If my dad sees you pulling that shit he will fucking blow your house up.

Doug blanched. You think it's dangerous?

After the drinking game devolved into a couple kissing, I bummed a couple cigarettes and went out to the back porch.

It was nice out. The house was one of those fifties bungalows with a small yard, away from campus on the edge of town, where I grew up—my parents' house really was only a couple blocks away. It smelled musty and cool and on the edge of rain, and though it was late there was still sunlight and some kids were playing catch a few yards over. We were close to the highway and there was a gentle, distant lull of cars.

Then I thought again about those two dudes, and a level of dread washed over me. That was stupid. Maybe it'd been worth it but it was just fucking stupid.

I lay back on the porch with my feet on the ground and let the beer and the smoke go to my head. The sky was orange and there were streaks of clouds. One of the kids got hit with the ball then insisted he was okay. When my first cigarette was done, I smushed it then flicked it into the corner of the yard and lit another. The wind was blowing again.

The door opened and a new girl I knew from work came out. She was stumbling and she went *awwww* shit you're my boss ohh is this *awkward?*

Girl, I said, not moving. I've been drunker at work then you are now.

Haaaaaaa! she said. I've kissed so many girls tonight.

Didn't even know you were a lesbo, I said. (This was probably unprofessional.)

Haaaa *yeah* well—*no* see I don't *exaaaactly* think I am?

Her head flopped forward and she lifted it back up. See I identify more, like, as *queer*, you know, like that feels more right, I just, I don't *give* a shit. About gender. I don't *see* gender, it doesn't *matter* to me I just see *people*. You know?

Yeah, I said to the sky. People.

I sat up and finished my beer and one of the other guys who lived here came up and hugged her from behind. She giggled and so did he then he squeezed her tits. She reached up behind her and put a hand in his hair. He saw me and said hey Carla!

I hated this guy. But I hated that he wasn't trying to do that to me. I had a picture in my head of both of them feeling me. It's not that I wanted them to do it, either. The image was just there, imagining them wanting my body. I wasn't even attracted to them. I can't make sense of why it ate at me, all the desire in this house, blowing past me like wind. I felt a tap on the shoulder and I turned around; it was a friend who worked at the diner Zeke and I went to. He liked to wear bow ties and give me very soft, light hugs when he was working and ask if I was doing okay. I nodded to him and then the guy who lived here. Hey guys, I said. What's up. We're gonna play a game. It's called gimme your beer.

I found Liam a bit later behind a couch in the living room on a pillow. There were weltlike hickeys on his neck and his pants were unbuttoned. Jesus. I kicked his shoe. Hey get up, I said. He lifted his head, waved, then lay back down.

Get up shithead, I said. I kicked his leg.

He made a noise.

You fucking slutbag cunt asshole get up! I said. Get up now! Come on!

Huh? he said. He propped himself up on an elbow. Whoa, whoa, hey chill out—

Fuck you chill out, I said. I was furious and I didn't care what I said about anything. Do you have your weed with you?

Yeah, but you shouldn't—

Fuck you, "shouldn't"! I said. I stumbled and leaned on the wall then threw my hands up. I never ask you for fucking anything, "shouldn't" my *tits*! *Shouldn't*. Shit.

He looked kind of sad but also frightened. It's in Doug's car, he whispered.

I rolled my eyes. In that moment, I wanted to see him shrink into the ground and wail. Well then, I said slowly. Maybe you could ask him for the key.

As we were heading out, Zeke materialized out of nowhere. Excuse me, she said, did I maybe hear you're getting weed?

We went out to the Jetta and an old man came out on his porch and turned his light on, blinking. There was only the sound of crickets and Liam slapped a lone mosquito. Smashed as I was, I drove a block forward just because. Liam broke the silence and muttered something to Zeke about finishing a story.

Oh right! Zeke said. I parked the car and Liam resumed looking for his bag.

So I knew this doctor in Minneapolis, Zeke said. I think he was part of a gay health project. I asked him if he'd ever taken care of any Mennonites. And he said he'd once worked out in South Dakota, during an early part of his medical training. This was in the early nine-ties. And he ended up taking care of this Hutterite man who'd gotten AIDS. He had been driving into the city to mess around or whatever. And when he was found out, they threw him out. Obviously. But when he was diagnosed years later the community let him back in. And this Hutterite guy, his ex-wife took care of him and took him to all his appointments and stuff and everybody cared for him until he died. And the doctor told me he always wondered: Did they let him go back to church? Did he have to go back to church? Were they nice to him or was it just cold, as in, did they not actually want to see him at all, but maybe considered it a duty thing?

To be fair, Zeke continued, obviously I wonder the same. But the odd thing about this doctor was that he loved this story. You could tell he hung on to it. And geez, you should have seen his face when I asked about Mennos in the first place. He said it gave him a really positive impression of my church and my community—which was weird because my family's not Hutterite but whatever—he said that it obviously showed they were, quote, "loving" and "forgiving" and they could make room for tolerance in their beliefs. To say nothing of the fact, right, that he had to hold this secret for years and then they'd kicked him out and shunned him for more. That couldn't possibly have played a part in anything, now could it have? No, that couldn't *possibly* have been the case! Never mind all the other fucking families that let their sons die without acknowledging their fucking existence.

Of course, she said hastily, not that I brought that up directly, exactly.

But like, she continued, the doctor had this story he told. You could tell he told it often. And that he loved us for it. I know it's ungrateful, maybe, petulant, maybe. And I love my people. I do. But. I can't stand that.

Carla, maybe that's what you mean when you told me once you hate tolerance, she said. Well, she added quickly, maybe it keeps you from being dead. So I don't think I exactly hate it. But it's not acceptance. And it's definitely not love.

I was silent. Then moodily I said, how do we use the word "tolerate" outside of this fucking subject anyway. You tolerate colds.

You tolerate toothaches, she said.

Flies.

If you can't hit them.

By this time Liam had found his weed. Zeke helped him break some up over a Kleenex.

My mom, she said. She once said to me: Well now, even though you were a bit different, our town treated you well, didn't they? They did. They were much nicer than they might have been.

Zeke swallowed, and for the first time since I'd met her she sounded close to crying.

And I said to her, Mom, my first memory of school is a boy choking me on a snow hill. And she said oh, well, yes, that's just boys though now isn't it?

I took her hand and nodded.

Liam finished packing the bowl. We toked up and inhaled long and hack-coughed for a while. The smoke kept recycling into our lungs so I rolled down the window. The wind was blowing a little harder. Zeke toked again.

Cold, Liam said.

Mmm, I said.

Zeke laughed like she'd heard the funniest thing in the world. Oh yes, oh so frigid, downright fucking *Arctic*. Here, have my sweater!

I laughed. It made sense to me somehow that Zeke would go zero to sixty when she got high. She giggled out of nowhere then cough-hacked again. Then she took another toke.

It *is* a nice sweater, I said. It really was, and I'd been meaning to say so all night, actually. It was cashmere and bright kelly green and hung on her in a way that somehow draped and hugged her stick body at the same time. Like it reminded me of the existence of expensive fancy clothes.

Thanks! she said. You know what rocked? BEING RICH.

Totally, I said. Wait, what?

Oh, well, she said. I'm not really—then she started hacking again. Never mind, she said. She shook her head hard and said never mind, never mind, never mind.

No, what, I said. You were rich once? Tell me about this! That sounds great. Tell me about being rich.

I was kidding, she said rapidly.

I tilted my head at her. No you weren't. Did you get that sweater here? It actually looks familiar. Are you a secret rich kid?

No! she said. I'm not!

I laughed, which seemed to make her mad. It was always so darkly satisfying to see her riled. Liam said, hey guys, what, what's the deal. And Zeke said, nothing, absolutely nothing, why don't we just move on, we don't have to have this conversation. And I said, *what* conversation?

Zeke toked one more time then reached for her bag. As she got out her phone, she accidentally turned the bag sideways and her wallet and my purple hair clip fell out.

Hey, I said, but she'd already shoved it back in. That's my clip, I said.

Oh, she said, her face fused in a scared smile. Is it?

Yeah, I said slowly. I've been looking for it for months.

Oh, she said, still with the dumb smile. Have you?

My heart slid into the deep end. Oh my God, I blurted, please don't tell me it was you who took our stuff.

Her face changed into a look of hopelessness. She took out the hair clip and put it in my hand and stuttered out a sorry. I was too stunned and stoned to speak or move. She fumbled for the door handle and then I was watching her jog down the road.

I took another hit and Liam said whaaaaat?

I watched her disappear into the black. Her placid face appeared in my head and I punched the window. Then I hit the side of the car like six or seven times with my elbow until I thought I heard something break.

Fuck, stop, said Liam.

I threw up everything in my stomach that night and I threw up the water and coffee I tried to drink the next morning. Beyond shaking, almost vibrating, kneeling in the bathroom of that wretched fucking house. Every patch of my skin was tingling and groaning and alive. My left arm too was really aching. It was all to the point that I forgot I was even angry. At first I was just dry heaving, just little bits of saliva, then after a few minutes some thick green liquid. That hadn't happened for a while. It passed across my tongue and through my teeth, more awful and alien than I ever remembered.

I'm not even sure why we were so angry about the passport thing. It's not like we used them anymore.

The hormones though. More I thought about it—that really did piss me off.

I had an email from her when I got home the next day: *I'm sorry about everything. I'm moving back to Canada. I'm really sorry. The cowardly truth, the awful weak truth of me, is that my parents had stopped talking to me and I was scared out of my mind. I can't even begin to talk about how sorry I am and I know I can't beg your forgiveness but please know—*

It went on like that for a while. *You became so important to me* blah blah blah. *I always knew in my heart that*—whatever. The girl had really made a scroll out of it. I didn't reply. It seemed like silence would eat at her most and I was good with that.

When you live in a small place, when your friends are stupid capital Q queers, you don't really have to make an effort to see most people. You'll bump into them sooner or later without much trouble. That was a thing about Zeke though. Whenever I saw her, it was always intentional. Like all the time she spent with people seemed part of a conscious choice. I rarely make that conscious choice myself. I see people at the bar, I go out with this guy from work after our shifts, Liam and I get bored and tell everybody to come over. It's not that I don't like making plans, it just works out this way. A weird thing with Zeke, thinking back, is that it was like she'd decided one day she was going to make friends with me: She came into my work, bought a book, invited me to lunch, then kept coming in and doing it over.

I liked that when I thought about it. And it made me think of this old crusty trans lady friend of mine, Lish. She bounced around in our town for a couple years but lives in Minneapolis now, and I never see her. It's dumb that I don't. She was one of my best friends, and I've got more means than she does to travel—but I never make the effort. Liam's not her biggest fan and I don't like leaving town alone. But still.

So, a couple weeks after Zeke left, I did. Just went to the station and bought a nonrefundable ticket before I could talk myself out of it. I caught an ass-crack-of-dawn bus out of town the week after; it still hadn't rained and when the sun went up the fields were the colour of dusted honey. I took some pictures and sent them to Liam. *Those are beautiful*, he said. Then: *Have fun today.*

When I got into the city at noon, Lish was already baked and going nuts about reuniting with some girl who drove for her when she escorted in the nineties somewhere up in Canada—or maybe that had been down here? I forget. Something about driver-girl's old cat. Anyway. I bought her lunch and we fucked around downtown 'til she put me back on the bus at nine. I hadn't been to the city for a long time. I told Lish about Zeke and she was like bitch, that girl's probably still got money, she probably got twenty grand for your passports, you shoulda clobbered her. Clobbered. I love that lady. Being a trans woman and a fuck-up means your number of living relatable elders are just this side of zero, but Lish is good people. Good for me, anyway.

When I saw Liam next, the following night, I came into the living room and he was reading a book of Sandra Birdsell stories, an author Zeke had really loved—rabidly, in a sort of creepy obsessive way, actually. Funny to see Liam reading that, though he'd been eerily silent about the Zeke thing. I guess he didn't know how to feel about it either.

I'm gonna watch a movie, he said. Do you wanna?

Not really.

He nodded.

You're going to be up for a bit? I asked.

Probably.

See you before I go to bed?

He kissed me on the forehead and went into his room and shut the door. I went to the kitchen and mixed a rum and diet. My left arm twinged.

If you watch the fizz of freshly poured soda from the top, it looks and sounds like TV static.

I took out my phone and looked at the email from Zeke. I finally typed a simple *Fuck. You.* and hit send.

Sipping my drink, I went into my room and considered what to read. The breeze coming in was solidly cold now, and I shut my window for the first time in months. I thought of her travelling north.

Aside from the recent trip, I've only been to Canada a few times, mostly between the ages of eighteen and twenty, obvie. Once, some friends and I were driving back from partying up there, in the middle of winter, on one of those perfectly clear and freezing nights. It was four in the morning and I was nodding in and out of hammered sleep, my vision mashed potatoes, we stopped so I could throw up at least twice. But as we drove with my face smushed on the window I noticed the field of snow along that stretch of the highway, all still and unmucked with. It looked brushed, almost. Or whipped. Designed. The patterns were the kind you'd see up close in a big rock. Sometimes you see that for far distances out here on the prairie, like a long white-blue sea. It's so gorgeous. And even with my brain's skeleton-crew state, I just thought, man. Everyone calls our part of the world bleak. But it's not bleak. I don't think it's bleak.

Every now and then I see a doctor and she's like, I do think you drink a little too much, and I'm like, you should see what too much really is, lady. I know I've got problems. But no one else really seems to get it. It's funny what people will latch on to. Like, I did some gross straight porn a while back and Liam felt kinda fucked up about it. And I was like, dude, when Tobi Hill-Meyer came to do that workshop on campus, you fell over your face in love with her. I know you're not anti-porn, so why are you so concerned?

And he was like, yeah, but—and then he stopped and said, that's different. I didn't need to hear any more though. *She's* different, he meant to say. What she *does* is different. And I could've gone into it and said, yes, I like queer porn too *but*. Yes Tobi's great *but*. But I knew his eyes, and I knew what he was feeling. And you can't fight every battle. So I cast my eyes downward and softly said, yeah, I know. I know. I pretended to sniffle a bit and hugged him and said, I know, but I can't talk about it now, okay? Okay? Please? Just be there for me tonight? Baby? And I knew he wouldn't push it after, instead he just hugged me and said, of course, of course babe, hey.

It's why I asked why was he *concerned* as opposed to the truth, which was why was he *angry*. It's sad how manipulable even the smartest of people can be. You just need to set it up for people, make them feel like they're decent fallible humans who had a choice and in the moment went and did something right. I've always thought, if you can give people that, they'll usually stop asking questions. I thought I had that figured out, but I guess Zeke did too. I had wanted to protect her. Part of me actually thought she was helpless. Though maybe in some ways she was. I dunno. Fuck. I bet her grandpa was actually loaded too. Everything pointed to it. Probably? Nothing about her made any sense, nothing nothing.

The random thing I really dwell on for some reason? Her neatness. Her place was always showroom clean the couple times I went over there. You could see your reflection in every counter.

How did she even know who to sell a passport to?

I hoped she wasn't going back to her town though, that at least she was going to a city of some sort. I wondered about her grandpa and it made me sad. I felt her there. It's shitty, but sometimes I wish my parents never talked to me again. Sometimes I'm not glad my mom and I have a relationship. It would be less confusing. Like when I call her and ask what's happening for my dad's birthday and she says well we're free the day before. A friend once said it's hard, letting that stuff go. I can't ever *imagine* letting it go. I wish someone could teach me how. I really do. I wish I knew if they would still be outright ignoring me today if I hadn't years ago started into a second bottle of whisky. But the question's unanswerable. Not unlike the question, I guess, of how much I really wanted to die.

People at the bookstore sometimes ask why I'm still there. Because no one else wants to fucking be here. But I'm happier in my day-to-day life than I ever was before. A lot of shit's still awful, yes, and I'm angry and negative most days, yes. But I love my job. I love my partner. (You know, most of the time.) I like our household. I do actually like how I've structured most of my life. I've started to see a future and it's got its shit parts, but it's also kind of really okay. Everyone sees me as a mess, Liam included. But I don't feel like a mess. I know what a mess feels like.

I sat on my bed and opened my laptop. Sometimes I—this might sound weird, but sometimes I put my computer on my crotch, right on my pubic bone. So I feel the heat on the top of my crotch but not my actual junk. I've never told anybody and it makes me feel embarrassed just saying it, but like—it somehow makes me feel like I have a vagina when I do that. I usually don't like thinking about that, it gets me too sad, it can set me on a spiral. But then I set this warm thing on this part of my body, and touch the soft folds of my neck. And I feel better. I can feel better.

A Carried Ocean Breeze

I'm going down to the beach today and I see a band playing in a parking lot downtown. By downtown I mean the kind where the buildings usually don't go above two floors and never five. It's an energetic band. They're fun, they're loud. The front man with the guitar has these crazed eyes that I like. The woman behind the drums is sweating like hell and the bass player doesn't seem to have any hair on his body. It's hot and somehow there's no breeze in this parking lot, so I take off my hoodie, paper thin as it is, and start rubbing and scratching my arms. Ugh, my arms. I go sit on a fence post, one that separates this parking lot from another one. As I'm sitting and watching, a girl with a bob of green hair parts through the crowd and starts yelling at the front man. It happens so suddenly: One second there's a band playing and now there's a girl yelling. The guy yells back. The girl with green hair screams something about how the guy fucks, and in response the guy does a hand flip and kicks a heel behind his back. I laugh a little without really meaning to. I spread my fingers and look at my nails. I'm really high. And it's good weed, good enough that I get trails when I make circles with my hands. Then I realize the girl with green hair and the front man—they're still screaming—sound strangely controlled in their fury, and the bass player and drummer look bored. Like, they're staring at the screaming couple, but they're also so obviously dissociated, unpresent. And the crowd seems on edge; they're engaged but no one's moving. A *performance*? I'm wondering. They're really screaming. Then I lean down to scratch my leg but my balance fails, and I fall off the fence post and scrape my ass and the back of my knee on the pavement and before I can stop myself I yell and my clothes and bag go everywhere and I blank out. Because I can feel the crowd, I know the two have stopped screaming, and I hear the laughs before they come; I can't believe I actually yelled, *fuck*, my vision tunnels and I scramble, getting up and getting my stuff, and people are laughing and a root beer bottle hits the ground beside my feet. I run a few blocks but no one follows or anything, and then I stop and look around and put my hoodie on again.

Usually I'd be rattled. But the weed truly is that never-dampen-me-for-too-long kind, and the breeze comes back and smells like ocean salt, like relaxed age. I even skip a couple times as I walk. When I get to the beach there are lots of people, but it's a weekday so the tourists aren't out, and the town just isn't big enough for it to get crowded otherwise. I'm a little nervous the wrong people will see I'm here but I want the water bad enough. I cradle my bag between some isolated rocks, take off my hoodie and sandals then go out to swim in my clothes. The water is warm, it makes lapping sounds as my body parts a path. I put my hands down and let them float and rise on the surface as I walk in deeper. I'm going slowly and I feel like I am in air.

Then my friend Elena walks by, wearing a Sunday tie and trailing her family. They're just walking down the road that goes along the water. I'm close enough to wave or call out to her, but I can't. I kick up and lie back in the ocean and feel myself in the water, preserved, rocking, my clothes puffing around me, like I'm floating away from my body. I only see the blue and white of the sky and my skin feels covered with a layer of fuzz. I can hear Elena walking; her shoes must be nice heavy church ones, and they're making this *click-clunk* sound on the asphalt. I let my eyes focus on the grey in the clouds. Her family looked so happy. Her little sister was pulling up a weed on the side of the road. Her mom was just walking. Her dad was cleaning his glasses, one of those kindly, too-skinny-and-meek-to-be-alive-but-still-sorta–*Father Knows Best* types. He volunteers at the food bank on Thursdays. Everyone in town loves them. Honestly, I want to love them too. I used to deliver papers and they were on my route. They'd leave me tips on Sundays. It wasn't all that long ago, really. But I guess these things have a way of seeming like much longer than they actually are?

I just wish the people who put on the we-pity-you act and say *but things are getting better* would also say to families like hers: *No. Stop.* Her parents know her name's Elena. They know I'm not a bad person. She and I would do this walk down here as kids. I'm tired of this. I'm not a fighter. I never wanted battles. I wanted to walk down to the beach with my friend, watch a loud band stage a screaming match and guess what's going on and make circles with our fingers and sit on fence posts and hear nobody laugh when we skin our knees and float in the water with real swimsuits and splash a little and point at the sky and get tugged and tugged and tugged by waves. Before I began to mortgage my liver and lungs, before I had friends afraid of cops and sidewalks, before I had dead friends, I just wanted to know what it was like to walk around with another girl and do that. I want to know what it's like to not be deathly worried about your friends. I'm so very tired of this. I can't stand it.

And me, like, I was doing bad for a while, but I'm all right now, or at least stable. You know? I have a job, my mom and I chat on weekends. It's not that I don't want to focus on these good things. It's not like nobody believes I'm a girl. Some people are nice. It's just that it all weighs on me. Is that an asshole thing to say when you're so young? I didn't have a bad childhood. There was a day as a teenager when a man threatened to break my head off and pushed me into the road and really, ever since, not a lot's been the same. There was a man who beat on my door begging to suck my dick, a man screaming when I was ordering food and banging on the window, a man who threw a bottle on the street and connected. It hurt. One guy followed me in a store the first day I ever went out in a dress. He said *What's the world coming to?! Those are for girls! Dresses are for girls!* Then he left me alone. It was the very first day I went out in a dress. I like to think I'm lucky nothing worse has happened. And I talk like I'm over this stuff. But I'm not. A man walked in on me in the bathroom at work the other day, just as I was pulling my pants up. We both screamed and he ran out of the store but I screamed for longer, everyone in the building heard me, and everybody wanted to know what had happened when I came out. You know. What went on in there. It took a lot to keep it together until the end of my shift. I kept my eyes on the door. I kept reconstructing the image of him so I'd know if he was coming. Dark hair, clean shaven. I fucked up almost all my orders. I gave back fifty bucks in change when I was supposed to give five. My boss yelled at me. He said I was going nuts. I went right home. It's been a few days so I guess I'm okay.

I just never really learned how you get back to normal. And even if I did. Even if I did pass all of the time, even if I could move somewhere no one knew me, even if I could get back to normal, it's just. I mean. These are still my friends. It exhausts me, it slows me down, it balls me up on the couch with movies and terrible food and it makes me weak. It's not beautiful or brave or redemptive. It's like a light case of mono that never goes away. I don't want to be brave. I want us to be okay. Sometimes when I'm here in the water I think what would happen if I screamed right now, and I imagine screaming and screaming and not being able to stop and going under and bubbles going up to the surface and gently popping without any noise and I scream and scream down until I'm lying on the bottom and I'm about to pass out and a second before all the black goes over my eyes I swim up, and I break to the surface, and I'm new and I'm strong and I'm actually brave and I'm actually redemptive and I'm ready to die and I'm ready to kill but the truth is really I'm floating away and remembering the stomp of Elena's shoes and she and her family are quieter and farther.

Winning

He's shivering, Zoe thought as she came in Robin's bedroom and saw his tall muscle-and-pudge body vibrating on the bed, blanket on the floor. She made to tuck the blanket back over him when she saw his face was contorted and his lips were moving like waves.

She said hey and softly rocked his shoulder. Robin gasped then his face turned instantly blithe.

Hey, sorry to wake you.

S'okay, he said. He stretched and his boxers made a ruffling noise on the sheets. You leaving? he said.

Yes, she said. Thanks for letting me crash.

Definitely. Boy, he yawned, I feel fucked up. Robin'd finished most of a magnum last night. Zoe'd had two glasses then switched to milk. She loved milk.

She giggled and said awww and mussed his wavy brown hair. It was silly, she realized, walking outside and zipping her hoodie up over her dress, but she had forgotten that boys even had nightmares.

It was mid-November, when in the Pacific Northwest the panorama of clouds stopped flirting with the sky and moved in and set parking brakes until May. A soft mist patter of rain was coming down as Zoe walked down the motel-like stairs of Robin's complex, then over to Eugene Station to take the 66 north. She got on and texted her best friend, Julia, back in New York: *Hi. You're beautiful and I miss you to fucking pieces.* When she got off the bus and walked up to Ayers the rain had stopped but the sky was still an ocean of pearl grey. Zoe hated this. *Humans aren't supposed to go months with all their sunlight broken,* she thought. She had actually loved the winters in New York. Everyone there complained about grey but to Zoe, New York had been sunny and bright.

Back at her mom's, the boxes in the kitchen hadn't moved. There was a note on the counter. *Gone to Farmers Market one last time. I need everything out of your room TONIGHT.*

Well, that was a new request. She still had a week to stay here, but whatever.

She went into her room and resumed clearing out her shit. *You can build up so much stuff when you have a room in a house you don't actually live in,* she thought. And Zoe'd always been a pack rat. Especially as a teenager. She would save a lot of things she thought regular families saved for their kids. She'd dumped most of that stuff now though, and there were only a few boxes left, orderly seas of social studies papers, choir programs, stuff like that.

Sandy came home as Zoe was mashing a basketball-sized paper wad into the recycling.

I bought some fruit for you, Sandy said.

I'm not hungry, said Zoe.

Don't give me that. Have you eaten?

I don't want any fruit, thanks.

Sandy washed a net bag of Bartlett pears and plunked it dripping on the counter. She put her elbows beside the bag and massaged her eyes. Better to tell me the truth, don't you think? she said.

Ever since Zoe transitioned, Sandy had become convinced that her daughter would develop an eating disorder, though Zoe was eating as little as ever.

No thanks Mom, Zoe said. I'm not hungry.

Zoe? Sandy said. The last thing I want to do is have to make you eat. It's not like I like having this conversation.

Sandy was trans too. Zoe had come out to her exactly eighteen months ago, on the phone, from her Brooklyn apartment, after she'd already been on hormones for a while. She'd meticulously taken steps to avoid telling Sandy, and when she did her mother had cried and cried.

Her phone pulsed and Zoe saw the text from Julia: *You're beautiful. I miss you.* Zoe picked up the biggest pear and took a gargantuan bite. What do you need help with next? she asked.

Sandy had done a lot to have Zoe with her wife at the time, Taya. This was back in the mideighties. Sandy'd sent a forged death certificate to the clinic where she'd banked her sperm, who then sent the samples to a friend of Taya's, a nurse practitioner, who then helped with inseminating. This was on the plains, where Sandy and Taya had grown up. They'd moved to Oregon to have Zoe, who was born downtown in an apartment off 8th. Zoe loved this story, and she never got tired of telling it to her friends back east. She liked to say she had been born loved. Though Taya'd left both of them when Zoe was eight, and Sandy hadn't always been the most stable of mothers, Zoe had always felt acres of love.

Can you go through the closet in the spare room? Sandy said.

No problem, said Zoe.

Hey, have another pear if you want it, they're completely yours! Sandy called after her. Zoe didn't respond so Sandy got out pita bread and hummus and went to her desk in the living room to do paperwork.

She passed well, her mother did. Zoe had always admired her for that, and she especially admired it now. In the old days no one had known about Sandy, and with her being six-one and broad shouldered and poor, Zoe thought, it really couldn't have been easy. I always wore jeans, Sandy told Zoe once, when Zoe was seventeen. It had been the fifth anniversary of Sandy's bottom surgery and she'd been unusually talkative. I always wore jeans, she said, almost never skirts or dresses. Because just in people's heads, subconsciously, the idea of trannies wearing jeans doesn't mesh. Zoe had listened to this raptly. They said I looked mannish, Sandy giggled, but they never thought I was a man! I tricked 'em. She sounded like she was gloating. She said, they just passed me off as some big earthy dyke. Well you know, that's okay.

From very early in her childhood, Zoe knew that Sandy had once lived as a man. Neither mom had hidden it from her, but it was also understood to be a buried subject, something gravely serious Zoe wasn't supposed to talk or ask about.

I did have some really pretty dresses, Sandy had said in that conversation. But I had to be very careful about wearing them. I just had to be careful.

They'd moved out of the apartment off 8th when Zoe was in third grade. It had been right after Taya left, and right when Sandy got her job with the county. That's when they got one of the few bungalows left along Ayers, on the north edge of town just shy of the city line. Sandy was from the country, and she missed the stars, she said. She missed the stars, and the quiet.

Robin called a couple hours later, as Zoe was muscling a box down from the top of the closet. Hey! he said. Do you want a job?

Um, Zoe said. Huh. Um. Fuck. I don't know. I want to go back to Brooklyn but I do need money and—then suddenly she sneezed, inflecting her expulsion up at the end like a squeak: *AAAA-choo!*

Jesus dude! Bless you, said Robin.

Um, thanks.

So what was that? You're going back to Brooklyn? Well hey, that's great, he said. I'm happy for you.

Zoe lowered her head and leaned against the wall. It made a thunk. No, she said to Robin, never mind. Yes. Yes I need a job. I would love a job. What's the job.

Oh! You're staying! he exploded. I love it! I love you! You will love it back here! You will love me! You will love everything! You will re-fall in love with the Northwest! I promise!

Zoe giggled a little. What's the job, dammit.

It's doing phone surveys for the government? Robin said, hesitant.

You're fucking kidding, she said before she could stop herself. Then she said shit, I'm sorry, you're being nice here. Tell me more.

It's eleven an hour, Robin said. It's not that bad! I did it when I moved back and it was a good way to get on my feet. It might be the same for you, he said. He stopped talking. Zoe stayed with her head against the wall not speaking.

Just thought I'd offer, Robin said. You wanna come out tonight? I could tell you more about it.

Sure, let's talk tonight.

Cool. Also you have to have more than one drink.

No I don't!

The rain patter was stronger and steady outside, the periodic thrum of these months that sometimes made Zoe think of a long, unbroken rustle of leaves. She showered, shaved, changed into a crinkly black-polka-dotted dress and sweater tights, put on makeup, and went to say goodbye to her mom.

You still wear tights this time of year? Sandy said.

Yup.

That for the boys?

Oh Jesus Christ, Mom.

It's just a question, Sandy said. Hey I forgot to tell you. I'm not leaving on the first anymore. Staying here 'til the tenth. Soooo you'll need to stay here longer.

Zoe nodded and said, I think I can make that work. Yes, that should be fine. She said it slowly, as if she actually had to consider her answer. Or as if she hadn't a month ago jettisoned her life and rent-indebted roommates back in Brooklyn to return to Oregon for the first time in years. It had been Sandy's suggestion; Zoe'd been talking about how broke she was and Sandy'd been like hey well look. Why don't you come back here for a bit. Get on your feet a little. I need help moving out anyway and I don't know what to do with all your stuff. It wasn't the first time Sandy'd asked her to move back home (I'd rather grow a second dick, Zoe'd once said, calm and icy, when Sandy wouldn't leave it alone), but she'd lost her job in summer and her debt was piling up and she'd crashed on a few couches but eventually she just didn't have a lot of options. And whatever, she'd thought, it'd be temporary anyway, she was a grown-up, she could stand living with her mom for a month or two and she could always leave if she had to. Maybe it'd even be good for them, Zoe had thought. Maybe it'd be peaceful, like they'd relearn some good parent-kid relationship things.

And to her surprise, so far, they generally had.

Now Sandy said cool, cool. Know what you're doing yet when I'm out of here?

Zoe shook her head.

Sandy sighed then caught herself and waved. Ah, she said, you'll figure it out.

Her mother was eating chips and salsa and spilling occasionally, thick blood-dot trails between her and the bowl. Zoe realized that she smelled pot.

Zoe'd hated weed as a kid. It did calm her mother, but it also made her forgetful and dumb. She'd flake on getting Zoe from school, leave the house without telling her, stuff like that. It used to scare Zoe, and then around high school it just made her angry. She'd made her peace with the stuff as an adult though.

It had cold-snapped today and Zoe put on her coat. I'll see you tomorrow? she said.

Sure sure sure, Sandy said. Just be safe, okay? I want you to remember to be safe.

I will, yes, I promise, Mom, Zoe said. She turned around and put on her gloves and hat and bugged her eyes once she was out the door. Waiting for the 66, she saw a younger girl in only a hoodie and scarf, shivering with her hood up. *It's like no one wants to dress warm here*, Zoe thought. As if because it almost never got *cold*-cold, people didn't want to turn on heat, put on coats, cover extremities. So they were colder here than they were in places that were actually cold.

Walking to the bar from the bus station, a girl younger than Zoe and wearing clothes that had all turned the same colour asked for a quarter and Zoe pulled a fingerful of change from her wallet. The girl mumbled a thank you and Zoe saluted with her fingers and said yeah lady.

It's gay night! Robin said when Zoe sat down at a table.

Eugene has a gay night now?

Yeah, that's what I thought too when I got back. But hey, there are drag queens, you'll like that.

Zoe looked around. Most of the twenty-odd people in the bar looked like Robin, young and punk-hipsterish and straight.

Wait, shit, should I not say that? he said. Are drag queens bad?

No, Zoe shook her head. Drag queens are great.

I can't tell if you're being serious or not.

Can we talk about something else?

Sure, sure, sorry, said Robin. They were silent then he said get a drink goddammit!

The bartender was a guy Zoe'd gone to high school with. She hadn't seen him since they'd graduated. She figured he knew about her transitioning. Thanks to Facebook, everyone knew about her transitioning.

HEY! said Zoe.

WHOA! HEY! said the bartender. *ZOE!* She liked that. Just Zoe. None of this Zoe? So … it's Zoe, right? Or her old name then Sorry! It's just weird to think of you as a Zoe! Robin had said that so earnestly and emotionally once and it had made her cry.

But the bartender. He was better-looking than Zoe remembered: Tall, with curly black hair, a slight beer belly. He was wearing a Huey Lewis and the News T-shirt. His name was—

Fuck why couldn't she fucking remember his fucking name?

Get a rum and diet? she asked.

He mixed her drink and stuck a purple umbrella in the glass. She ran through memories of people they'd had in common. There was Frankie—

Oh holy fuck. A lightning bolt of memory went through her. *Frankie.* Frankie Pringle was a girl Zoe'd been close with but drifted apart from after high school. Well hey, here's a weird question for you, Zoe said.

What?

You still see Frankie at all?

Frankie Pringle?

Yeah.

No. Not for years. We fell out of touch, there was just, y'know, some bad shit.

Zoe nodded like she was trying to be thoughtful. Yeah. Bad shit.

I know she's back in town though, he said. Last I heard she was getting in deep with the nose candy.

Really? Zoe said. She'd known her share of cokeheads back in New York but she'd never have guessed Frankie … Okay, Zoe said, thanks anyway. Just curious.

The music got louder. You like the umbrella? he hollered and smiled huge.

Zoe giggled. Yeah! she said. It's flashy! Thanks! She did a small wave and said good seeing you, then went back to the table.

So apparently, Robin said suddenly, some like, student-bro types have been shooting homeless people lately.

Zoe opened her mouth and swizzled her drink. What? No, she said. Jesus Christ.

It's weird, dude, he said. It's weird. Like, they used BBs, not bullets. But still. You'd think it's such a quiet little town, you know?

You'd think, Zoe said. She looked at Robin's face, open mouthed, almost awestruck, and she turned sour. She took a long drink. So what's this job about, she said.

Robin gulped his beer. Okay. So it's like, you come in, they tell you what survey you're doing that day, you read a little sheet about it, and then you call the numbers on your list. And some people do 'em and some don't. It's not hard. They pay you eleven an hour no matter what.

That's good. How many hours? On average? she asked.

Twenty-five.

Not bad.

You'd have the job, Robin insisted. I know it. My boss loved me, like, he *really* liked me. I guess who's to say but I'm pretty sure I was one of the best people there. If I called him tomorrow and told him how awesome you were? He would probably hire you.

Thanks ... Zoe drifted off. I don't know. I do need money, I just don't know if I want to—

Oh for chrissakes, she thought. Even if she was sure about going back to New York there was no way she was getting there soon, and talking on the phone was as appealing as shovelling shit but whatever, there were worse jobs out there.

You know what, she said. Sounds great. Thanks. Sign me up.

Cool! Okay. Hey, how're you doing back here anyway? Robin had that serious, concerned look on his face that sometimes drove Zoe up the goddamn wall.

You always ask me that, honey! Zoe said. I'm fine.

Robin and Zoe had known each other since they were little, but they'd gotten tight in high school because of theatre. They'd both been drawn into tech, she lights and he sound, and they ended up board op-ing something like six shows together. They'd been kind of a duo, actually. They were known for a lot of wiseass shit. Once during a full tech run for the spring musical they'd interrupted a climactic scene in a church by overlaying death metal and a wash of blood red.

Robin'd been a gas-station-jacket kind of emo kid back then so a lot of people thought he was into dudes, to which he'd say no, Zoe was the one guy he'd ever go gay for, and to which Zoe would say stuff like that's sweet but I hope your dick grows bigger. Most people didn't question it. They were those boys. They weren't besties, they just had their thing. They'd given each other flowers at graduation. And Robin'd always stayed in touch, in his own way, posted dumb videos on her wall, sent a little *Whoa, congrats girl!* message when she transitioned. Zoe'd always liked that he did those things, and she liked how the two of them hung. She liked how their friendship could be close without being intimate.

Hey, see that bartender? Zoe said.

Robin shifted in his seat. You mean Al?

Al! That's his fucking name! she said. I've been trying to remember.

Robin snickered. You forgot about Al?

He's cuter than I remember, said Zoe. Robin laughed awkwardly and said ha, that's funny. She took another drink. *Hey!* she said. Shit. I can't believe I haven't asked you this yet. Do you know what Frankie's up to?

HOLY SHIT! Robin pounded a fist on the table. He wasn't even drunk, he could just get that excited. I never told you about her! Fuck man. Okay. You know we lived together?

Zoe shook her head and he said well we did. It was my last place in Portland before I came back here last year. But I didn't get all my stuff out right away so I went back a few months after to get it, and dude, Frankie was pregnant.

Zoe's mouth unhinged slightly. Yeah, Robin said. Like six or seven months along. That was this February, so she must've had the kid by now. Zoe blew a tuft of black hair out of her face. It was weird, Robin said, to see her that big, you know? Zoe nodded; Frankie had always been sickly skinny. Apparently, Robin continued, she gave it to some super Portlandy gay dude couple in Sellwood? That's the rumour anyway. Who knows.

What do you mean the rumour? You didn't talk about it?

No, said Robin. I tried. I said are you keeping it? She said no and I was like hey I know we're not really friends anymore but do you want to talk about it? And she just lit a cigarette—in her own fucking apartment too—and went into her room. And then her boyfriend or whoever he was, some dude—not to be mean, but you know how Frankie's always had some dude—this dude just sitting there, he squinted at me like *I* was some sort of asshole, so I got my stuff and left.

Oh.

Robin frowned and rubbed the side of his face. Yeah, no one's heard anything solid about her since. Like I said, there's rumours, but I don't know for sure. Sometimes I wish I'd done more, I dunno, but shit. She just fucked up, like, a *lot*, and not just with our rent. You heard about her dad, right?

Her phone buzzed. It was a text from Sandy. *Your room is a shithole. I love you!* She scooped the phone from the table and dropped it in her bag.

I know he's gone, said Zoe.

Frankie's dad had been great, a kind and gentle older man. He'd gotten cancer and died a few years ago. It had been sudden and sad. She'd left a message on Frankie's voice mail but couldn't fly out for the funeral.

Robin shook his head and said she abandoned him. She wouldn't leave Portland to see him. She had all these excuses, like, about work or how her uncle was looking after him, but she almost never went down. She saw him like three or four times. It was fucked up.

What?! He was like the best dad ever! That is really weird! Zoe said.

Yeah. I just didn't get it, I guess.

Zoe had sometimes wondered what Frankie would think of her now. She wondered if Frankie would have wanted to hang out with her, if she would talk to her the same way, if she would—Zoe hated admitting this to herself, but—if Frankie would still think she was pretty.

Frankie'd been this tall girl, roughly Zoe's size, with small tits and bright-blue chest-length hair. Zoe'd go over to her place on Willakenzie and Frankie'd loan her clothes and teach her things like how to cover her beard shadow, line her eyes so it was just barely noticeable. And how to flat-iron her hair and deep-colour coordinate and all that shit.

She was the only one Zoe ever did that with in high school; she'd never said anything about wanting to be a girl either, and Frankie never asked. It just kind of happened one day. They were hanging out in her room and Frankie said, okay sorry if this sounds weird but I was just thinking you would look really good in this one thing I have.

And it went from there and it was like they both knew better than to talk too deeply about it. Zoe'd never told anybody about this stuff, not even later in New York. It had been so surreal at the time that it never took up the front burner space of her memory. Only a few times a year, even after transitioning, would she remember snatches of being in Frankie's room. It always startled her. How easily she could forget it happened at all.

And Frankie once had looked at Zoe and cupped her chin and said God, you're beautiful. She was never exasperated with Zoe's tics or—as a lot of cis women would later be to Zoe—bitter or nasty or bitchy or jealous or any flavour of mean at all, really. She'd only taken care of Zoe, sisterly and lovingly. But then Zoe'd gone to New York and Frankie'd gone to Portland, and they tried to keep up with the odd text and call and stuff, but they were never back home at the same time and Frankie hated Facebook and pretty quickly their contact just petered out.

Zoe returned a text to Julia then said to her mom *Sorry, I'll fix it, I love you too.* People finally started to fill the bar, wet with rain and their hair stringy. Zoe remarked on this to Robin.

It's probably because the Ducks just finished playing, he said. Zoe let out a hoot. Dude, she said. Only in Eugene are all the gays at the football game.

⚬

The supervisor at the survey place interviewed Zoe for ten minutes and told her to show up the next day at four.

The following afternoon, Zoe put on a white button-up blouse and a purple pencil skirt and got there early. Hey hey new girl! said the supervisor. He seated Zoe at a desk with a stack of green carbon papers and a list of numbers and a phone. She made her first dial and drew a long line on a piece of scratch paper. A cheerful man from Elgin answered and she talked to him about his hay cuttings. She had drawn a lot more lines on the scratch paper by the time he hung up. She made a second phone call and the man swore about Obama so intensely Zoe got flustered in her questions, and then the guy yelled now wait a minute, am I talking to a boy or a girl? A girl, sir, Zoe said weakly. He hung up a lot sooner. She pressed a hand to her cheek and looked around; everybody else was busy calling.

On her third call, she stuttered a bit because the man on the phone, a surly dairy farmer outside Pacific City, sounded exactly like a man she'd known back in New York, a guy with layered blond hair who ran a bar in Williamsburg wallpapered with covers of Gaddis books. They had gone out for dinner, then out dancing. He'd been amazingly charming, gentlemanly. She'd accepted all the drinks he bought her and back at his place he'd begun squeezing her nipples and slipping his hands south and her last memory was of mushily shaking her head wait, hold on, I like you, I want to, just like, wait. And when she woke up she was on his bed, alone, and he was at his desk on his computer, and both sides of her bottom had a dull, vomit-spurning ache.

How many milk-giving cows did you say? said Zoe. I'm sorry? Including heifers that are not ye—

Fifty. Two, said the man. Now do you have it this time or do I need to repeat it again! You tell me here! and Zoe said yes, of course, of course sir, and by nine o'clock Zoe had covered the scratch paper with black-and-white pencilled swirls and shapes, criss-crossing paisleys and hectograms and triple helixes and the outlines of faces.

Some of the faces resembled her mom.

Her mom.

Zoe had always seen Sandy as dimly gorgeous. She had short coiffed ash-blond hair, like Sharon Stone in *Casino*, wore blue or grey skinny jeans, tank tops with shiny satin edges that showed off lightly muscled swimmer's arms, and long earrings that skittered around her collarbone whenever she moved her head. In winter she wore cable-knit zippered hoodies. Zoe, on the other hand, kept her hair black, liked dresses with stripes or polka dots, see-through blouses over camisoles, patterned sweater tights in winter. She sped through tubes of eyeliner and lipstick; Sandy maybe used a little mascara once in a while. Even as Zoe took no part of her own style from Sandy—if she had to be honest, she dressed a bit like her other mother Taya, who now spoiled her with clothes on visits—Zoe did admire the way Sandy looked.

She admired a lot about her mother, really.

She admired the way she hadn't hid from Zoe the pain of Taya leaving her, but she rarely badmouthed or castigated Taya herself.

(And given that Taya had departed with a load of their money and a note including the words "Like anyone else would have loved you," she would've had plenty of reason.)

She admired how Sandy'd treated Zoe's boyfriends in high school, the ones she dragged up from South or the U of O (no gay boys were out at her own school), and how Sandy welcomed them and cooked for them even when sometimes they were snotty to her.

She admired the sex talk Sandy had given her when she was really young, before puberty. Sandy had told her: Now, this is a thing teenagers and adults like to do and they get to do. Kids don't, it's not a kid thing, you won't even want to do it and you shouldn't. But this is what'll happen when you're older. And it can be wonderful. But it's important you're safe. There's a safe way to do it and an unsafe way, it's like driving without a seat belt, where if something bad happens you can die but if you're safe it gives you freedom, you can't imagine, the happiness and the freedom. When you're older, I will help you and we can talk about it. This is something I want you to do right and it's something I want you to look forward to. I want this to be a good and healthy part of your life. Zoe really admired that, especially when she found out about all of Sandy's friends who'd died during what she'd only refer to as "the plague." Zoe remembered a few of them, from when she was a kid. But only faintly, and only a few.

Thanks for your time sir, Zoe said to her last call.

Yeah, yeah, good night ma'am, the man grumbled. Zoe folded the drawings she made, thought of sticking them in her bag, then dropped them in the trash—not the recycling, the trash.

So New York, huh?! the supervisor asked as they left the building together. Why'd you come here?

Zoe was tired of answering that question and lately she'd just been snapping, I'm helping my mom! in a tone that made everyone think her mom had a deadly illness and needed Zoe to tend to her last days. Or something. It usually got people to leave her alone. But when she said that now her supervisor just said huh. Do you like it here though, like do you think you want to stay here?

Zoe considered how to answer that to a stranger.

Well, I grew up here, she said softly.

Walking down darkened, slick Willamette Street with her hoodie up in the sprinkle-mist rain, it occurred to her that she'd often walked these streets late since coming back to Eugene but hadn't been prop-ositioned or harassed once. Or been made to feel unsafe in any way, really.

When Zoe was a kid she thought she lived in a great town, she thought no place was better than this little city (a term Taya had liked to use, oh, this little city.) Zoe didn't like the neighbourhood they'd ended up in, a weird little bumpkin-and-religious-yuppie enclave, but she loved downtown and she loved the U of O and she even loved the dumb political battles that played out in the city: Bike paths through the Catholic school, the cross on Skinner's Butte, where to build the new hospital; all the little clashes between right and left, hippies and Mormons, developers and enviros. It had felt like that stupid idea of what America was supposed to be. And no one was from there. It was a place you moved to. Even from middle school on, it seemed like being born in town put her in the minority. When she was a teenager, leaving just didn't occur to her, like, why would you do that if you were lucky enough to be *from* here? She thought when she left home she'd just get a room in a house back downtown by the WOW Hall and go be a stupid Duck for four years, then get a job and a little house of her own then there she be, there she be! as her mom would say, in one of her few kept Midwesternisms.

Zoe was rarely bitter about being trans; if you needed to believe in the possibility of unbitter trans women, Zoe'd be your girl. But she knew she wouldn't have left if it hadn't been for that. She would've stayed, gone to the Country Fair, signed on with a co-op, checked in on her mom, lived the Beautiful New Liberal American life. It had been so close. Hell, on the face of it, the town in its current era had been designed specifically for someone like her, like, who else if not for the fag kid of a woman like Sandy, queer and transplanted and a hippie to boot. Zoe had really always thought it was a great town. She'd never hated it growing up, never, never, never. But she knew staying meant a boy future, a pretend-to-be-cis future; she didn't have the strength to figure out the gender thing around everyone she'd known. She knew that in part from her mom. You couldn't transition and keep everything else in your life the same. Couldn't happen. She tested it a bit one summer by telling a few friends about Sandy, the ones she thought would react the best and ... the *looks* on their faces—especially her boyfriends—of revulsion, horror, the *things* they said about her mother. One just said simple dumb stuff like, oh gross she's your *dad* that is fucked up, that is *fucked up*, and another said, hah, well, she was too pretty to actually be real anyway. *Hey* maybe he'll be a *penguin* next huh? Though the worst was a girl, a close friend, who'd looked ashen then said: You know, it sucks, I knew she had problems but I still looked up to her as this strong woman. I thought I had this strong woman in my life. I thought you had this strong mother. Zoe clammed up about it after that, she didn't even mention it to Frankie. And so, when fall came and she applied for and squeaked into a fancy school on the East Coast, she saw for the first time in her town a void, endless black. She would be forever grateful she grew up here, but the future she saw was for some willowy gay kid, lovely but not her.

And then everyone's fucking attitudes about trans stuff changed so quickly after a few years. Chaz, Thomas Beatie, all those fucks. Had she been born five years later, she thought sometimes, she might've felt like she could've stayed.

So. Zoe was bitter about that.

She looked away from her supervisor and adjusted her bag. I don't mind it, she said quietly. There's a lot of worse places to be.

Oh geez, said the supervisor, you have no idea! I love it here! He started talking about his hometown in Arizona and how there were grocery stores and bars here in Eugene he just loved and you'd never find that where he was from and just even the people were so nice, like, they gave a shit about being humans here, you know? He had grey eyes and they kind of sparkled as he talked. Zoe said uh-huh, totally, and decided to picture Al lubed and naked until they got to the bus station, where she returned some texts from Julia and the supervisor got on the 24 going somewhere south.

The next day Zoe was finishing cleaning the garage when Sandy walked up to her from behind and hugged her and burrowed her head into Zoe's neck. Then Sandy said, I love that you're my daughter, and both of them shook and cried a little in the most delicious, healthy, loving of ways, the way that only mothers and daughters can. In a way that really, in a sense, Zoe had wanted to touch her mother for twenty-four years. They stood in the garage, cold, holding each other for a long time. She thought of Sandy's parents, estranged since before Sandy had even left home, and wondered fleetingly if it was possible to love so fully, as Sandy had, unless you had been cut off at some point from that love yourself.

She texted Frankie as she was going to work: *Hey Frankie. This is Zoe Quist. I had a different first name in high school, though you can probably figure out who this is anyway. I heard you're going through a tough time. If there's anything I can do please know you can call me. Or if you just want to hang out, that'd be nice too.*

The next evening she went to the bar with Robin and one of his lady friends. Zoe had a couple and went to shake it on the floor. She felt loose and free, in a rare silly mood. After a few songs a bro started creeping on her, dancing up close and touching her sides, her ass. She turned and gave a come-hither smile for half a second—the dude's smirk lit up—then she scrunched her face and shook both her head and forefinger. The dude scowled and went away. Zoe laughed and decided to get a third highball. The bar was crowded. A guy in a Crass shirt reached out his arm and started running his fingers through her hair. She smiled seductively at him too then took his hand and placed it on his chest. *No*, she enunciated.

I just like your hair! the guy hollered.

That's great, honey! Zoe said, smiling. You're not going to touch it! Nice shirt though!

Well give me a hug then! he said. Zoe laughed and did the smile-scrunch-head-and-finger-shake thing again. The guy's face crumpled in confusion. You'll say you like my shirt but you won't hug me? he said.

What can I say! Zoe yelled as the music got louder. It's a rough life!

Growing up Zoe was pretty deferent around boys, but a few months after the Williamsburg bar owner guy she started taking some pleasure out of messing with them like this.

A space at the bar opened. She shoved against it to flag down Al.

Zoe! said Al.

She smiled. *Zoe!*

Rum and diet? he asked.

No actually! she said. Gimme a G and T!

You got it!

She watched him pour. It was strong. She sipped the drink and tipped him big and said thanks!

Yeah!

He lingered in front of her for a second. She felt a glow surge to her face. Hey! she said. I know you're at work and all so this is weird but—Al grinned and nodded hard and one of his curls fell into his face—do you want to hang out sometime?

He hesitated. He didn't turn his head but she could see his eyes dart from side to side. Then he said sure! Can I find you on Facebook?

Sure! she said. Then she said you know what, actually no, fuck that! Fuck Facebook in its motherfucking penis! Gimme a pen! Al obliged. She took his forearm and on the inside steadily wrote her number in small script, ink shiny against the fish-white underbelly of his skin. There! she said. Call me when you want? I'll wait. Al smiled and then the guy in the Crass shirt yelled for beer.

Later, much later, Zoe and Robin and Robin's lady friend were coming out of the bar, veering in the direction of Robin's house. The rain was the lightest of mists and none of them put their hoods up. Zoe looked at a text from her mom (*KID I AM SO STONED*) and she giggled. Like oh, oh, this life. Zoe saw the hot dog cart on Olive and Broadway and snorted and said look at that shit.

What? Robin said.

A hot dog cart in Eugene! she laughed. Robin and the lady friend looked at her with blank drunkenness. Zoe felt her phone go off and looked at a text: *Hey! This is Al! Now you have my number! Let's hang soon.*

She smiled big and toothy at her phone and they crossed the street and a man with coal fingernails and missing teeth came up to them, pulling down a homemade bandage on his arm to reveal a thick unbleeding open wound. Hey! he said. Do you maybe have some money for some beer, this tweaker bitch just stabbed me! He was smiling as if it had happened to somebody he didn't like. Robin and the lady friend's faces went glossy and said no, no sorry man, and Zoe's face crinkled and she said holy shit that sucks, yeah, hold on.

She opened her wallet and took out her only bill, a five. Here you go man I hope—

Thank you! the man said, then continued seriously, it was for *no reason*, she was *just a cunt you know, my God she was just a fucking CUNT YOU FUCKING! CUNT!* and went back to the curb where Zoe caught a glimpse of Al outside the bar, smoking a cigarette and peering at her standing in the middle of Olive Street with her friends frozen and blinking a block behind her and her wallet hanging open like an unattended lip.

As Zoe lay passed out and cold on Robin's couch, Julia made her phone light and buzz through the night.

03:16: *Hey lady, woke up for work right now yr probably sleeping but I wish you were still here <3*

03:26: *Milton and me talking last night how we miss you a lot, like really miss you. We had Thanksgiving other week and propped up a pic of you on the table. We kept telling you to shut up. Good times*

03:59: *Ugh I hate the fucking subway. I wish you were here with me gorgeous you could clear the path ha ha*

04:14: *PS Lost your address and I wrote you postcards!! send again?*

The next morning Robin's lady friend gave Zoe a ride home. She slouched against the window the entire ride north. She felt sick. Fuck, she had promised to help her mom this morning. And really—she felt bad about being so teasy to the guy in the Crass shirt (though fuck the bro who groped her). *Classy*, she thought darkly about the whole sexy-smile-scrunch-finger-wave thing. *Classy classy classy*. And then, *you can be nicer. There isn't always harm in being nicer.*

Hey party animal, Sandy said when Zoe walked in. She was at the kitchen table eating some grainy cereal with strawberries in it. Zoe tried to open the fridge and take out the milk.

No, no, Zoe pleaded wearily.

You're hungover, huh, Sandy said. She looked tired and pissed.

I'm sorry. I'm sorry. What do we need to do today? Zoe said. She set the milk jug on the table with a thump and tried to sit down, but when the chair stopped her body's descent, her head kept going south and she face-planted in slow motion on the tablecloth. Fuck, she said.

Sandy got up from the table. Jesus Christ, she said. Stay right there.

Okay, Zoe said into the tablecloth.

Sandy came back with four ibuprofen and a tall glass of water. Take these and drink all of this, she said.

Zoe obliged then said what do we need to do today?

Well first you're going to sleep for an hour, Sandy said. And no more.

Zoe stood up and made visibly strained efforts to stay vertical. I'll be fine, she said. I'm sorry, just. Gimme. A few minutes, I'll be fine.

Kid. Stop, said Sandy. You're going to bed. I am setting my alarm for an hour from now and then you may help me.

Zoe blinked and somehow stumbled without moving her feet.

When she was little, Zoe had nightmares; she had them all through childhood and far into adolescence. Before Sandy began falling asleep earlier than her, if Sandy heard Zoe thrashing, as Zoe often did, Sandy would come into her room and sing. She usually sang the mockingbird song—Hush little baby, don't say a word—but sometimes, especially if Zoe was crying, Sandy would sing, I'll love you forever, I'll like you for always, as long as I'm living, my baby you'll be.

Zoe still had nightmares, though not quite as often. But she had one this morning where she was on the ground in a basketball court and a man was running at her from a long way to get at her and hurt her, he had two hands with long knives, three- or four-foot-long knives, and there was a car she could get to but her legs couldn't move and she couldn't—

ZOE!

Zoe's feet kicked the wall as she was shocked awake.

Yeah? she called out.

Hey! yelled Sandy from the living room. You've snoozed long enough, huh? I let you go 'til noon! Now come help me!

Zoe rubbed her eyes and searched for her bra and yelled coming! then rushed out her bedroom door.

Her mother's face softened when Zoe stumbled in and she said, you should eat something before we start.

No.

They opened the boxes Sandy'd taken down and started sorting. They made piles of stuff to keep or throw away or give to goodwill. It wasn't exactly fun. Besides being hungover and ferociously hungry, everything Zoe saw just made her sad: Christmas-gift sweaters with moth holes in them, pictures of Sandy's birth fam that Sandy cut to pieces without pausing, a pretty sheer yellow blouse Zoe reached for to keep for herself but Sandy balled it up and said this is like a whore uniform from the fifties, what was I thinking.

They came across a few old pictures of Taya, and Sandy looked at them moodily then said so, you should keep these, and turned them face down and slid them toward Zoe on the floor. Zoe did like that. She and Taya'd never been close—probably wouldn't ever be, really—but she liked seeing pictures of her, especially from when Zoe was a kid.

When they were done, Zoe took the car to drop stuff off at goodwill. She saw a woman there pawing through jeans with marks under her eyes dark as football paint. It made her think of Frankie, who hadn't gotten back to her. She wondered if maybe her number was different now so she texted Robin and said *Hey can you give me Frankie's number?*

He texted back as she was pulling out. *I can, sure, but why?*

I'll tell you later?

He did and the number was different so she retyped the same message and sent it. *There*, she thought. The rain got stronger as she drove home and became one of those true downpours that happened only every few weeks or so, a car wash–grade spray that slowed every vehicle's speed by fifteen and turned everything from damp to just plain soggy. Back at the house, she bundled her coat and put on knee-high boots and went to ask her mom for a ride, but she had started day drinking—Sandy did that sometimes—so Zoe trudged down to the 66 and by the time the bus came every move she made was a squelch.

Months after she graduated college, four years into living in New York, Zoe had called her mother to tell her she had been on hormones for a while, that she was a girl, and, well, that that was that. Sandy'd made a high choking sound then said oh no.

A beat went by and Zoe said oh no?

Well what do you think, huh?! Sandy yelled. "That's that," you think it's like you got a job or a boy or something? Zoe made a chok-ing noise of her own and then they were both silent for a long period in phone time, like twenty-five seconds, and then Sandy said, I'm sorry. I'm sorry. I'm sorry. You know what, I'm sure you want to talk. I know you want to talk. But I can't do this now, you'll need to give me some time.

Mom, Zoe said. I'm sorry.

I always wondered, Sandy said quietly, after another, shorter silence. So hey, there she be. But you'll need to give me a few weeks on this, kid.

Okay, Zoe said. I can do that. I'm sorry.

Kid, Sandy'd said. No apologizing. No apologizing. I can tell you that right now.

Okay.

They were silent some more and Sandy said yup, I'm gonna go. Don't call me for a while.

Okay.

Then Sandy said, well actually, hey.

Yes?

What's your name?

It took her a few seconds to understand the question.

Zoe, she said. My name's Zoe.

That was when Sandy'd started crying heavily. Okay, Zoe had said, sitting on her bed with a hand on her face. Sandy hung up. The thing with the Williamsburg bar owner happened a week after that. Sandy didn't call her back for months. It hadn't been that great a time.

Do you work today? Sandy asked the next morning.

Yeah, at four.

Well, she said. After I go for a swim, I'm going to go to the mall and get some new clothes. Do you want to come with me? Get you, I dunno, a new shirt or something?

Oh sure! That'd be great! Zoe said. The two of them hadn't gotten out of the house together much.

Great, said Sandy. Maybe you can help me out with a new pair of jeans. I may actually get something with colour today.

What? Sounds like an *abomination*! Zoe said. Sandy laughed and gave her a little slap on the shoulder and went out the door. Old joke. Once in middle school they'd been out with Sandy's girlfriend at the mall, and a woman saw Sandy and the girlfriend holding hands and cartoonishly loud-whispered to her husband, an abomination, I tell you. So for a few years everything was an abomination. Mom, can I have some Nutella? *What? ABOMINATION!* Hey kid, how do you feel about a movie tonight? *Movies? ABOMINATIONS!*

Later, in the car, Sandy said so. You know it's different now that there's two of us.

What do you mean?

You really not know what I mean?

Zoe sighed. Mom, I do not know what you mean, so why don't you just explicitly tell me what you mean.

Oh, well, I ... Sandy muttered, oddly flustered all of a sudden. You just—you tend to get more trouble in groups, that's all.

What?

Don't you know that?

Oh, said Zoe, well yeah I read that somewhere once but I didn't really—

Dammit it's true, Sandy said, suddenly aggravated. And I'm glad we're out doing stuff but Zoe, you can't be so cavalier. You can't.

The sky was breaking outside and cylinders of sunlight were lighting up mist like specks of silver. Sandy said, you can't just sail through the world all charmed and oblivious anymore, all right? It sounds depressing but it's true, *all right?*

Mom I do okay, Zoe said, feeling tiny.

Sandy concentrated on traffic but she looked pissed. Zoe stayed quiet.

Being pretty won't always protect you, said Sandy.

Zoe looked out the window. Stop it, Mom.

I'm serious! said Sandy. They'll find out you used to be a man!

Mom! Zoe cried. I don't! Want! To have this conversation! And I was never a *fucking man*, okay?

Sandy snort-laughed, then she choked. Then she laughed, kinda unable to breathe for a few seconds: *A-ha! A-ha! A-ha!* She sounded like she was trying to pass something. Ohhhh my God! You think you just stopped being my son, don't you? she said. Do you think that's how it works? Do you think you went to a fucking wizard?!

Zoe put a hand in her hair and the other over her eyes. And Sandy said c'mon, tell me more, kid. She reached out her arm and pushed her daughter's left cheek like she was trying to wipe something on it. No! Zoe said. I don't! And Sandy said come on! Look. I'm here, aren't I? Sandy went on like that for a bit and Zoe said no Mom, stop, just stop, then they got to the mall and out of the car.

The sun was still glinting through sky cracks and the few people in the mall didn't give either woman much of a glance.

Zoe never got those kinds of glances, actually. Bodywise she'd been born as lucky as a lot of trans women would've ever hoped: She was tall but not Amazon tall, had slight bones, narrow shoulders, a naturally high voice and only a hint of an Adam's apple. Her facial hair was blond and even before electro never cast much of a shadow. She waited 'til she was ten months on hormones to go full-time, and she never heard an unkind word in her direction about it. Not one episode of street harassment or threat. Of the trans variety, anyway. There were a few months where people stared like they weren't sure what was up, and she was mute in public for a little while, but that was it. She was lucky, she knew it; none of her friends back in New York (like Julia, fuck …) could say that. But she'd more or less passed from the moment she wanted to.

They were silent in the mall as they walked to a clothing store. A man with a neatly trimmed beard smiled at Zoe and said to Sandy: Ma'am, if you don't mind me saying so, you have a beautiful daughter. Sandy flushed and said well thank you.

Sandy and Zoe were looking at jeans—Zoe generally wrinkled her nose at pants, but her one pair of black jeans was falling apart—when a clerk walked up and made a clearing noise in his throat and Sandy looked up unblinkingly and said yes?

Um. Can I help you, said the clerk.

No, my daughter and I are just fine thank you, Sandy said curtly.

The clerk stared without responding for a couple seconds. Then he said yes, yes, of course.

In the dressing room, unzipping her skirt and sliding her hands down inside her tights, Zoe remembered when she'd told her mother she liked boys. She was thirteen. Though she'd been raised by lesbians, Zoe'd been nervous. She had imagined Sandy stormily yelling oh, so now you want to be different *too*, huh? or maybe saying, Lord, they were right, they all said it would end up like this … or maybe, she'd thought, Sandy would just slap her. Sandy was generally pretty hands-off but she had slapped Zoe a couple times. Once she'd thrown a video game controller at her.

But Sandy hadn't done anything like that, and she'd even appeared to be in one of her bad moods at the time. Immediately she'd smiled, as if something glistening had been poured on her face, and she opened her arms and said, I love you. Come here. She hugged Zoe tightly and said well, what do you know, you're one of us. Isn't that just the greatest.

On the ride home from the mall, Sandy started on how Zoe's tits were falling out of her shirt. Zoe tuned her out and stared out the window as her mother got going again and didn't look back at her, not once, not even when Sandy screamed *LOOK AT ME!* and dug her nails into Zoe's thigh.

Right before work ended that night Zoe texted Al: *Are you busy tonight? Would you want to hang out?*

She put her cell away and made one last call that devolved into arguing about the farm bill with a man outside Rickreall. She was about to leave the building when Al texted back. *Hey lady! Yes I do! I'm off in an hour, meet me at the Horsehead?*

Zoe groaned. Another fucking bar. She really was drinking way too much here. Oh well. The guy was a bartender and all.

As she walked down Olive she saw a homeless girl who looked like Frankie. It wasn't her, Zoe was pretty sure—well, but how could she know, she supposed, she hadn't seen Frankie in so long. Was it her? No, it didn't look like her. The hair was wrong and her eyes were a different colour—maybe? It really could've been her. Zoe passed the girl and gave her a dollar. *No*, she thought, *it probably wasn't her*.

The mist coming down strengthened into steady rain and Zoe put her hood up.

OOGA-BOOGA! said her supervisor.

AH! Zoe wheeled around. She noticed for the first time that he had an arm tattoo of a kraken.

Sorry! he said, looking embarrassed. I didn't mean to scare you. Um, hey there. He put his hand on her shoulder and she shivered and shrugged it off.

There was an awkward couple seconds then she said where are you going?

Jameson's, he said. You?

Horsehead.

Oh so we're going the same way. Let's walk together!

Zoe thought of pointing out that both bars were exactly a block away then thought better of it. They walked over and parted ways and she went inside and ordered a Diet Coke. There. She didn't even *have* to be drinking in a bar.

She sat in the corner and took out her book. No one bothered her. She had learned a default public bitch face in New York and she still had it, which honestly she didn't really like. She had liked living there, but she'd picked up some habits of hardness, too, that she wished she could give back.

Then Al was in front of her plunking down a PBR. Hey! How's it going, lady?

Great! Zoe put her elbows on the table and propped up her head with her fists. How are *you*!

Awesome awesome. Wow—damn. I haven't actually talked to you in a really long time! Al said. You were in New York, right?

Yeah! Brooklyn.

Okay, I've been wanting to say this since I saw you again. But not while I was working, because that's creepy, right? But you look *really* good. Like, you look fuckin' *hot*. Shit can I say that? Is that okay? Like fuck, dude, good job.

Thanks. She blushed. Thanks, you're very nice.

Hey, don't thank me, speak truth to beauty, right? So what made you leave New York?

Uh, I was broke. And my mom needed help moving to Seattle for her new job. And all my shit was here. And I was broke.

I hear it's just a little expensive out there.

A month's rent here is like a … bag of apples over there. Or something.

Mmm. So tell me, you been the belle of every ball since you came back?

She scooched closer to the table. Oh pray tell what does *that* mean?

Come on lady, he grinned, you were en fuego at my bar the other night.

Oh please, that was, like, my one night off my butt. I'm really boring. Look. She picked up her drink. Diet Coke. I am the janitor of every ball, I am the DD of every ball.

Oh whatever, stop that! Al said. I don't believe that for a second! He said it in that weird way guys can that sounds mean and protective and attractive all at once. Then he softened and said, I'm sorry, I get it, I'm sure dating's really hard for you, I can't imagine.

Zoe blinked and said it's not actually—well, whatever. What about you?

Well—Al smiled sheepishly—actually I've been meaning to say, I can only hang for so long, I have a date in a couple hours.

Ah, said Zoe. Yeah no problem. *Goddammit.* He nodded and she nodded for far too long and then she said a date at midnight? The fuck are you going to go, Shari's?

She works at Dough Co., he said.

Got it. She smiled. I think you should go to Shari's. Three-dollar-ninety-nine pie, mmm! The bathrooms are good for blowjobs too, I bet you'll have a great time! She was trying to laugh and sound cheery and silly but it really wasn't working.

Uhhh I'm sure, Al said, taken aback.

What, don't you like blowjobs? She tried to laugh again but she just sounded like a bird.

Uhhhhhhh, he said. Then his face made a tic and his eyes lit up, then fell into something soft and kind. And pitying. Oh … he said. You didn't think …

Mildly contrary to the upbringing she'd had, as well as the neighbourhood in Brooklyn where she'd spent the last few years of her life, Zoe had never wanted to live even a little bit wild. Her natural state was to wake at seven and be reading in bed by ten, and her lifetime ratio of cups of milk to units of booze was probably around fifteen-to-one. She liked it that way. She definitely wasn't boring, you could never call Zoe that—she loved to travel, she liked sex in quantities mass and frequent, she read books others only pondered cracking and when she made the time she sewed beautiful clothing from scratch. But wild she wasn't. Whether it was here or Brooklyn she had only ever wanted a few rooms and a sweet dependable guy and, like, some plants. Shit job, loud dirty town, rainy town, whatever, all of that could be fine, she never minded, she just wanted the regular indoor shelter of a nice dumb quiet life, not boring, just quiet. When she was growing up she'd thought that was here and then she thought it was Brooklyn and now she thought it might be here again.

So as much as her vision had blanked with disappointment, and as she briefly envisioned unquiet reactions—taking a bunch of shots, going across the street to her supervisor, just kissing Al anyway, fuck it—she knew she wasn't that kind of person. Not in the least. She just said, sorry, no, don't be silly! Of course not! It's okay. Sorry, I was being weird, I was being really weird just then. And she smiled politely and listened to Al talk about his girl then took the last bus home after he left. *It's funny*, she brooded, face pressed at the window looking over Coburg Road, her vision travelling the dark-dark-neon-dark pattern of closed stores and parking lots, the Dari Mart, the Trader Joe's, the Albertsons, the Dairy Queen, the Burrito Amigos, the closed American Family Video, the Safeway and the Papa's Pizza and her old dentist's office, *it's only when they reject you that it really sinks in just how much you liked them.* She walked up Gilham and the sky was rainless with a scrum of thin clouds lit from behind by the moon; when she turned onto Ayers the rain returned again and the moon turned opaque, into a soft faraway light, as if covered by quilts. She entered the house and put away the chips and salsa Sandy had left on the counter. She wiped the pot ash off too, then scrubbed off her makeup. She changed into pyjamas and poured a glass of water in the kitchen, then noticed the saucepan sitting on the stove with crusts of hardened oatmeal rimming the sides and bottom. She looked at it for a long time then laid it quietly in the sink and filled it up with water.

∽

Hey Taya! said Zoe when she opened her phone.

Yeah hello! said Taya. Well? How the heck are you?

It was far enough into December now that the trees were bare, and Zoe was raking the last leaves on the lawn. It was raining steadily and when a car sped past over on Gilham the water it kicked up looked like smoke. She put the rake down and sat on the front steps of the house.

Well, I'm getting rained on! said Zoe. How are you?

Getting sunned. Come to California.

I'd like to soon, Zoe said, I really would.

You probably wanna go back to New York though, huh, Taya said. Maybe.

How's Sandy? Taya asked.

She's great. She's just great. About to go to Seattle. How's the beau? she asked. Zoe always called Taya's boyfriends beaus. She started playing with the rake.

He's good, Taya said. Lots of new clients. We're trying to set up a home office dealio at the moment but we need a bigger house.

Ah. Well, that sounds tough, Zoe said blankly. She tried spearing a single leaf without getting any others on the tines.

So, any boys I should know about? Taya said.

Zoe rolled her eyes and said you can't see it but I'm rolling my eyes. Taya tittered.

Thought of you when I got this new dress yesterday, Taya said after a silence. It's lime green and has polka dots on it and I just thought ooh, Zoe would love this, this is a *Zoe* dress.

Cool, Zoe said. She tried to flip the rake around so she could remove the leaf with her teeth.

Well, it's good to talk with you, said Taya. Please keep in touch!

Sure, Zoe said. They hung up and she had a singular text from Julia: *Woman! Where are you? Yr killing me!*

⁂

Robin and Zoe were eating at Burrito Boy after Zoe got off work. So what're we doing tonight? said Robin.

Can we please not go to the bar? Zoe said.

Tall order, said Robin.

Well we can, she said. I just don't want to be there for long. Like one drink?

Robin said yeah. There's a girl I wanted to say hi to there. How about we go quick, and we'll be out of there in an hour. An hour cool?

Sure, Zoe said quickly. Even if it ends up being more than an hour, just, like, promise me we'll end up back at your place early enough to watch a dumb movie and be in pyjamas and stuff? Please?

Promise.

When they got to the bar, Zoe's supervisor was there. He came up and chatted with her and Robin then bought a round of shots for the table. He was young to have grey hair, Zoe thought, couldn't be past his early thirties. Beyond the kraken tattoo on his arm Zoe noticed another one, near his shoulder, of a boy reading on a floor. She liked that. Then he excused himself to the dance floor and said hey hey, join anybody?

Zoe made a weighing motion with her hands and gave him a cute smile, then sucked on her rum and diet. The supervisor blew kisses at her and Robin and went to dance.

Hey, she said to Robin, does he know about me?

Robin immediately shook his head. No. If he does, I didn't tell him.

Thanks, she said. You're a good friend.

Robin smiled happily and said it's none of his business!

That's right, she said.

Robin went to the bathroom and Zoe watched the supervisor on the floor. *Someone overlearned "dance like no one's watching,"* she thought. His eyes were half closed and his limbs were kicking everywhere and he had a chunk of the floor to himself pretty quick. Zoe sat and watched him for a whole song. She liked watching men in moments like this. Like they were both self-possessed and not.

She went to the floor and tapped him on the shoulder. He turned around and Zoe made some jazz hands. The supervisor laughed. He was drunk. He hugged Zoe and they danced for a couple songs. Then Zoe said hey, let's, like, talk. Outside. He put on a serious face and said yeah, sure, hey, whatever you need, you know.

Zoe led him around the corner and behind Lazar's Bazar then turned and kissed him; she kissed him for what she figured was a minimum pretense of time and then dropped her hand into his waistband and then she was kneeling with her back against a chain-link fence. It was raining the lightest of mists again and she latently felt her hair gradually turn from dry to not dry to damp. She sucked him methodically, quick, almost mechanically but not in an unpleasurable way. After a couple minutes she took him down to the base and then pushed on his behind to guide him a bit; he started fucking her mouth and she made sounds to signal *Yes! Good!* though who knows if he really heard or paid attention to them or what. After he came she hugged him, same position, her arms wrapped around his legs and his emptied cock in her throat, breathing in through her nose, out through her nose, in through her nose, out through her nose, in through her nose, out thro—

He slipped himself out and she almost fell forward from leaning.

He helped her up and hugged her and tried to finger her but she'd already locked her thighs tight. Kiss me, she said. Kiss me. Kiss me. They kissed and kissed and she touched his face all over, and in a smooth motion he lifted her hands in his against the fence and leaned her back while pushing his body close to hers. She wasn't expecting it and he was smiling and then he stopped smiling and said oh.

Zoe flinched and pivoted and took a step back, then she poised, she was ready to run or scream but she was too tipsy and tired to feel fear, really. She was more weary, defensive. Like, *okay. So. Now this is a thing that's going to happen.* I guess I could've seen that coming. But then he just put on a stupid smile and made a stupid little laugh and said ha ha in a tinny voice and then said well I guess I'll see you at work soon.

An hour and a few drinks later Robin said sorry I took longer. Let's go?

The weather turned nasty when they left the bar, another rare heavy spray. They both only had hoodies and then Zoe gave hers to a shivering dude with a soggy cardboard sign—she had a job now, whatever—so she was especially cold but soon they were both at underwear-squelch level anyway so it didn't really matter.

Fuck Oregon! she yelled over the sound of the rain.

Yeah! Robin yelled back. Fuck this fucking state!

I don't ever want to see water again!

Let's live on milk! he hollered.

Now you're talking!

After twenty minutes they got to Robin's place and Zoe found out the pyjamas in her bag had gotten wet. Shit, she said, showing him as he shucked off his clothes. Can I borrow something to sleep in? Robin said sure and went to his room.

An oversized band T-shirt and grey billowy mesh shorts sailed into the living room and landed on the couch. She eyed them; they were faded and threadbare, she actually remembered Robin wearing both these things in high school. She changed in the bathroom with her back to the mirror. Back in the kitchen she heated up warm milk for the two of them. You'll like it, she found herself saying. Shhh! Just let it happen, let it happen, she said, and at that Robin laughed.

Hey, Ye Olde Supervisor really seemed to like you, he said. He hadn't noticed them stepping out, he'd been talking to that girl and he'd only seen that the two of them had been dancing.

Yeah, he seems like a nice guy, Zoe said. Don't think that one's a good idea though.

Oh right, of course not, duh, Robin said, tapping himself on the head. Work boss relationship. Thing.

Then he said hey, speaking of that, I know it must be tough for you with, like, dating and all. So, uh …

Mmmmm? Zoe said.

Robin's upper teeth appeared to rest on his lower lip. Well, he said, I know this dude who wants to go on a date with you. If you wanted me to set you up. He's seen you at the bar and stuff, he asked me if you were single.

Sure, Zoe said blandly.

I don't know if you'll like him, he said quickly. I don't know if *I* like him, but I figure maybe it's hard for you to find guys and I know he's into girls like you and so maybe it's not my place and I should just connect you with him anyway.

Do it, give him my number, she said, shaking the saucepan a little. She didn't look at him. I really don't care.

Okay, cool, Robin said hurriedly. I just have to say that, you know, for my own conscience, but like I said maybe it's not my place.

It's okay, Zoe said, pouring the milk and beckoning him into the bedroom. They sat on his bed shaking off the chill, and as she watched him close his eyes to drink—he had such long, pretty eyelashes—suddenly Zoe said you get nightmares a lot, don't you?

Sometimes, Robin said softly.

Aw, Zoe said, drawing a finger across his cheek. The rain was making bullet sounds against the air conditioner outside the window. She caught her reflection in the dresser mirror. The oversized T-shirt and shorts filled out and enlarged her little frame. Her eye flickered like she'd taken a swallow of something utilitarian, like cough syrup or bottom-shelf gin.

A childhood memory of her mother suddenly settled in her head, like a fallen balloon. In it she was dutifully standing by Sandy's desk as Sandy was crying and talking to her. She said a lot of things, but all Zoe remembered was Sandy saying please don't ever look up to me, and Zoe saying okay.

Nightmares of what? Zoe asked. Why? Robin closed his eyes and his long eyelashes fluttered a bit, and he shook his head and Zoe said you deserve something to make that better. She stroked his wavy brown hair.

You're a good friend, Robin said, curling away from her and lying on the bed, then swaddling himself in blankets. You're a good, good friend.

This is the last bit, Sandy said as they went down to the laundry nook of the basement. Once we get this corner cleared out, you're free. I release you.

Cool, said Zoe. I'll probably stick around 'til the weekend. If that's okay.

Do whatever you want, said Sandy. You know where you're going yet?

Zoe shrugged. Look for a place here? I guess? Robin knows a few people who need roommates. And it looks like I can crash on his couch until then.

Sandy scrunched her face like she was confused about a smell. You would hate that, wouldn't you?

Extremely, said Zoe. Can't be a princess all the time though.

I've been waiting years to hear you say that.

Shut up!

They cleaned the machines as best they could then started on the cabinet above the dryer. Hey, Sandy said thoughtfully. So I've seen you reconnect with some of your old friends here. Have you seen Frankie at all?

Funny you ask. Nobody really knows where she is, actually, said Zoe. She picked up a leaking bottle of detergent with a logo she hadn't seen since high school and dropped it in the garbage. Oh my God Mom this is gross, she said. The sink needs to be on like right now.

Sandy turned on the hot water in the big industrial sink and slime glided off Zoe's fingers. What do you mean, no one knows? said Sandy.

Well, I know she had a kid.

Sandy blinked. What.

She gave it up for adoption is what I hear, but she fell off the map after that.

Oh my God, Sandy said.

Supposedly she's back here in town. I tried texting her, said Zoe. But she never responded. I'm worried though, I think I might've seen her on the streets the other day, like, panhandling.

What about her dad? Sandy said.

Oh fuck. I never told you. He died. Cancer.

Fuck, Sandy said, more softly than her daughter.

Yeah. Then Zoe's face clouded and her tone turned mean. *Apparently*, she said, Frankie never even saw him while he was dying either, she just skipped out. *And* I heard she got really into coke too, I mean, Jesus.

So you're telling me, Sandy said, that one of your old friends who no longer has parents and just had a baby who she had to give up is possibly on the streets right now and possibly has problems with serious fucking drugs and all you did was text her.

Zoe was silent.

She could be dying, kid, Sandy said.

Zoe looked at the floor. I guess I just, she—

Oh shut UP! Sandy said, throwing the detergent bottle on the floor like she was spiking it. Zoe jumped and screamed, immediately scared. She backed against the wall and her mother continued: None of you get it around here! You don't know what friendship means! No, it could never mean life and death, could it? Humans aren't fucking games where you just try your best! Okay! Every night you've spent— she stopped and said, why am I about to waste time yelling. Let's get in the car.

Why are we getting in the car? said Zoe.

We're going to look for her.

Zoe's mouth opened and Sandy moved to the stairs. She ducked her head under the door frame and put one of her wide, chapped hands on the railing, then glanced back at her daughter. The whites of Sandy's eyes were glossy and nicotine yellow, and Zoe could see her calves tense on the first step with spiderweb strands of pain. She was getting old.

That her mother could walk through the longest desert and keep walking was a thought that entered and exited Zoe's mind. We will find her? Zoe asked. Who knows, Sandy said. Let's get in the car.

When Zoe was little, like nine, a kid in her school had once said on the playground, your mom's a *man*! Don't you know your mom's a *man*! My dad told me, he told me everything, you're not even homos you're like freaks for homos. He was a strong kid, an older kid, and he used to slap Zoe—not really hard, he just did it a lot, around the face and arms and sometimes in the nuts. He went on the whole your-mom's-a-man thing for a week and never said anything to the other kids or teachers, who knows why; maybe he figured no one would believe him. Zoe had told Sandy about it that weekend, a Saturday, and Sandy'd put her head in her hands and said what's the kid's name. Zoe told her and Sandy said his dad's name is Don, right. Huge guy. Loud guy. Zoe said yes, and Sandy said okay and left and was still gone when Zoe went to sleep, and the next day Sandy spent all day in bed and wouldn't talk to anyone, called in sick the next day and stayed in her room again, though she called Zoe in before school to kiss her on the head, and Zoe could hear her moving around when she left the house and at school the kid wasn't bothering Zoe anymore and then on Tuesday Sandy got up and went back to work.

Zoe was still in the basement as Sandy stopped for breath on the stairs. Then she shook something final out of her body, and followed her mother up.

Youth

She is shaking in her sleep, but I am only half awake. We are on her futon, in her mother's house, though her mother doesn't know I am here. Laura, I say. I try to rock her gently. Laura. I worry I do this too roughly. I don't mean to. It's okay, I say. You're having a bad dream. It's okay.

When she wakes with a start (I did rock her too roughly) she turns on the futon and puts her head in my neck. Her hair is in a long A-line, and the short part at the back gently prickles my fingers when I rub her head. We were watching *Buffy* on mute as we went to bed and now green text from the DVD menu is making auroras on her wall. One of her hands moves and clutches mine. We're both wearing T-shirts. The first time I stayed over, she said, apologetically, that she didn't like to sleep naked. That's okay, I told her. I really mean it, that is totally totally okay.

In an hour I'll wake up, walk to my car, drive home, and pretend to get up again. Two hours after that, I'll see her at school before class, and then before lunch we have the same free period.

Tomorrow night she is at her dad's. Her dad is not a good man. What she watches, what she wears, what she says, will be under intense scrutiny. So I hear, anyway. I have met the man once (he is intensely religious, I put on a sweater and khakis for the occasion). Myself, I don't understand why it puts her in depression. But it doesn't matter, I just want her to feel better. He won't leave me alone, she says desperately, I feel like shit when I'm with him. She feels her fattest and ugliest there, she says. She cuts herself most there too. She usually cuts her thighs but sometimes her stomach. She has cut herself when I'm at her mom's house, in the other room. She confided this to me after the fact. I hate that I cannot make her happy enough to stop.

She kisses me now and I say: You are so beautiful. Her eyes go up and sideways. Thanks, she says. I tell her she's beautiful all the time, there really are few things I mean more. The featheriness of her skin, how shirts travel over her breasts, the smallness of her forehead as it meets her hair, the way her thighs rise in curves then taper to her knees—I really do mean this, I know it sounds cheesy and like crap to her. But it's how I feel. I want so badly for her to understand I'm not lying. I find absolutely everything about her body beautiful, almost holy.

I pull her closer, and I feel her hip bones with mine. Softly I say: Did you have a bad dream? She doesn't speak. I say: What are you thinking? She shakes her head in my neck, she says, *Mmmm*. She says: You always ask that! You always ask that! I'm sorry, I say. She says it's okay. I think of what else to say. I am always thinking and planning how to be around her so I can do the right thing.

I have never been close to a girl before. I'm only sixteen, she is seventeen—but her body is so gorgeous, I really meant it. It's alive. I think alive's the best word I have. Her bones and skin give heat and energy in a way I didn't know bodies could. I said this once; she didn't believe me. She said I was an evil man, that I must want sex or money with the way I talked, that I couldn't possibly mean it. I wasn't angry she'd think that of me. I know how awful most men are. But I hated myself that I couldn't say it so she'd understand, and I put ribbons in my own thighs the next day, something I don't usually do. I want her to love herself more than anything in the world. I can't understand her self-hate. It exists with such fury. I don't particularly like myself, but I don't hate myself either. I can't say I feel too strongly one way or the other, honestly. I'm just this guy who found a really amazing girl.

She kisses me again, which makes me happy, because that means I didn't say anything wrong. She puts her hands on the sides of my head then kisses me furiously, and I kiss her back. She loves to be touched. I cup her breasts and she breathes sharp. She fumbles under my shirt and then my pants. She said once she loves hearing me gasp with pleasure, so I do at the right moments.

Soon I have to go. She hates when I leave. I do too. I get up and put on my oversized hoodie, my jeans. I kiss her and kiss her on her futon. Stay with me, she says. I wish I could, I say. I love you. I love you too. I touch her gingerly because I'm afraid of being rough again, and I am also so genuinely possessed by how her body moves (sometimes to the point where I go oh geez dude, you are being a creep, yes, you love her, but c'mon don't let yourself get creepy).

I drive home as the dark night breaks into mist and light winter grey. I park on the street and climb into my window and stretch on my bed. I make an X on my mattress. Even though I already miss her, it feels nice at first, splaying myself out untouched. My muscles untense and I set my alarm for an hour forward.

My mother is worried. She says Laura and I are too intense and I spend too much time over there. And of course she doesn't know I'm there at night too. I understand where she's coming from, I guess I'd be worried about me too. It's just—I love her. I hate not being around her. And I worry about her so much, I do. I worry one day she will kill herself. She has tried before and I worry she is that close again. I worry about the next three days she will spend at her father's. I am always worrying about this.

I wonder which verses she will have to discuss out of the Bible tonight. Last week it was something about a fountain of youth.

We pretend we are Mimi and Roger from *Rent*. I am a boy version of the former, the one vying for Laura to live, to love life, love herself, because life is too short. (I, myself, am doing exactly that, I think. I am living for love and I have no regrets.) She is a girl version of the latter, the one who hates to leave her house and face the world.

She is an artist, a painter, and she has talked about painting on me. That is so cool! I said. I would love that, I said. I really would. I want to sit on her floor, beside her futon, and feel her brushes move across my back. When she brought it up, the feeling was so powerful I almost didn't believe she was serious. So I waited for her to bring it up again. But after waiting for weeks, I said to her (and for a few hours before, I rehearsed how to say this): Hey love? I just wanted to ask, do you still want to paint on me? Just because I still like that idea, I said. And I do. Some boyfriends might not like that idea, but I am a boyfriend who does. And I'm proud of that. She says maybe soon. Maybe on a warmer day, when it's not supposed to rain, when we can open the windows and do it in her room. That'd be nice. I dream of a day when she is happy, when we can exist together and just be, when I can wake up in the morning with her hair in my face, whole and entwined. I'll wait for that. I think of that day and I know that we will be all right.

I think I would be content and peaceful for the rest of my life with her painting on me. Like our bodies would be so connected that I would forget the sense of how I feel in my own. I can't think of anything more perfect—though I admit I don't understand why she would want to put art on someone so ugly and awful. I know I can't really do anything for her. I'm too terrible and stupid and I'm so scared one day she'll see that. I'm sinking my hands in my mattress right now wanting to be back with her so she'll assure me she'll stay. Sometimes when I'm without her I don't want to exist, I feel dumb, I feel gross, I feel like—I don't know what I feel like. My mother always told me to look in the mirror every morning and say, I am enough. But I do that and I just see an alien. Who looks in the mirror and sees an alien. Do you hear what I'm saying? Am I getting through to you? Please listen to me. Please try to understand. In this awful world, you might get love. Let me go with my luck. She's what I'll dream of. Lying on the floor, a sunny sky coming in through the window, under the pure of her eyes and the turn of her hair, giving myself to her brush, forever, without wish to go forward or leave.

AFTERWORD

One spring, a friend gave me a card she'd found in a coffee shop. The card was a call for submissions for an anthology of short fiction with transgender themes by a new publisher, Topside Press. It was 2011 in New York City, and I was finishing up an MFA. I was writing about trans stuff, but it was non-fiction—I wanted to write personal essays and journalism. Fiction? I thought, what the hell.

Over the next few months, I wrote "Other Women," the first story in this book, and it unlocked something inside me. It was frustrating and hard to write, and especially once I touched on sexual trauma, I felt something grim settle onto my skin—but all in a way that said *yes, you're getting close to something, and you should probably keep doing it.* The week before the submission deadline, I was particularly single minded. I devoted all my time outside work to finishing it. By then I was out of school, working retail in downtown Manhattan and living in West Harlem. Hurricane Irene hit the city that week, and the evening before it did, with the subway shut down, my roommates walked all the way to Times Square to see it wet and empty. I stayed at the apartment, writing. That night, I woke up at 3 a.m. to a red sky that was churning and spookily quiet, an image that has since stayed in my dreams.

Days later, I sent in the story two minutes before the deadline. And almost right away, I went, *OH MY LORD, WHAT HAVE I DONE?!* I had written a trans character with weaknesses and shittinesses who kept getting way too drunk and had explicit sex scenes—I was mortified that I'd made us look bad. That was the phrase swimming around my head: "made us look bad."

Earlier that summer, in fact, a prominent older trans writer had found personal essays of mine published on the *McSweeney's* website and tweeted that they were "creepy" and "not helpful." I emailed that writer immediately, and she apologized to me, which she didn't have to do, and explained her concerns, and we hashed it out. But she said a thing I still think about, not because it represents her so much as it represents a dominant paradigm, I think, that can hound nervous minority artists who suddenly get a spotlight. She said: "The more you can make us seem like thoughtful, complex, sweet-hearted people, the better ... trans people are still in the very, very early stages of our movement ... we have to be as noble and thoughtful as we can possibly be."

I disagree with those notions now, for reasons I can articulate: I wish for trans artists the freedom to be as strange and difficult within our work as anybody else, and I do not believe encouraging the portrayal of trans people as consistently noble and thoughtful is conducive to that freedom. Also, trans resistance has a very long history, and I do not agree that it was in its early stages in 2011. Back then, however, I was wrestling deeply with these concepts. Most of the sparse trans culture I had imbibed at that point played by such rules that what made us Look Palatable was of high concern. (Which isn't to say there weren't exceptions to that culture—just that I hadn't found them yet. I had encountered a few: *Stone Butch Blues*, Elena Rose blogging as "little light," *Whipping Girl*.)

It's easy for me to look back and say, heh, my fear of making us "look bad" with one short story in an indie press anthology was a little silly. But it just didn't feel that way at the time. Most trans creations I'd seen had cis standards in mind; they delicately balanced what they had to say with upholding mainstream sensibilities. This was before *Nevada*, before *Pose*, before Janet Mock on Piers Morgan and Laverne Cox on Katie Couric. I thought maybe this story I'd written was, like, irresponsible.

But Topside accepted "Other Women" and published it. And my friend and fellow writer Donna Ostrowsky (to whom this book is dedicated, rest in peace) came up to me and said, "Something like what happened to Sophie happened to me." We had just spoken to a class of cis people who'd read our stories—they'd expressed confusion about "the erotic ending." Donna, I never told you this, but it meant the world to me that you could see how messed up I felt after we did that class. (I miss you, by the way.)

And since then, many other trans women have told me similar things. Trans women's experiences of sexual assault is something we still don't talk enough about. If that's you too, all I can say is you're not alone—I promise you're not—and I love you.

I left New York soon after that, and I kept writing fiction. I wrote the overwhelming majority of the book you hold in your hands during a frenzied two-year period between 2012 and 2014. I began "Not Bleak" in my high school bedroom in Eugene. I wrote "How to Stay Friends" almost entirely in one shot at the Kopper Kettle restaurant in Morden, Manitoba. I finished reading Sandra Birdsell's *Night Travellers* during the polar vortex winter in Winnipeg, and I immediately wrote "Youth" as an emotional response. Topside Press accepted the book, and I sent the last proofs off to them in April 2014 while sitting at the Toad in the Hole Pub, after which I got rip-roaring drunk and hooked up with a surly middle-aged guy in a leather jacket who bestowed on me my first experience with cocaine, then freaked out at my new vagina's tightness and screeched, "*Are you a hermaphrodite?!*" (Subsequent book send-offs have been far less eventful.)

I was nervous as the book seeped into the little queer and trans worlds of which I was part. I can't begin to tell you how grateful I was (and still am) whenever someone approached me at a reading or left a message in my inbox to say that what I'd written resonated. Especially when it was other trans women. It's been maybe the most meaningful thing in my life. Thank you. ♥

I've published two more books of fiction since: *Little Fish*, a novel, in 2018, and *A Dream of a Woman*, another story collection, which I finished back in New York City in the spring of 2021, an exact decade—almost to the fucking month, actually—after my friend passed along that card from Topside Press and I thought, what the hell. These three books also contain many interconnected characters, and that's intentional. On one hand, I've always thought that there are only so many of us out there, and it made sense to me that these women might know each other, might drift in and out of each other's lives. But also, these books have all felt somewhat a piece of the same idea. I'm not sure what I'll write next. But I do think of these three titles together—*A Safe Girl to Love*, *Little Fish*, and *A Dream of a Woman*—as a trilogy of sorts.

Looking back, I think I spent a decade working on a very particular project of depicting young trans women growing up and making lives for themselves—or trying to, despite the efforts of the world around them, as well as their own flaws. And ever since that grimness settled upon me when I was writing "Other Women" and I realized, oh, this is what I'm doing, and it's perhaps *not* irresponsible, and ever since I understood that determining whether my art "made us look bad" was neither within my capacity nor my job as an artist, I resolved that if I was going to write fiction, I was also going to incorporate the specific truths of transgender life as I personally have witnessed and thought about it.

I really want to emphasize *personally* here; I don't mean to say my books are about "what it's like" or whatever, because trans people vary too widely for that, and my characters have their own specific concerns and idiosyncrasies. (Sidebar here to paraphrase Meredith Russo: if you're trans, and you don't see yourself in these people, that's okay. They're not real, and you are.) Further, I'm a white millennial who transitioned at twenty-three, and I think my work likely reflects that. What I have resolved to do is not elide or compromise my own truths the way I as an individual have known them, even when they get a little desolate or sad.

And you know, I'll give some credence to that older trans writer from above; I do hope to be thoughtful, strategic, and politically conscious about my professional *conduct* as an artist moving around this shitty world. But I don't believe in doing so through the art itself; I don't think that serves the art much, or the world, for that matter. But maybe that's a whole other essay.

Okay, what else? I would be remiss to leave out the fact that after I wrote "Not Bleak," I spent much of the following year imagining it as a movie whose entire soundtrack is from Taylor Swift's *Red*. The opening scenes are to "State of Grace," probably with nice shots of the landscape. The trailer is to "I Knew You Were Trouble." Carla and

Zeke's burgeoning friendship over the summer is to "Holy Ground." The drive from North Dakota to Manitoba is to "Red," natch. On the drive back, as Zeke opens up to Carla, it's to "Treacherous," and the bridge kicks in when Carla gets home and kisses Liam. The last scene with Zeke in the car is "The Lucky One." The end credits are to "Stay Stay Stay." Taylor, if you're into this idea, call me!

I have people to thank profusely for this new edition. Enormous gratitude to the ever-sterling crew at Arsenal Pulp Press for pushing this book back into the world: Brian Lam, Robert Ballantyne, Cynara Geissler, Catharine Chen, and Jazmin Welch (thank you for designing such a gorgeous new cover! Not to mention its links to the Carly Bodnar original). Thanks to Imogen Binnie, as well as the good folks at Consortium Book Sales & Distribution, for the help navigating reclaiming my rights to the book. To Riley MacLeod, who was the main editor for this book back in the day, thank you for all your work on it so long ago—I can never thank you enough. And to some very certain trans women I met in New York back in those early days, who through example and conversation showed me there was a different life for myself if I chose it, I can never thank you enough either: Katherine Cross, Red Durkin, Julie Blair, Jessie Lee, Amelia Yankey, Bryn Kelly (rest in peace), and Imogen again, and Donna again.

Lastly, when I began all this in 2011, trans people were mostly absent from the larger culture, save as villainous jokes or perfect martyrs. We were certainly on few politicians' radars. And now …

Well.

I am writing this during a week when a children's hospital is receiving death threats because they provide health care to teenagers. The issue is those teenagers are trans. I am writing this during a year when over twenty-five bills that forbid people, primarily children, from existing in public life—from accessing health care, going to the bathroom, playing sports, or doing something so innocuous as to tell someone their name and hear it repeated back to them—have been signed into law across the United States (not just introduced, but signed into law). The issue is that these people are trans. What these bills target—could it be more innocuous? Any old person walks up to the coffee counter. "Name?" You tell them. They write it on a cup. They call it when you're needed. Someone asks, "What's your name?" and you tell them. That's the level at which they pass laws forbidding trans presence (so often, trans *children's* presence) in public life. Do you think they'll stop there? They already haven't. They're phoning a kid's hospital with death threats. They've stripped away the right to medicine. They didn't stop at a simple name. Someone asks, "What's your name?" and you tell them. Can you imagine it being that simple?

All this is to say that I am horrified, enraged, and sometimes deeply depressed by the current right-wing backlash to the existence of trans life. If you are a trans person feeling hopeless right now, you're not misguided for feeling that way. Also: We have always been here, and we always will be. The annals of our history and our present are filled with dread and grimness, and so are they filled with nearly infinite examples of how we survive. We don't always survive, but we survive a lot. We will always be here, and we must not stop fighting—for survival and dignity and the right to make our own lives. We must not and we cannot.

Where does literature fit in? Yeah, a good question, isn't it? I didn't write my books with hopes in mind of what they might actually do in the world—I just wouldn't have been able to create that way. And you can't control what people do with your art. My favourite example: Oliver Stone intended *Wall Street* to be a screed against the evils in high finance, but instead he inspired a generation of Gordon Gekkos. No writer really gets to dictate what the thing *does* once it's out there, you know? But no writer gets to check out of politics either—and if they think they do, they're fooling themselves. Our work enters the same world that existed when we started, and that world can be rough out there. So, where does literature fit in? When it comes to my own books, I usually say that's up to you, the reader. And I do mean that. But if I press myself for another answer, if I really press myself as to my hopes for what my books might offer specifically to my trans readers, my mind goes to two quotes, both from *Meanwhile, Elsewhere: Science Fiction and Fantasy from Transgender Writers*, which I co-edited with Cat Fitzpatrick.

The first is from our editors' afterword, which we ended by saying we hoped to make "a book of stories that allow room for the heroic everydayness of real trans people's lives … and we hope that it might, in a Janus-like fashion, act as both an escape from the current world and manual for your own possibilities."

The second is from the ending of Jeanne Thornton's "Angels Are Here to Help You": "Pretend that the rest of your life was the aberration. Pretend you have the confidence you need. Try, try so hard."

CASEY PLETT,
AUGUST 2022

ACKNOWLEDGMENTS

Thank you everyone who read pieces and said things about them. Tall Girls especially: Cat, Red, Julie, Jessie, Annie, Katherine, Janis, but also Lindsay, Yardenne, Madeline, Sarah P, Alex, Stephen, Courtney, Alison, Calvin, Rachel C, Dana L, Erin B, and foremost and especially Callan, whose love and support and late-night talk-throughs and dozens of readings were irreplaceable, you are amazing. Thank you Riley and Tom at Topside.

Thank you Columbia workshop folks. Thank you everybody way back in Dangerous Words. Thank you McNally Robinson for such consistent, active, kind support of this book. And thank you Katie for Low Standards.

There was always someone there in a rough spot, know you're in my heart: Tara, Brent, Carly, Kate, Amelia, Glo, Dad, Olivia O, Ari, and Sarah P again, and Callan and Jessie again (and again and again). And thank you, Stephen, for getting me at the subway.

Those who put me up and helped me land in and out of a million places while I was writing this with money or muscles or both, thank you thank you: Mom and Harold, Dad and Linda, Devin, Russell, Merrill, Phiona, and the whole Doerksen clan.

To which: Grandma, I took this name thinking of you. I hope you don't mind. I still pray and I still don't believe that things talk.

Casey Plett is the author of *A Dream of a Woman*, *Little Fish*, and *A Safe Girl to Love*; the co-editor of *Meanwhile, Elsewhere: Science Fiction and Fantasy from Transgender Writers*; and the publisher at LittlePuss Press. She has written for the *New York Times*, *Harper's Bazaar*, the *Guardian*, the *Globe and Mail*, *McSweeney's Internet Tendency*, and the *Winnipeg Free Press*, among other publications. Winner of the Amazon Canada First Novel Award, the Firecracker Award for Fiction, and the Lambda Literary Award twice, she has also been nominated for the Scotiabank Giller Prize. She splits her time between New York City and Windsor, Ontario. *caseyplett.com*